ERRANT WINGS

BY S. JEAN

ALSO BY S. JEAN

Hymn of Memory
The Devil in the Woods
Forevermore
Born of Scourge
Wherever the Stars Call

ERRANT WINGS
BY
S.JEAN

STAR★CADETS

CONTENT WARNINGS
arson, self-destructive behaviors, sexual situations, references to underage drinking, smoking, language

To those who need a reminder:
your life is yours,
no one else's.

1

Blood

DAWN'S LIGHT PUSHED across the hilltop and shined through Asher's window as a brushstroke of brilliant gold, except that wasn't what jolted him awake.

It was the sudden, excruciating pain.

Starting at his shoulder blades, it followed what had been a dull ache the night before, but was now white-hot, like a knife being dragged through. It quickly eclipsed his entire back, like his skin wanted to split open to free what was inside.

Not here. Not in his room.

Asher swung his legs over the edge of the bed and stood so fast, the room spun. The muscles in his back spasmed, something within making room for itself, and he lurched forward. He caught himself on the doorframe and afforded himself a moment to reorient. A moment for a deep breath. The pain was so bad, he wanted to retch it out, but he couldn't. Not until he got to the bathroom. Just two doors down. He could keep it together until then.

He just worried his back wouldn't.

The hallway darkened between blinks, black spots from the pain threatening to take over. He thought it would happen, that he'd pass out, but then his bare feet touched the cool tiles of the bathroom. He blinked and met his panicked expression in the mirror. He exhaled.

He'd made it.

Pressure built at once, like permission finally given, then released just as fast as the skin across his shoulder blades split open.

Blood splattered across the bathroom—the walls, the seashell decorations Judith had hung up, the bathtub, the seaside curtain holding on from summer, the mirror—*everything*. Asher's legs folded underneath him, numb, and he caught himself on the sink.

That's the worst of it, he told himself, mouthing the words when his voice failed. Both Raum and Amy had warned him that the pain literally felt like it exploded until the wings were free. So, this was typical.

Except, had there been this much blood when their wings sprouted? The blood's sticky warmth trickled down Asher's back and pooled around the rim of his sleeping pants. Slid down the walls and mirror it'd splattered across like a horror movie.

Asher's mind was too numb with pain to remember clearly, but he knew one thing for sure: neither Raum nor Amy had screamed. Asher must have; his throat was raw.

Judith's voice carried through the house as her steps thundered up the stairs. Addam's heavier ones followed just as fast. They'd know. Asher nodded to himself, delirious. They'd tell him if this was normal.

Asher forced a shaky smile on his lips and lifted his eyes to catch himself in the mirror, so he could see *his* wings. Three years late, but this pain meant they were here.

The smile fled immediately.

White wings had sprouted from his back, each feather coated in his blood. Much more formed than they should have been. His mind emptied of everything he was going to say as Judith and Addam came in. Their forms were blurry in the mirror, from his pain or tears, Asher couldn't say. The strength left his arms and he slipped. Darkness encroached and he let it have him this time.

"Angel wings," he exhaled and passed out.

Foundlings were parentless children who sometimes appeared on doorsteps. Every country, county, and city had them. Sometimes with generations between appearances. Origin stories ranged from something more mundane to the more supernatural, but there was no concrete proof where exactly foundlings came from. The only way everyone knew they were not normal children simply abandoned shortly after birth were their peculiar purple tongues. It marked them different from other children.

Instead of burdening unlucky individuals (there was no rhyme or reason as to who were gifted the children), the problem of foundlings became a government issue. Most cities created foundling houses and employed house parents to raise the children as though they were normal. At least until their sixteenth year, because by then, every foundling grew *wings*. Either full of feathers like birds, or with the soft velvety texture akin to bats.

Most of the time, anyway. Rarely a year earlier, but sometimes a year later. Except Asher.

Three years and some months had gone by since his sixteenth birthday and each one had ended without his wings. He'd begun to think he'd never grow them, despite x-rays showing them beneath his skin. Unfortunately, doctors weren't allowed to extract them with surgery. There was still too much unknown about the wings, so no one wanted to chance forcing them out. Some superstitious bullshit.

So, Asher had waited. And waited. And then waited some more.

He'd hated it. He'd grown up with two other foundlings—Raum and Amy—and they'd gotten their wings at sixteen and had long since left the foundling house for what was deemed as their calling. Then there was another flock of much younger foundlings, a quartet. He'd worried even they'd get wings before he did.

They didn't, as it turned out.

Finally, he had his wings. He should have been doing cartwheels. Throwing a party. Eating fucking cake or something, but there wasn't any fanfare.

When he finally regained consciousness—sometime around noon—all he got was *pain*. It felt like knives pressing into his shoulder blades before it spiderwebbed down the length of his spine. The weight of the wings made his skin stretch and burn.

He was laid out in bed, drenched in a fevered sweat, and begged to pass out again. Waking up wasn't worth this. Fuck getting wings. It wasn't supposed to hurt *this* much, was it?

Voices drifted inside from the hallway.

"It's because we waited," Addam argued. He was the house father, a stoic but kind man. Asher liked him. He'd let Asher vent and vent and vent, and simply nod in understanding.

"I know," Judith replied, her voice tight. She was the house mother. She dealt with all the governmental bullshit. "I know," she repeated.

They must have often had this argument out of earshot. Each time, it reached the conclusion of inaction. Asher's wings *shouldn't* have taken three years to breach. They'd clearly been growing underneath the skin given how heavy they felt now. Judith had a background in medicine, she could have extracted the wings herself. Except she'd insisted they wait like they were supposed to. Everything was by the book with her and, more than ever, Asher hated it.

There had to be stitches along his shoulder blades. Asher couldn't look, but the way his skin burned? Definitely felt like stitches. He had some delirious memory of waking up in the midst of Judith doing them, but he wasn't sure if that was a nightmare born from the pain or if it'd actually happened. He wanted to ask Judith about it later, although he doubted she'd give him the truth if she thought it'd be too traumatizing.

What bothered Asher the most beyond the pain, however, was that they were worried. Asher wanted to raise his voice and tell them he was okay (even though he doubted he was), but all that came out was a pained breath.

Addam responded quickly, coming inside just as Asher's vision became spotty and blurry. Then there were pain pills and water and Asher gave into the darkness crawling across his vision, just so the world would stop hurting.

He came to sometime later in the afternoon when Addam was checking his temperature. At least Asher was still at home. He'd thought it'd have been the hospital next. Not that the hospital would touch foundlings under normal circumstances (always touting the same superstitious bullshit). The pain was considerably less upon this awakening. Maybe the painkillers were finally doing their job.

"How are you feeling?" Addam asked, pressing his hand against Asher's cheek and then the other.

"Like I got run over," Asher grumbled and quickly added before Addam could frown, "but a little better."

He'd hoped to see a betrayal of emotion from his house father, see how bad this really was, but like always, Addam remained stoic. It was cool, most of the time, but right now, annoying. Judith was the more outwardly emotional one in their marriage and while she was just as calm and collected most of the time, she wore her emotions on her sleeve.

They'd been married for years, but had no plans for biological children. Addam had told Asher once he and Judith always wanted to take care of the children who didn't have parents. That led them to being in charge of the foundling house when the couple before them had grown too old to keep up. The trio Asher was part of had been Judith's and Addam's second set of foundlings. The first had been more spread-out with their ages and had already left by the time Asher had formed real memories.

According to Judith, Raum and Amy had come together from the same frazzled bachelor who had no idea what to do with them. Asher came a few years later, a toddler by the time the young woman he'd been given to couldn't take care of him anymore. She'd visited a few times after giving him up, like she wanted to make sure he'd do okay without her, but Asher hardly remembered her now.

"Is this normal?" Asher finally asked, afraid of the answer. Addam had moved on to looking at his wings. A cold chill touched them from an unseen washcloth. Must have been cleaning them again. "D-Did you have to do this for Amy, too?"

Amy had feathered wings like him and they were what people had colloquially dubbed as angel wings. Raum, on the other hand, had the bat wings and thus called a devil wing. The names came from the more religiously minded folk and it varied in different countries, but most people here used the terms regardless of their religious affiliation because it was easier. The connotation was always problematic, however. Unfortunately, the city fully leaned into it.

Angels were good, devils were bad.

Asher tried not to think about it. Not right now. Not while he was delirious still.

In any case, Asher was sure neither Amy nor Raum had been this bad; although maybe his excitement that they'd gotten their wings at all made him forget.

Addam didn't answer. He just washed Asher's feathers. His hands were gentle as he manipulated Asher's wings. They were incredibly sensitive to the touch, but it wasn't long before the pain melted into something Asher distantly realized was pleasure. Deft hands moved across the joints of his wings, gently but firmly holding them still. It made Asher shiver. He hadn't realized how *good* it'd feel to have someone touch his wings like that.

On second thought, he should have known. Raum was always very vocal about it when Asher manipulated his wings. Quickest way to turn him on. Asher had honestly thought it was a devil wing thing, though. Amy certainly hadn't mentioned anything like that. Then again, Raum was Asher's boyfriend. He'd probably be way more forthright with that kind of information than Amy.

Right now, though, with the source of the pleasure being Addam, the foundling house father? Embarrassing. Asher was just glad he was lying on his stomach and nothing gave him away. He hid his face into the pillow and tried not thinking about it. It sure beat pain, at least.

Addam didn't comment, thank god, and continued working diligently until he was satisfied with the state of Asher's feathers.

"There," he said when he finished. He wrung out the washcloth in the basin and Asher glanced over. The water was tinged with red ribbons. "A little more white, this time."

Asher hid the scowl twisting his lips and pressed his face into the pillow again. He didn't want to think about his wings. Not yet. Not ever. He just wanted to be happy that they were out.

Addam gently squeezed Asher's shoulder. "It'll be okay."

After he left, Asher eased out a soft sigh and turned his head so he could see outside his window. The sun had come and gone, leaving a deep violet to peel across the sky.

Asher had *angel* wings. And, if that wasn't all, his feathers were *white*. Some pure shade of fucking white from what little he'd gleaned from quick glances. Someone would look way too much into that, even though it didn't mean anything.

Except having feathers at all meant everything he'd planned would change.

X-rays had only ever shown their shape. Nothing about feathers. No one knew what wings a foundling would get, but people liked to say you could guess by how the foundling acted.

Between Asher delighting in making trouble, his stubbornness, and how he eschewed rules if he could have fun, everyone—even himself—pegged him as a devil wing. He wasn't straightlaced like Amy, after all. She was the prime example of what everyone thought angel wings should be. Rule-abiding, a good listener, and kind to a fault. Raum, on the other hand, had liked making trouble with Asher, was always a willing participant in mayhem, and time and time again, was up and down with Asher in the city until dawn to find trouble for the hell of it. Devil wings made sense for Raum. It should have for Asher, too.

So why did he get angel wings?

The question made the pain worse. All his plans had hinged on him being a devil wing. They weren't doable as an angel wing. So much more bullshit came with having fucking feathers, for some reason. People expected shit from you.

Just acknowledging it made the pain flare hotter. He wanted to scream in frustration, but he needed to show Addam and Judith he was doing better so they didn't worry. He muffled the sound into his pillow, wishing everything was different.

Days blurred together as Asher waited for his back to recover. All he wanted to do was drag himself to the house phone and call Raum, but he couldn't stand long enough to dial the number. He needed help getting to the bathroom; he didn't want to have either Judith or Addam having to linger while he talked to Raum. Besides, his boyfriend probably already knew what kind of wings he had. Judith would have told him and she also would have told him not to come by until Asher was completely healed. Asher wished Raum hadn't listened to her. Just to give the days blurred with pain some meaning.

It was a week before the pain and fevers finally broke. When Asher pulled himself out of some delirium induced sleep, it was past midnight, leaving his room once again in soft violets. Weak bursts of orange glowed from the fairy lights Addam had left on. Amy had wrapped them around Asher's headboard when he was ten and afraid of the dark. They'd been brighter back then. Now, they were but dim stars. One day, they'd die. Asher would probably leave them up anyway.

Asher thought about rising to eat something

beyond the breakfast shakes and oatmeal Addam had been bringing for him, but putting pressure on his arms made him want to cry. So much for less pain.

He collapsed on his bed again and seethed. The breeze from the window fluttered across his back, and thankfully, felt nice. Cooled the fevered sheen of sweat left behind Late autumn air whisked itself through his room, smelling of crisp leaves and the bonfire Addam must have had going earlier in the backyard. It was the time of year for them.

Maybe in the morning, Asher could convince his body to be fine enough for a shower. The heat would be nice on his back. Maybe he'd even have a real meal. Go on with normalcy. Get it over with.

As he closed his eyes again, content with his plan, he felt weight on one side of his bed, close to the window. Then the weight pressed down near his other side, like someone was gently stepping over him as they came in through the window. Asher couldn't have hidden the smile crossing his lips even if he'd tried.

"Raum," Asher breathed his name as a pleased exhale.

Raum's lips on his cheek made him shiver and he opened his eyes to take his fellow foundling and boyfriend in. Soft tawny skin dusted in freckles, auburn hair pulled back so its feathered strands fell down the nape of his neck, and always dressed in something befitting his job at the tattoo parlor downtown. He had a black bridge piercing, a gunmetal gray nose stud glinting in the dim light, black rings lining both ears, and a tongue ring he liked to show off. Capping it off were his brown devil wings. They really suited him.

His wings had come at the stroke of midnight on his sixteenth birthday, like some sort of fairy tale. Asher and Raum had been cuddling, drifting off against one another, when Raum had suddenly lurched off the bed and made the same scramble to the bathroom. He'd only reached the hallway before his skin broke, releasing the wings. Asher had been quickly exiled from Raum's room for a few days while Judith and Addam handled the aftercare, but when Asher had seen him again, Raum was proudly showing them off like they'd never hurt. They'd started pretty small, but had quickly grown to match the span of his arms. They were just big enough where Raum could wrap them around Asher if he'd wanted to.

He hadn't needed a week of downtime to recover. He hadn't ruined his back with wings grown too big underneath the skin. Not like Asher.

"Hey you," Raum whispered, his voice a soft tenor that ran shivers up and down Asher's entire body.

Raum settled on the floor beside the bed and dropped his bag in his lap. When Asher managed a little grin at him, Raum pressed a palm to

Asher's forehead.

"Addam's been keeping an eye on my fever," Asher said, leaning into Raum's hand. "I think it finally broke."

"You're a little warm. Amy and I had fevers too." Raum traced his fingers lovingly down Asher's face. His thumb stopped at the scar on Asher's lip and he touched it softly, like always.

The scar had come from Raum by accident. He'd had his canines sharpened in the spirit of being a devil wing and had gotten overzealous. Asher didn't mind. He liked the teeth and Raum had grown way more careful since.

"I meant to come by sooner," Raum continued, "but Judith kept thwarting my attempts. I think her mom-senses finally went slack. I brought you something."

"Hmm?" Asher raised his eyebrows, curious.

Raum pulled open the drawstring on his bag and Asher tried to push himself up on his elbows to look. Nope. Not happening. His wings spasmed hard, knocking the air out of him, and pain sunk deep into his back. Raum gently led him back down to the bed.

"Easy, Ash," he said and pressed a chaste kiss to Asher's tattooed shoulder. It was entirely black, almost all the way to his elbow, courtesy of Raum. "Gotta rest up, remember?"

The next kiss pressed against the crook of Asher's neck, where the tattoo ended, making Asher smile. Raum stopped there, but if Asher hadn't been in so much pain, next would have been the delightful press of Raum's teeth against his skin in the same spot. Understandably, Raum skipped that part of the game tonight.

As Asher settled back down, a little disappointed he couldn't reciprocate the kisses, his boyfriend took a jar from his bag. It wasn't much bigger than Raum's hand and was filled with a creamy mixture.

"It's the pain lotion Amy got from another angel wing. It should help." Raum unscrewed the jar and tilted it toward Asher. A little lumpy, it looked like someone had put it together in their kitchen, but if it worked, it worked. The aroma of lavender and mint spilled into the room with the lid off. Asher breathed in deep, hoping the smell alone would help.

"It'll be a little cold. It reminds me of menthol. Want me to rub it in?"

"Yes, please do." Asher breathed out. "I could go for a cigarette, actually."

Raum chuckled. "Stay awake, then."

It wasn't hard, not when Raum left his coat and boots on the floor and crawled onto the bed to straddle Asher from behind. Obviously, he did it this way to tease Asher, but Asher wasn't going to give him the satisfaction of acknowledgment. He stayed quiet, letting Raum work, and did his best to hide his delight.

Pleasant shivers worked their way through his back as Raum massaged the lotion into the area where the skin had torn. His hands followed the motions Addam had made cleaning the wings, spreading the lotion across the sore joints too, and Asher's body reacted the same. The pleasure burned much hotter this time and Asher let out an easy sigh.

"Mhm, you like that?" Raum whispered.

"More than I should. I liked it a little too much when Addam was washing my wings," Asher said and tried not to shudder as the lotion cooled his skin. It *was* cold. "I was *so* glad I was on my stomach."

Raum cackled. "Remember that crush we both had on him as kids?"

Asher made a face into the pillow. "Don't remind me."

"Just saying. I had to deal with him washing my wings too, you know."

They were silent for a little bit as Raum worked. It felt heavenly as his fingers moved; he had the same precision as when he used the tattoo gun. It made Asher think of other things Raum was good at using his hands for and quickly brushed those from his thoughts. Not right now. Not with this pain.

Raum's fingertips ghosted Judith's stitches. Asher's skin burned at the touch, making him wince, and Raum retracted his hand. Asher still hadn't seen them yet, but it must have looked ghastly enough to give even Raum pause.

"There's a lot of stitches," Raum whispered.

"That bad, huh?" Asher asked.

"It's neat, but you might get a scar. I can tattoo it after it heals, if you want."

"I'd like that."

Alongside the black shoulder and arm, Asher had become a willing canvas as his boyfriend learned the ins and outs of tattooing. Between them, they had sketchbooks filled with what was slowly becoming a tapestry across Asher's skin. Many geometric shapes, wide mystical looking eye, and the occasional little sparkles. They'd been planning an intricate work for his back, trading sketches back and forth for ideas, but all of them were based on getting devil wings. The idea just wouldn't work with angel wings.

Raum's lips met the back of Asher's neck, bringing him out of his thoughts. The attention made Asher's wings twitch. While the sudden movement stung, the kiss was worth it. He'd missed feeling Raum's lips on him.

It'd been a while since the last time. Not for lack of trying, though. Raum was busy at the tattoo parlor and running errands as expected of well-behaved devil wings for extra cash. Asher was... well, more depressed than anything else waiting for his wings and hadn't felt up to much of anything the past few months.

"You like that, too?" Raum asked, the soft movement of his lips brushing against Asher's skin.

"Yes," Asher said and hated that it came out like a whine. He closed his eyes and focused solely on how electric Raum's touch felt. How the heat of the kisses slowly made their way downward along his spine. "If I wasn't in so much pain, I'd say take me now. You're making it worse."

Raum withdrew his hands and Asher refrained from pouting as Raum took his entire weight away. Not Asher's intent. Before he could insist Raum could stay exactly where he'd been, Raum settled on the floor beside the bed again. He leaned his head against the mattress next to Asher's, brown eyes twinkling in the dim light.

"Maybe when you feel better." Raum winked and if Asher could have lifted his arm without his entire back hurting, he would have thrown a pillow at his boyfriend.

Raum must have seen the attempt; he took Asher's hand in his, always gentle, and laced their fingers together before he kissed the tattooed moons across Asher's hand.

And yet, his gaze flickered to the wings for a split second. A worried line worked its way into his brow. Asher tightened his fingers around Raum's.

"Everyone's disappointed, aren't they?" he whispered.

"Hm?"

"That I got angel wings."

Raum smiled sadly and folded his wings around himself so they resembled a dark cape down his back. Angel wings couldn't do the same.

"I'm not. I think they're cute. Has Amy come by yet?"

The quick diversion didn't go unnoticed, but

Asher left it be. It shouldn't have mattered if anyone was disappointed or not. Asher had angel wings and that was that. Everyone would just have to deal.

"I think Judith's keeping her away too," Asher said and tried to shrug. All he ended up doing was wincing, pain digging deep. Raum released his hand and placed it on Asher's back. His fingers went around it in a gentle circle, right between the wings. It felt heavenly.

"Most of the week's been a blur, anyway," Asher said. "If she has, I don't remember."

Raum rested his head close to Asher's again. "Bet she's been doing cartwheels, though. I might owe her five bucks."

Laughing hurt, but Asher couldn't help it. The bet had come about because Raum and Amy got their wings within weeks of each other and assumed Asher would be next. Then he wasn't. And wasn't. And wasn't for an entire three years.

Until now.

Raum pulled away, the absence of his hand stark, but Asher held his complaints as he watched his boyfriend take a pack of cigarettes from his bag. A godsend. They were both supposed to be quitting, but Asher didn't care right now. If it dulled the pain, made right what felt wrong, he'd do anything at this point.

Raum fished one out, lit it with practiced ease, and let Asher have it first. Asher shook more than he thought he would putting it to his lips, but he managed and took a deep drag. When he exhaled, he gave it back to Raum. Judith would probably lecture him about smoking inside, but it wasn't like Asher could sit on his windowsill right now. He'd apologize later.

The silence between them was easy. Cozy. It always was, ever since Asher and Raum first cuddled together in one of their rooms without Amy present. She was never interested in relationships or kissing, so she hadn't minded giving them their space.

One summer night, one of them had kissed the other (they always argued about who'd made the first move) and ever since, they'd been in a relationship.

Asher had thought for sure that when Raum had gotten his wings and left the foundling house, he'd want to move on from whatever their relationship was. It would have been easy to say it was simply a product of their past and now was the time to explore other possibilities. Asher wouldn't have blamed Raum, but Raum hadn't. He'd continued sharing his affections with Asher. Like nothing had changed.

Asher sometimes wondered if it should have, but he just as quickly brushed that thought away. He couldn't imagine life without Raum at this point and, quite frankly, wouldn't want it any other way.

He nudged his boyfriend gently and Raum lifted his eyebrows. "Are you staying the night?" Asher asked.

Raum glanced at the door as he took the last

drag on the cigarette. Everyone was fast asleep around them. The younger quartet of foundlings had rooms on the ground floor and were tucked in until morning. Judith and Addam's room was near the stairs on the other side of the second floor and they were huge proponents of early to bed, early to rise. Asher's room was on the same floor, but on the other side of the house.

Raum nodded. "I don't think Judith will mind, just this once."

Ignoring that there had been *many* times Raum had sneaked inside Asher's room late at night without anyone the wiser (at least, Asher hoped no one had known). It had been a while since the last one and while Asher was in no state for their usual activities, he was glad Raum was here.

After foundlings got their wings, it was customary for them to leave. Judith and Addam honestly wouldn't have minded if foundlings needed to stay for another year or two, but city officials would accuse them of either coddling the devil wings or obstructing the supposed divine right of the angel wings.

Besides, staying longer made it harder to leave.

Knowing that every foundling would leave one day, Judith did her best to make sure each one had funds and networking to help them find their footing. She acted as mediator between the city officials and angel wings to find the best place for them to do their duty, and kept money and connections to halfway houses ready to go for devil wings. Amy had lingered longer than Raum, but only because he'd already had another devil wing eager to look after him. Freedom was always Raum's goal and he'd taken to it with ease. Amy, meanwhile, had craved structure and found it doing exactly what the city expected of her.

Neither of them had ever truly been gone, but their visits had become infrequent. More times than Asher wanted to admit, he'd been left lonely in the foundling house. He'd never hold it against them, though. They had their own lives. He'd just wished for three years, he'd been part of them.

"Is that a yes?" Asher asked, smiling.

"I can't resist that face." Raum put out the cigarette and gave Asher his own smile. "You know that."

Raum leaned closer and pressed their lips together. If only Asher wasn't in so much pain; he wanted to feel the warmth of Raum's lips for so much longer. All over his body. Make up for lost time when they were too busy to meet up. But even as their kisses turned heavier, dragging soft sighs out of each other, Asher couldn't keep up. The pain was reaching across his shoulders again. Boring into them. Making it so hard to just enjoy himself with his boyfriend.

Asher had to part first, seething. Raum was always understanding. No matter what kind of mood Asher was or wasn't in, he had so much grace and patience. Asher had no idea what he'd done to deserve such a boyfriend.

"Sorry," Asher whispered anyway.

"When you're better." Raum kissed his cheek. "Want me to curl up with you?"

"God, yes, please. I can at least move over."

It was embarrassing that Asher needed help doing that too, but his limbs felt so weak. Raum gently moved him and squeezed in close. His shoulders had filled out since leaving the house and he'd had a small growth spurt too, so he didn't quite fit in Asher's bed like he used to. Asher was scrawny and short in comparison, but at least it made it all the easier for Raum to wrap him up.

Until wings got in the way. What was once easy for Raum to wrap his wings around Asher in a kind of second hug wasn't happening tonight. Asher winced when Raum tried, the tips of his boyfriend's wings brushing painfully against the stitches. Raum whispered an apology as he got himself resituated. He draped one arm across Asher's waist and slid the other one underneath the pillow instead of curling it beneath Asher to pull him closer. Raum left his wings laying off the side of the bed, but Asher missed their usual squeeze.

"Better?" Raum asked softly.

"Much." Asher kissed him. "Thank you."

As Asher rested his head against Raum's chest, he breathed his boyfriend in as deep as he could. The leather lingering from his riding jacket, the comforting scent of sandalwood from his cologne though faded from the day, and the smell of ink. It was all Raum. Soothing. Warm. It wrapped Asher right up, making him really believe that maybe everything would still be normal when he opened his eyes in the morning.

2
Dawn of a New Day

RAYS OF SUN found Asher's window at the break of dawn, and this time, it really felt like the dawn of a new day. The pain had lessened to a dull ache and, more importantly, Raum was there. It had grown cold overnight, but that only meant Asher could snuggle closer for warmth. He was content to close his eyes again, thoroughly enjoying this fuzzy time where he and Raum had nothing to do, but then his door opened.

Judith sighed, loud enough for Raum to jerk awake, and the door latched shut again.

"All right, Raum," she said from the hallway. "Be gentle. He's still healing."

The floorboards creaked as she walked away, almost deliberately as though to make sure they both knew she hadn't lingered outside the door. Asher bit back a laugh and Raum smothered his own against Asher's black hair.

"Gentle, huh?" he said and kissed the top of Asher's head.

Asher's body shook with more stifled laughter and his wings twitched involuntarily in response. The motion sent pain darting through his back, but one he could deal with. He wasn't going to let it ruin this. "Do you think she knew when we sneaked into each other's rooms?"

Raum cringed. "I don't want to think about her knowing when we were fooling around."

Good point. Neither did Asher. He made the same face as Raum, eliciting a chuckle from him. It faded quickly and Raum cupped Asher's chin to kiss him. Chaste and quick, not at all like the one from last night that still sent butterflies through Asher's stomach. This one was a promise for later.

"I have to get back." Raum peeled himself away and Asher hid his disappointment. "Judith probably wants to talk about everything coming up anyway."

Asher flopped onto his pillow, sighing. "Don't remind me."

"It won't be so bad." Raum bent over to kiss Asher's cheek this time. The stubble lining his jaw was scratchy this early in the morning. Asher had missed it. "Call me if you want me to sneak over again, all right?"

Asher struggled lifting his arm to wrap it around Raum's neck to pull him closer. The pain stretched out across his shoulders, making him huff, but Raum got the picture and leaned in. Asher kissed him on the cheek.

"I will. When I can walk, I'll come by to visit the shop."

Because after everything—all the talking, planning, and healing—Asher knew he'd need time outside the house. If only to pretend everything was normal for a little longer. It'd be even better if it became alone time with Raum.

Raum nodded, planting another kiss on the top of Asher's head, and withdrew to pull on his boots and jacket. Another kiss found its way to Asher's cheek before Raum deftly stepped over him to get back to the window.

Whenever he visited, Raum liked climbing through Asher's window. Something about it being more romantic than the door. Asher indulged him, of course, and left the window unlocked every night. There was a lattice fence against the wall that neither Judith nor Addam had taken down yet and Raum took full advantage of it. Although Asher was sure if it hadn't been there, Raum would have found a way into the shed and hauled out a ladder.

When Raum was outside, ready to descend, he stretched his wings proudly behind him. The dawn light caught them just right, outlining them in gold.

Show off. Asher snickered as Raum began his descent, a knowing grin on his lips. His boots clunked with each step and it was a wonder the trellis could still hold his weight.

"Raum!" Addam's frustrated voice came from the back patio. His very *what the hell are you doing'* voice. Raum and Asher had heard it too many times as kids. "Use the door like a normal person, would you?"

"Next time!" Raum called back and Asher imagined the way Addam shook his head in exasperation. "Promise!"

The rumble of Raum's motorbike soon sang through the air, becoming a soothing rhythm as it sped off into the city waking up for the day. Raum's bike would be lost to the sounds of traffic before long. Asher listened for it as long as he could until he had no choice but to let it go. What Asher would have given to be speeding off with him, with devil wings instead of his angel ones.

He closed his eyes, hoping to drift off into a daydream where that was reality. It felt like no more than a second, imagining the wind through his hair and the autumn sun kissing his skin, before a knock resounded from his door. Not Judith's; she knocked with purpose. This was softer than that.

Asher opened an eye as his door creaked open. His fellow foundling, Amy, was peeking her head inside.

Well, fellow angel wing now.

They made eye contact and it was enough of an invitation for her to let herself in. Asher didn't mind; she was like a sister to him. In her arms was her usual basket and on her lips was a hopeful smile.

Like Raum, she was tall and it felt like she always had been. Unlike Raum, however, she had a willowy frame that never quite filled out. Maybe it was an angel wing thing; Asher was in similar straits. Delicate with angular limbs.

Her brown wings brushed in behind her, the

longest feathers reaching down to her fingertips. The sun always had a way of making her wings almost gold too. Her hair matched her wings, golden shimmer and all. She kept it pulled back in a high ponytail with a number of wisps always escaping despite her efforts otherwise. Her skin was pale, but splashed with freckles the same as Raum's.

"I see Raum already sneaked in," Amy said, eyeing the jar of pain lotion on the nightstand. "Maybe I should have scaled the lattice, too."

Imagining her climbing it made Asher snort and he covered his smile. Raum was always the athletic one of the three of them. He wasn't sure Amy could have done it.

She plopped herself down where Raum had sat last night, tucking her legs beneath her skirt, and by then, Asher had managed to sit up on his elbows. Not as much pain as before. Maybe the lotion was working.

"That obvious?" Asher asked.

"I heard Addam scolding him." Amy wrinkled her nose. Right. The cigarettes. Any other time, she'd pull a Judith and comment on it, but instead, she forged on with her mission and held up her basket. "I brought you more goodies!"

Asher smirked at her. "It's not even my birthday." Amy sighed and flicked his shoulder. "Raum gave me the lotion. I think it's working. I'm not nearly as miserable."

"Think you can stand?"

Trying did *not* go well. Resting on his elbows was one thing, but standing was another.

He collapsed back on his bed after the attempt, pain pushing its way up and down his spine, reminding him it was definitely still there. Amy apologetically smoothed another handful of lotion across his back. Swift with precision, her hands didn't linger like Raum's did.

Once he was settled, the chill seeping into his back once more, Amy sat on the floor and retrieved the items from her basket.

A small hairdryer. A spray bottle filled with a clear liquid. A bag of gummy bears. And, lastly, a handbound book.

Amy placed the gummy bears on the nightstand. "Obviously, for eating. Judith said you weren't able to keep down much food at first. I hope it's better."

"It better be," Asher said, eyeing the colorful bag. They were his favorite brand, too.

Amy held up the hairdryer in front of him before he could rip open the bag.

"This is for your wings," she said. "Small, easy to use, and it's battery operated, but I have a plug in here too, just in case." The hair dryer was black with a toggle to adjust the heat. Just like any other hairdryer, then.

"The heat feels *really* nice, believe me. When you wash your wings, you want to make sure they're thoroughly dry. Sometimes letting them air-dry doesn't quite work."

Asher frowned. "Devil wings have it easier in the department, then."

"Devil wings aren't good for warmth in the winter," Amy shot back, like she'd expected the comment, and Asher chuckled. Her wings pulled close to her in a protective huddle. "Just imagine: sitting and watching the snow with a cup of hot cocoa in your hands, your wings around you. It's comforting."

She had a point. "I'd rather have Raum around me," he said and she made a dramatic show of rolling her eyes. "Although, it *does* sound comforting."

Amy's wings lifted behind her. When he set the hairdryer back down, resolving to use it when he could handle standing long enough for a real shower, she held out the spray bottle.

"A coating for your feathers," she said. "Just spritz and pat with a towel. Keeps your feathers from getting too dirty while out and about. White wings have a bit more trouble staying clean than mine would." She spritzed the air between them and Asher sniffed. Pine trees. "I tried to find a more manly scent. Patrons usually gift me flower scents. Is this okay? I can probably find another one if it's not."

"It reminds me of when the three of us used to run through the woods," Asher said. "I like it."

"That's what I thought too." Amy stared at the bottle and her wings drooped until they'd spread out on the floor around her. She wore her emotions on her sleeve, and her wings made them much more obvious. "I miss that."

Asher rested his head against his pillow, leaning toward her. "Me too."

Foundlings hardly ever made friends with normal children. While the city insisted foundlings get the same education as others while they waited for their wings, no one wanted to interact with them beyond manufactured niceties. Everyone knew their lives were transitory. Once they got their wings, they'd likely never see their peers again. Asher honestly wished Addam had homeschooled them, and always wondered why he hadn't. It would have saved them the pain of dealing with others.

When the other children didn't accept Asher, Amy, or Raum, the three of them had taken to exploring the woods along the hillside near the house. It had felt large and mystical as a child, but as they'd grown, the city had built over bits and pieces to make more suburbs. Wildflower groves had given way to manicured lawns or concrete parking lots. The woods still existed, a sliver of it, but it was a mere park at best with a paved path going through it, ruining some of the mysticism it had once held. It was now a space the city controlled.

Asher glanced at Amy. Like the woods, she'd become something the city controlled too, but that came with angel wings. Thinking so dragged his mood down even further, the silence between them growing taut. Amy must have seen it too. She wouldn't look at him.

Angel wings lived their lives in service to the city. They were expected to take residence in one of the many 'nests' the city built and, while there, listen to the confessions of the masses and help guide them somehow. Supposedly, through giving a confession to the angel wing, whatever was wrong would be absolved and the confessor would go on to live a better life.

It sounded like bullshit to Asher. A holdover from some religious doctrine with no basis in truth. Just confessing something didn't make it better. It just made the angel wing some divine symbol to be controlled. Gawked at.

And it was what awaited Asher.

He twisted his fingers into his bedsheets and tried to push out the thoughts. Amy loved being a typical angel wing. She liked helping. It wasn't her fault that Asher didn't share her sentiments. That he'd thought of himself like that tiny park, once wild and free, now manicured and controlled to fit the city's whims like he would be as an angel wing.

Amy didn't deserve him taking out his frustrations on her.

Slowly, he reached out and touched Amy's hand. To comfort her. To find something for himself to hold onto, even if only for a moment. Anchor him back to some reality where things weren't as bad as he was making them out to be.

"Sorry," she said. "Just nostalgic today…" She cleared her voice and turned to the final item. "Last, but not least, I brought you this." She presented the handbound book to Asher and he couldn't help but smile warmly at it.

One of her hobbies was binding books. Asher already had plenty; all of his sketchbooks had been bound by her. If he ever needed another one, she'd have it whipped up in a day.

"I wanted to give this to you sooner—you

know, before you got your wings—but then you went and got them. I might have rushed it at the end."

Neatly written out in her practiced calligraphy was the title: *Wings Tips & Tricks*. Pride swelled in Asher's chest. There wasn't much material for angel or devil wings to learn about themselves. If they found a diary secondhand, great, but there was nothing officially written. This was as close as Asher—any foundling after him—was going to get. That Amy had put it together all on her own was sweet.

"I figure if I was lost... others would be too. Like you." Amy sidled closer and propped the book open between them. "Raum helped me fill out the devil wing parts. We're actually rather similar, deep down."

Not that Asher needed to be told. They were just wings people assigned meaning to, regardless if that meaning was correct or not.

"I have a section for pain management and stretches too." Amy paused and drew her gaze over his back. She made a face. "Although, I guess I'm a little late for the pain management part."

"You think?" Asher teased and she giggled.

"The stretches help though!" she insisted. "Wings can feel heavy sometimes, so make sure you do them! It'll strengthen your back muscles."

"I'll just have Raum carry my wings."

Amy snorted and slapped his arm gently. "He can't do that! Come on, Ash, I'm serious."

"I know, I know!"

Her feathers ruffled and she moved to the next section. "I had Judith write up a how-to for mending your clothes. I even made the illustrations!" She flipped through the book and stopped at the detailed sketch of a wing's skeletal structure.

Out of the three of them, Asher and Raum were the artists, but it was nice to see Amy had picked up a few things. She was very good at replicating what she saw, though she had trouble coming up with something totally on her own. Raum had drawn a few illustrations beside hers, and his were done with surer strokes.

Asher wished he could have helped—no one had even asked—but he bit the jealousy back. It wasn't like he would have known what to contribute, especially since he'd spent much of the year depressed and frustrated over his lack of wings.

Before Asher could compliment her sketches, she handed the whole book over and scrunched up her shoulders, embarrassed.

"I'm sorry, I'm rambling, aren't I?"

"Aw, I think it's cute."

"I know." She smiled shyly. "I just made it to help you. Anyone, really. You don't have to keep it if you don't want to."

Asher gently flipped through the book on his own. The pages were neatly typed and smelled like the ink ribbon of an old typewriter. Typical Amy.

When she was younger, she'd steal away with Judith's typewriter and use up all the ink until Judith knew something was up. Then, Amy had begun hoarding ink ribbons in her room. There were many times when they were younger that she'd have to hide ink-stained fingers behind her back so Judith didn't know how often she'd used the typewriter. Asher and Raum had always been her lookouts.

Judith had probably always known just how often and began leaving her reams of paper.

As it was, her book looked professional and was impressive. It was so like Amy. She lived the ideal angel wing life, putting her heart and soul into anything helpful.

"I want to keep it," Asher said quietly and Amy's wings perked up. "You do have copies, right? I'd hate to keep this from the kids."

Amy nodded. "I went to that new print shop down my street and made a bunch of copies. I thought you should keep the originals." She took the book back and pointed at the spine.

A chain stitch binding kept it all together. It was precise and neat and she was clearly proud. The sketchbooks she'd made for Asher and Raum back in the day were... Well, they were clearly made with love, even though the stitching was loose and messy now. This, however, was practically flawless.

"I'm getting better at this part. Next, I'm going to try making hardback books."

"And they'll look amazing," Asher said. "Do you remember the little booklets you made at school? Those were your first ones and even they looked great."

Amy's cheeks flushed and she attempted to cover her face. The booklets had actually been a rant about how callous their peers were after a group of them had held Asher down in the schoolyard to see if he really had a purple tongue. While the rant didn't have much of an impact (Raum beating everyone up did), it had shown everyone that Amy *could* bite back. The kids traded those booklets for days before they eventually disappeared from the classroom.

With the gifts doled out, the easy distraction from the obvious faded. The room became silent. Amy unburied her face and peeked at Asher's wings again.

Sighing, she thumped back against his nightstand. "White angel wings," she finally said. "I honestly didn't believe it."

"Think any watcher will have me?"

She didn't answer. It was kinder than saying no to his face, at least, but the rejection still stung. With his reputation, however, he'd already figured as much.

To help angel wings perform their duties, the city gave them watchers. Once, before the city became more secular, watchers were religious leaders appointed to the role. Now, they were individuals voted on by the city council.

Same difference, really.

Watchers worked as liaisons between the city and the angel wing, making sure if the angel wing had a problem, the city would fix it. They were also in charge of taking care of the angel wing's needs and their nest.

Nests were small buildings across the city with a confessional on the ground floor and a small apartment for the angel wing on the second. Those who lived nearby (or even tourists from other places without angel wings), would be encouraged to visit and if needed, confess some malady they'd done or seek advice. A little money would be donated and that money would cycle back into the system, being used on whatever the watcher deemed necessary for the angel wing. Be it upkeep on the nest, to help the community at large, or even to line their own pockets. Amy insisted watchers didn't actually do that, but Asher had his doubts.

When Amy got her wings, every watcher without an angel wing had tried to push one another aside to partner with her, even some from cities away. She was what they believed every angel wing should aspire to be: kind, a good listener, and most of all, approachable.

Asher doubted he had any of those qualities, but that had been the point. He'd tried to game the system being everything an angel wing wasn't to ensure he'd have devil wings, and the universe decided he'd pay for that.

It wasn't even like the devil wings had it easy. They had freedom from expectation, sure, but the city treated them like burdens to endure. No homes were given to them, they had no real way to better their lives, and they were blamed for everything that went wrong. As a result, most devil wings acted out. Why bother being nice when the city and its people had already decided you were wrong? In more religious circles, people liked to say devil wings were the city's sins personified, but that was bullshit and everyone knew it.

Still, Asher had wanted to be a devil wing because it'd meant *freedom*. At least then he'd have been in charge of his own life.

"I don't know," Amy said finally. "Judith always has a plan."

"When we're predictable," Asher said and inclined his head toward her. Absentmindedly, she reached out and gently ran her fingers through his hair, brushing it back. "You got room in your nest?"

Amy considered him sadly. They both knew it didn't work that way.

By design, angel wings were solitary. Being away from others supposedly meant they could listen more effectively. Realistically, it was easier to control someone who was alone. Asher was sure if Amy's watcher was more of a hard ass for tradition, Amy would have been discouraged from coming back to the foundling house at all. Small miracles, Amy could come and go as she pleased.

Devil wings, on the other hand, tended to stick together, creating small crews that haunted whatever city they resided in. Sometimes, they'd do odd jobs for cash, but other times they caused mayhem for the hell of it. Most knew how to toe the line so cops never got seriously involved. Besides, most cities didn't like to lock up too many devil wings, like it was bad luck or something. Other undesirables also joined them, of course, but it was more the merrier after a certain point. They'd look out for each other.

Sounded much less lonely than what awaited Asher as an angel wing.

"It'll work out," Amy whispered. "I promise."

Ever the optimist, but she had to be. Every problem had to have a solution, according to her. Asher wasn't so sure. The only thing awaiting him was a watcher who'd lock him in a cage and force him to play the part when all he wanted to do was spread his wings.

Silence blanketed the room once more. Asher wished he could believe as much as Amy did. It'd be easier. Maybe then the dread of what-ifs wouldn't have filled his stomach. Maybe then he wouldn't feel like his life was ending. He was being dramatic, but he couldn't imagine what his life was going to be now and he hated it.

Easing out a sigh, he reached for the gummy bears. Sugar would keep the dread at bay. He took a handful and gave Amy the bag so she could take her own. She smiled at him, her expression tinged with her own exhaustion, and took a handful.

By the time the bag was empty, Amy was stealing glances at the digital clock on the shelf. Almost noon. Each angel wing set hours for when they'd be available. Some liked to always be available, but Amy had the sense to make strict times. Noon to five and then a short seven to nine for those with typical day jobs.

She unfolded herself and stood. "I have to go

or they'll panic when I'm not there to say hi." She bent over and kissed Asher on the forehead. "You rest up. Have faith in Judith."

Asher smiled at her as best he could. "I'll try."

Because that was all he could do. Amy looked like she wanted to say more, words obvious on her lips, but she swallowed them back. Instead, she took her now empty basket, nodded, and left without looking back.

Resting was easy, at least. Asher only wished having faith was. He sunk his head into his pillows and closed his eyes, begging for sleep so he didn't have to think. To worry. To hope he'd wake up and find the angel wings were a lie and that he'd had devil wings all along.

Sleep never came and reality persisted.

Foundling Blues

IT WAS ANOTHER day before Asher managed to sit up without help. And another day after that before he could stand without immediately wanting to lay back down. The pain was still there, stark when he reached too far, but when he managed pulling on a pair of jeans instead of old shorts, he figured it was time to get on with his life.

Food had stopped coming right back up, thankfully, and he needed more than oatmeal and gummy bears. Cereal sounded good today. Perhaps the eggs he could smell wafting through the house. He could manage that much. Or, at least, he'd make himself manage it. Life was too boring drifting in and out of sleep. Fantasizing about what he'd do to Raum once he felt well enough took only so much time.

Judith hadn't come in to talk to him about everything yet, but she had left his newly mended shirts folded on his dresser. Each shirt had slits in the back for his wings. Judith had the stitching down to an artform. Amy's shirts had been embroidered with flowers while Raum's had spirals resembling ink. Asher was, thankfully, not left out; she'd given him geometric designs along the slits—diamonds, triangles, and even the eyeball design he had tattooed on his right shoulder. The embroidery was sweet.

The first attempt at getting his wings through his shirt ended badly. He'd tried pulling it on too fast and ended up pushing his wings flush against his back, aggravating the stitches.

The second try was not much better. He was gentler this time, but trying to reach around to maneuver his wings through the slits made hot tears collect in his eyes.

The third try, he didn't even bother. He just grabbed one of the tank tops Amy had left behind. It went over his head and tied up the sides. Easy. The slits for the wings were basically holes, not really decent for going anywhere, but it'd be fine for around the house.

Asher caught himself in the mirror hanging off his closet. Yep. Still looked wrecked. Black hair a mess, barely tamed with his fingers. Green eyes betraying how exhausted he was despite all the sleep. He tried smiling at himself just to feel normal. There was the typical crooked lift of his lips where the scar was. Usual Asher awkward smile. How he looked in most photos. It wasn't like he didn't know *how* to smile; there was a candid shot in Judith's photo album that someone had once gotten of him and Raum with real smiles. Not like this one. Today was not a real smile day.

At least he was dressed and decent. Even if the white wings made him want to smash the mirror.

Downstairs, the house was waking up for a normal day. The quartet of foundlings—the knee-high ankle-biters as Asher liked to tease—were accosting Addam in the kitchen while he made breakfast. Scrambled eggs with sausage and toast. Special breakfast today. Usually, it was cereal and bananas. Maybe he'd been hoping to entice Asher downstairs.

It worked, even though Asher immediately had second thoughts seeing the kids.

Asher was... not good with children.

They were sticky, asked way too many questions, and made it a point to never give him peace if he stepped out of his room. Amy and Raum had been the perfect distraction (they were great with kids), but since they'd left, the quartet was bolder. No longer held back by a grimace, if they felt the need to, they'd assert their presence and Asher just had to deal with it. It was a wonder none of them had disturbed his bedrest.

The four of them were raven haired and pale, and although they looked related to each other, they weren't. No foundlings ever were, even if they were dropped off together. Scant research had been done years ago by some curious geneticist and all they'd gleaned from it was that foundlings were not related to each other. They weren't related to *anyone*.

The one with the freckles all over was Aubrey. She insisted pink was the only color that *ever* existed and typically wore pink everything. She took the leadership role amongst her foundling siblings; if one of them needed something and was too shy to ask, she'd do it for them.

Caroline and Liberty liked to pretend they were twins, always endeavoring to wear the same thing to confuse onlookers, but their faces gave them away. Caroline had a wide nose and small eyes whereas Liberty had a small nose and wide eyes.

The last one, the shy boy who liked books and enjoyed existing silently with Asher when he got the chance, was Claude. Glasses balanced on his nose, a little too big for his face, but it was cute paired with the freckles across his cheeks.

As usual, Aubrey was watching Addam so closely, she must have been trying to learn through osmosis. Asher figured she'd be an angel wing, but corrected himself. It literally could be random. If she was a devil wing though, they'd suddenly be organized and that'd be a real terror for the city. He silently hoped for it.

Caroline and Liberty sat at the table and stared so intently at each other, they must have been having a staring contest. Neither of them blinked, at any rate. A little scary, but kids did whatever kids wanted to do to have fun.

Claude was the only one who'd picked his head up when Asher came in. His eyes darted to the new angel wings and his jaw dropped.

Aubrey turned, likely some foundling sibling sense alerting her to confusion afoot, and
her eyes went wide upon seeing Asher. It was
only then did Liberty blink, allowing her and
Caroline to stare at him too.

"Oh my gosh!" Aubrey squealed, ducking
around Addam's attempt to stop her so she could
come closer.

Shit. Asher had no time to move; in seconds,
the four of them were upon him. He turned,
keeping his wings away from Aubrey first and
foremost. Of the four, she was very touch first,
ask questions later.

She huffed and pointed instead. "You really
got angel wings! I thought Amy was kidding!"

"They're pretty!" Caroline said and attempted to pet them. Asher spun again, getting
away from her, and intercepted Liberty's hands
as she tried to pet them from his other side.

The four of them had still been pretty young
when Amy and Raum got their wings, and
nowhere near as bold. As he kept his eyes on the
three girls, ready to intercept them again, a
gentle hand petted Asher's wings from behind.
Asher took solace that it was only Claude.

Unfortunately, moving as quickly as Asher
had to avoid the others reignited the pain. He
seethed, trying not to snap at the foundlings.

"All right, all right." Addam finally swooped
around Asher. Aubrey's hand was in his and
Caroline was quickly under one arm. Because
Caroline was contained, so was Liberty. She
raced after Addam as he deposited the caught

children at the table now full of breakfast. Claude lingered another moment before he hurried to join his foundling sisters.

"Eat before you're late for school." Addam straightened his back as the kids dug in and he nodded at Asher. "I fixed you a plate, too."

Stomach grumbling, Asher happily took it. Fluffy eggs done just the way he liked them (probably on purpose), maple flavored sausage, and toast smothered in jam.

Asher settled pointedly at the counter next to Addam as the man cleaned the dishes. The kids had run of the table and Asher would not risk sitting with them. Addam didn't seem to mind; there was a smirk on his lips.

As Asher took a bite, the foundlings grew quiet, their eyes trained on the door to the hallway. Asher swallowed, grimacing, and looked too. Judith stood there, watching him hopefully.

Asher sighed, thumping his head against the low cabinet. Now that he was up and about, she took it as time for the Talk. Get his entire life sorted in one single morning. Couldn't even let him eat breakfast first.

Honestly, their Talk should have already happened. Raum and Amy had healed quickly and had their lives planned mere days after getting their wings. It made sense to do it now. Get what was stalled for three years and some months rolling again.

The one bite of eggs he'd managed burned in his stomach, but he forced it to stay down, and slipped off the counter to follow Judith. Her office was past the living room, just off the stairway landing on the far side of the house.

Judith's office had been the sunroom once and still looked like it if one ignored her desk and shelves. Windows lined two of the walls, letting in natural light. The raised garden beds were just outside, blooming their last autumn flowers before winter arrived.

The room was always clean and tidy, matching her as a person. Everything had its place. Bookshelf near the door with books on different subjects, the city's history with angel and devil wings, and some psychology mixed in. Next to that was a cabinet of toys and board-games Asher, Raum, and Amy had raided too many times to count. Simpler times.

Judith's desk was against the far wall, perfectly illuminated by the sunlight streaming in, and another bookcase sat behind it with all her files and folders neatly shelved. There were packets detailing her previous foundlings, maps of the city around each nest, and binders full of places that would be happy to give a devil wing a place to stay while they got their footing.

In the center of the desk, she had Asher's folder. His entire life summarized. Though he was curious what exactly she'd written about him, he ignored it for now (he'd learn eventually) and sat in the plush stool facing the desk. He would have rather had the armchair she'd pushed aside to make room for the stool so he could curl up in it, but on second thought, his wings would get in the way.

Judith settled in, sorting a few papers that had gone askew, and Asher studied her.

A serious woman with broad shoulders and a soft face of gentle curves and deep-set eyes. Black hair seldom left down and, instead, pinned in a tight bun. When not acting as the professional she was with a muted color pantsuit pressed perfectly for the day, she'd wear cozy sweaters with jeans and sneakers. The perfect mom look.

Asher wished he was staring at the foundling house mother, but she was the professional today. Ready at a moment's notice to meet with city officials on Asher's behalf like he was a kid still.

Not like he wanted to meet with them on his own. Not enough patience on his part.

Judith hesitated, silent, and then eased out an exhale. "I'm glad to see you're eating."

"I feel a little better," Asher admitted, placing his plate on the desk. He poked at his eggs with his fork. "I'm kinda screwed, aren't I?"

"I'm not saying that."

"But you aren't saying that it's not true, either."

She didn't try to placate him with lies or a fuzzy truth. Never had. Sometimes Asher appreciated that about her, but not today. He could have used a well-meaning lie right about now.

She stared at him, silent, and her eyes pierced right through him. All her plans—hell, all of Asher's plans—had rested on him getting devil wings. He'd already secured himself a place to go, but he'd had to wait for his wings.

It would have been above a small gardening boutique Asher had found accidentally. The owner had already said yes. He'd even saved up money from odd jobs to make the move easier. Raum had even been ready to look after him.

All of it ruined with feathers of all things.

Angel wings didn't just live anywhere in the city. They had a purpose, whether they wanted to fulfill that purpose or not, and that purpose was inside a nest. Except who would want Asher? He didn't want them.

The silence grew uncomfortable and Asher's wings chose this as the time to spasm. He winced, the pain working its way through his shoulder blades, and Judith looked ready to get up. The wings calmed down all on their own and she settled back in, still worriedly watching them.

He had to convince her he was fine. As a show of normalcy, he took his toast with a shaky hand and nibbled on it.

He didn't want to be there. He wanted to be in his room again with Raum, cuddling in the morning twilight where reality never mattered as much as it did now.

Judith leaned back in her chair with another sigh, this one resigned, and she peered down at a page on top of the pile. Asher refused to let his gaze flit across it. He already knew it didn't say anything useful. Names and numbers scratched out.

"Only one watcher has returned my calls," she said slowly. "The rest haven't responded."

"Because I'm not Amy."

Judith pressed her lips together. "Asher..."

She'd never outright blame him, but Asher knew it was entirely his fault. After Raum got his wings, Asher wasn't shy about riding with him and other devil wings through the city, being a menace simply by association. He and Raum had been up and down the streets too fast on Raum's motorbike without a care in the world, their laughter carrying on the wind.

Hell, they'd even made a game of going to the junkyard and smashing shit for fun. Not to mention all the graffiti art Asher had graced the city with to give his anxious hands something to do. Many times, he'd crawl through his window near dawn with paint all over himself from an entire night of art.

Sure, he technically never made legal trouble for Judith—or got caught in anything that would have—but he'd toed the line enough times that people would rather reject him outright now than trust him as their angel wing. No one liked empty nests, but it was apparently better than trusting an angel wing once known as a nuisance.

"I'm still getting in contact with other cities," Judith suggested slowly, watching Asher for a reaction. "They might be more willing."

"They'd ask around here and find a reason to say no," Asher said and looked away. Besides, he didn't *want* to go to a whole different city. His entire life was right here with Raum and Amy. With the streets he'd long since memorized.

Judith nodded, understanding his hesitation

without him having to explain it. She pulled papers from her stack. "In that case, Watcher Bartholomew seemed interested." She slid over a business card and a photo.

Asher almost said no on the name alone—that sounded too stuck in the past—but he gave Judith the benefit of the doubt and looked.

Bartholomew was a middle-aged man with thinning blonde hair and dark eyes. He didn't look like he enjoyed photos any more than Asher did. Though his expression was a little dour, there was a certain pride with the way he'd held himself.

"He made a case for Amy as well, although she felt Wendolyn fit her needs better. He's been here for twenty-five years now and the city holds him in high esteem," Judith explained.

Asher resumed picking at his eggs. They'd grown cold. He ate one of the sausages before replying. "Is this how it went with Amy? You handed her business cards and photos and she picked someone she liked?"

Once more, Judith made a calculated pause. "Well, there are meetings too," she said. "More were open to hosting her, and she had a pool of good candidates and streets to research." She clasped her hands together on the desk. "As of now, you only have Bartholomew, but I am trying to reach out to more. Maybe they just weren't expecting it. There are three empty nests, after all, surely one more will be amenable to you."

The city was large enough to be divided into

six districts, although they were only called that to make it easier to situate angel wings and their nests. Smaller cities obviously had less. Sometimes only one. Watchers looked over their districts and answered to an elected board, but Asher didn't know much about that.

Besides, reaching out to the watchers who hadn't bothered contacting Judith yet would only prove Asher's fears. No one wanted him. Even though the city believed nests *had* to be filled or the city would suffer—superstitious bullshit, honestly—watchers knew there were four other foundlings after Asher. Chances were, two of them would be angel wings. Why take the chance on an angel wing known for causing problems when they only had to wait a little longer for someone who wasn't a nuisance? Addam and Judith were probably watching the quartet a lot closer than they'd ever watched Asher so they didn't have a repeat of this.

Thinking about it left Asher sadder than he wanted to admit. One watcher curious and it was the one Amy didn't choose. There had to be a reason beyond Wendolyn was simply better, and chances were, Asher wouldn't like the man.

He swallowed his dread and set the plate on the desk. There was still one more option.

"Could you just... sign my independence over to me?" Asher tried.

Judith made another calculated pause. A tenseness tightened her shoulders, giving away her discomfort. It wasn't entirely unheard of, Asher was sure. Foundlings were wards of the city and remained that way until they got their wings. Then they were either free with the caveat of nowhere to go (devil wings), or signed over to the wardship of a watcher (angel wings). There had to be some middle ground.

"That's what you were going to do if I didn't get my wings by my twentieth birthday, right?" Asher continued. "You were talking about it with Addam a few weeks ago."

"I was..." Judith said slowly. "I didn't know you were awake."

Asher shrugged. "So? Can't you?"

"You have your wings now," Judith explained and Asher frowned. "Asher, that was a just-in-case because I knew you were getting restless here. Now that you have wings, and angel wings at that, the city won't accept the request, especially since there are nests to be filled."

"Nests that don't want me," Asher argued.

"One's open to you."

Asher bit down on his lip and glanced away. "And it doesn't matter if I don't want that one?"

That was the real question and stopped Judith's next reply. She wasn't callous enough to say out loud that no, the city didn't care about what Asher wanted. Even though it was the truth. He was trapped within this system by virtue of having feathers.

"All right," he said, throat stiff. "I-I should talk to Belle at her shop, then. Tell her I'm not the devil wing we thought."

Not much he could do about the watcher situation. Might as well do something about the situation he *could* influence. Even if it just meant telling the gardening shop he couldn't stay there.

"Actually," Judith said slowly, thinking, "you should ask her if she'd like to host you."

Asher lifted his eyebrows. "Excuse me?"

Judith searched for paperwork buried under others. Some photocopy of a photocopy from an old book. The text was grainy and hard to read. Judith squinted at it.

"Technically, the apartment Belle set aside for you *could* be considered a nest. It fits the dimensions," she explained. "Since the city has become more secular about angel wings, it's not like you need to be above what was once essentially a chapel. And besides, this isn't unheard of. There was a case a few years ago where the city had no open nests and the angel wing didn't want to leave. So, the angel wing became the ward of a very nice stationary shop owner and had their nest there. They still performed their duties to the city, although I'm not sure exactly how they arranged it, but it proves it's possible."

Not quite freedom, but it sounded preferable. Especially if it'd be with Belle. "Really?" Asher asked. "They'd let me do that?"

"It never hurts to ask if she'd be willing." Judith put the papers down and nodded. "I want you to have options, Asher, and we are coming up incredibly short. Maybe Belle will shuck off tradition. Once I have her permission, I can use that to make the case. No one wants you miserable, Asher."

If anyone in the city would shuck tradition,

Belle would. She was already a huge advocate of the devil wings and did what she could to support them. She made them little care packages if they graced her shop, supported them in town-hall meetings when the rest of the city was ready to use devil wings as their usual scapegoats, and even helped collect funds for the few that were interested in furthering their education.

It left her a little ostracized from the many that wrote devil wings off as worthless, but she got by with her wife just fine and supported devil wings anyway.

Asher found himself nodding and kept nodding as he stood. It wasn't a bad idea. Not perfect, but much better than what he'd been dreading. He was brought out of his thoughts when Judith came out from behind the desk.

She was smiling, the professionalism melting into the softness he'd wanted when he'd followed her in.

"Thank you," Asher said.

"We'll figure this out." Judith gazed over his back and tilted her head. "Did you want help getting into one of your mended shirts? I know it's hard while your back's healing."

"I'd like that." Asher chuckled and picked at his shirt. "A little too cold to be running around in this old thing, huh?"

Dressing with Judith's practiced hands guiding his wings went well. A black tee went over his head and wings were gently guided out of the slits. The dark burgundy flannel slipped on just as easily. He hoped he didn't need more.

Trying to pull on his paint-stained denim jacket was a nightmare and he promised Judith he'd be warm enough without it.

With both the shirt and flannel on, he looked a little more put together. Judith even assured him that removing everything was easier alone.

"I can drive you, if you want," Judith offered, following Asher through the house.

"It's fine," Asher insisted. "I'd like to do at least one thing on my own."

Besides, if Belle rejected their idea, he didn't want Judith to see him cry.

Judith hesitated, like she wanted to insist for her own peace of mind, but she acquiesced with a nod. "I understand. I'll be meeting with city officials this evening. Addam will be taking the kids to their baseball event and then ice cream afterward with the team. Will you be all right on your own later?"

Asher nodded and smiled. "I'm standing and walking. I think I'm over the worst of it."

A walk by himself was what he desperately needed. Not the reminder she'd bring that he'd screwed up his entire life by not being careful enough before he got his wings.

She saw him to the door and he headed off alone.

4

City Streets

THE LATTER HALF of autumn made the wind brisk, the skies gray as sunlight pierced through the clouds, and Asher breathed it all in deeply. Filled his lungs with the world around him, and not the worries for the future and his past regret. The breeze even felt nice on his wings, giving them a delightful shiver the first gust through.

The walk from the foundling house hill took him through sloping downward neighborhoods that quickly turned into strip malls and corner stores as he closed in on the main boardwalk through town. Lampposts had been decorated for the yearly autumn harvest festival. It was more tradition than anything else; farms weren't even close by anymore. Oranges and reds were strewn from post to post among the late autumn flower baskets still in bloom. Cars flanked the streets, each one parallel parked beside a meter, and the ones on the road leisurely made their way down the streets. People went up and down the sidewalk, busy and absorbed within their own lives.

It was quaint this time of day. Not too busy, but not a ghost town either. Toward late afternoon and dinnertime was when the streets were packed with cars and people both.

Honestly, Asher wished it was quieter. Very quickly, he felt eyes on him. It made him twitchy. Literally. His wings spasmed with jerky movements until he got the hang of keeping them close to his back. He'd taken out a poor kid walking with her mom before he'd managed it. His wings were like extra arms, but also not. They still didn't feel real and actually attached to him by muscle and bone, but he hoped that came with time.

Anyone who glanced at him must have known he was a fresh angel wing, one with the face of someone who had no business being one. A sham. Most people were protective of the angel wings who took residence in their district because of some weird sense of ownership. Like angel wings were little celebrities. Very quick were people to drop everything and help one in need, especially if it was their own. Asher doubted he'd garner the same respect.

Whispers reached Asher's ears—some curious, others acknowledging him shyly, and most of all, worried that someone like *him* could be an angel wing. He was the punk that hung out with Raum—a known devil wing—one who never hesitated to flip people off if they tried interrupting him making out with Raum in public.

Hell, they'd probably also watched him tag the blank walls down the many alleys between buildings. Turned their nose up at it, even when Asher had permission.

He was a troublemaker, even with wings that should have indicated otherwise. Maybe they were worried because he was proof that the whole idea of what made a foundling an angel wing or a devil wing was a lie.

The attention made him fidget, and fidgeting made his hands pat down his flannel. Brought the same shaking hands to the hidden stash of cigarettes and lighter inside the interior pocket.

Screw the image he was *supposed* to have. Everyone had already made up something in their heads. He needed to calm his nerves before he found himself having a panic attack or, worse, punching someone out. It could go either way.

He lit up the cigarette, breathing the taste in deep, and exhaled. Easier. There went some worries. Another drag and there went the thoughts that begged him to turn back and go home. He'd make it to Belle's shop, see what would happen, and be home before he knew it. He just had to repeat that to himself.

Belle's shop was past the packed city center, across the bridge over the man-made river cutting underneath the outer edges of town, and down a street of buildings so close together, it was like they were huddling for warmth. Cars couldn't come down this way—it was too tight— and Asher always enjoyed the walk.

There were new age stores, a stationary shop Amy loved, a cute café that didn't mind serving devil wings, and a grocer at the far end who carried local, in-season stuff. Not like the supermarket that had opened up off the main road.

No one stopped him as they normally would have stopped Amy when she was out and about. It was never for anything nefarious; usually to wish her well, or sometimes to give her a small gift as thanks for looking out for them. Her nest was on the other side of the city, unfortunately. What he wouldn't give to have her walking beside him today. This place had its own angel wing, but Asher couldn't remember their name right now.

Thankfully, Asher also didn't see any of the usual devil wings that prowled about the city edges. They were a rowdy bunch that leaned happily into their mayhem roots, but they'd looked after Raum when he'd first gotten his wings and for a while, Raum stayed with them. They didn't even mind Asher hanging out too, totally believing he'd be a devil wing like them.

Maybe it was a good thing then that ever since Raum had gotten the job at the tattoo shop, he'd been too busy to run with them. Asher never had reason to hang out with them alone. They'd probably be disappointed seeing the feathery mess sprouting from his back, anyway.

Asher didn't want them to see his wings before he was good and ready. On the chance they did reject him (and they would), what they thought didn't matter. All he needed in his life was Raum and Amy. Everyone else could screw off as far as he was concerned.

He arrived at Belle's Gardening Boutique by the end of his cigarette and flicked the butt into the nearby receptacle. The storefront was made with white slats with the large windows she'd filled to the brim with all sorts of plants for the season. Most of what she sold came from the community garden a few streets down and the money was shared amongst everyone who worked on it. Above her shop was the small apartment that she'd been keeping empty just for him.

If he'd gotten devil wings.

Could still be a nest for an angel wing. Asher tried to shake out his nerves. All he had to do was ask.

Belle was open for the day, getting the pumpkins ready to go out. Her shop was a slapdash of different things from grown plants, packets of seeds that changed every season, and also the garden paraphernalia that always held a mystic flavor. Many enjoyed her unique finds. During winter, she made a killing bringing in miniature pines from a local tree farm.

It was a good store, and Asher prayed Belle would agree. With an exhale, he strode inside.

He regretted coming immediately. There were little devil wing decorations strung across the walls, and hanging from the ceiling were little bats. No one had told her which wings he'd gotten. Belle must have bought out some clear-ance section of old autumn decorations to celebrate with him.

He was staring, speechless, when a party popper spewed confetti over the corner counter. He jumped and spun to face it.

Belle was a large woman who gave the best bear hugs and somehow always hid in plain sight behind the counter. Her head was crowned in fuzzy blonde curls and her eyes were a warm brown, ready to accept whoever you were. She always wore cozy flannels and jeans, weather permitting.

Her eyes grew wide behind her thick framed glasses and the smile morphed into a silent *'oh'* as her gaze flicked to the wings protruding from his back.

When Asher's wings hadn't come at sixteen, he'd been listless. School had been torture under normal circumstances, but it'd become much worse when Raum and Amy left. Everyone always knew who the foundlings were and knew they left at sixteen when they got their wings. So, when Asher's birthday came and went with no wings, they took it as reason to treat him worse when no one was paying attention.

Thankfully, Judith had let him finally drop out when he angrily argued for it. He was already failing all his classes by then since grades didn't matter. Angel wings were intellectually isolated, cut off from higher learning, and devil wings usually weren't accepted into it either unless they made really strong cases for it.

So, with nothing else and bored out of his mind, Asher had gone on a graffiti spree and ended up at Belle's blank wall near midnight. How she'd had the sense someone would be there, Asher had no idea, but she hadn't turned him in. She'd actually liked the thorny vines in the shapes of devil wings he'd done, and offered to give Asher a job in her shop.

Though he'd been hesitant at first, he'd quickly realized he liked having something to do outside of himself. Loved it, even. It was a small quiet space in the world that accepted him as Asher, not an angel or devil wing to be.

And Belle had been ready for Asher for years, making sure the apartment above the shop was prepared whenever he got his wings.

Except now they were the wrong kind. Panic kicked back in, making Asher's heart race, as Belle stared at him.

"Those are not devil wings," Belle said, more to herself than to him. Her shop was in its lunchtime lull and Asher wondered if he'd rather have had the conversation somewhere more populated. Just so he wasn't tempted to cry. Maybe he should have brought Judith.

"I know." Asher tried to make his wings move, to show her they weren't fake, but all the motion did was make him wince. "Came last week-ish."

"I figured when Judith called and said you needed some time." Belle came around the counter and waved him closer, away from the door, and he let her look at the wings.

She stared for too long, like she'd see devil wings somehow hidden beneath the feathers.

"God damn," she whispered finally.

Asking couldn't hurt. It was all he had.

"W-Would you be willing to host an angel wing instead?" he asked, eyes already flooding with tears from the rejection he knew was coming. "Judith said technically, the apartment you'd set aside meets the dimensions of a nest and if you give her the okay, she can make a case that I can still be here."

The immediate silence told Asher enough. Panic seized him deeper; it felt like he couldn't breathe.

"Oh, sweetie." Belle gently turned Asher to face her, but he couldn't. Not directly. He stared at the counter behind her. It kept blurring as he blinked back hot tears. "I can't."

There it was, her rejection. Asher forged on anyway. "Why not?" he asked, his voice cracking. "Judith said..."

"It's not as simple as that," Belle explained slowly. "A devil wing isn't anything to anyone and they don't have rules on where they can stay. Angel wings..." She hesitated, searching for her words. "Are different. We have an angel wing a few blocks down and he's very good at what he does. People—the watchers included—will think I'm trying to replace him."

"Except we're not," Asher said, looking up at her. "I wouldn't even want a confessional. I just want to work here. I don't want to do any of that bullshit. I just need a nest."

"I know, but that's not how the city's going to see it." Belle's expression was twisting in regret. Or pity. Either way, Asher hated it. She was willing to rock the boat all she wanted for a devil wing, but not for an angel wing.

"I could be asked to relocate my shop. They could force you out of here. Asher..."

Asher felt like an asshole. He was expecting her to choose him over her livelihood. She made just enough to stay here. If she took the chance to shuck tradition to let him stay, then she could have been asked to relocate. Then, if the city wanted to, they could orchestrate it so rent would be too high to reopen anywhere else, just to punish her for trying.

He squeezed his hands into fists, his entire body trembling. He shouldn't have come out here by himself. The panic of failure raced through him too fast. He felt sick.

"M-Maybe in another year or two," Belle tried, uselessly. "Lance has been here almost nine years now, he might... he might..."

She didn't finish her sentence because everyone knew what happened to angel wings after ten or fifteen years. They disappeared. Always did. Devil wings did too, but no one paid their sudden disappearances much attention.

No one really knew *why*, but theories holding on from more religious times said that when angel wings fulfilled their duty, they ascended, and took a devil wing with them. How the angel wing fulfilled their duty was always left vague and handwaved away.

It was terrifying when Asher thought too deeply about it. Ten or fifteen years in service to the city, shut up in a nest like some sort of prize, only to be gone afterward. Like he never existed at all.

Whether the angel wing Belle was talking about had another year or two didn't matter. Asher needed somewhere to go now. Options. The city wasn't likely to let him wait any longer.

Belle must have noticed the slowly building panic. One moment, her hold relaxed, and then the next, her arms were wrapped around him in the tightest hug she had in her.

"Oh, sweetie," she murmured into his hair. "Everything will work out. I know it. Come back and paint my walls anytime, I'll never say no." She withdrew and ran a hand through his hair to push it back. Looking at her was hard. She was all blurry. "I can introduce you to Lance, maybe he can help?"

Asher quickly shook his head. "N-No. I'd rather not bother him," he said. Most angel wings were *not* willing to talk to him; Amy had already tried to introduce him to some when he was waiting for his wings. His reputation as a punk was too widely known.

"I-I've already got Amy to talk to." Even if she also wasn't much help right now.

Belle studied him, like he might reconsider, and pulled him in for another squeeze. "I'll try to find a way to do something for you. You are not alone, I promise." She withdrew again and held him at an arm's length. "You don't have to be a stranger, okay?"

Asher nodded, sniffling. "Okay." His throat

tightened, all the despair bubbling up. No. He couldn't break down in front of her. Not in front of anyone. It wasn't her fault he'd fucked his life over by just being himself.

"Thank you." He cleared his throat for some modicum of control. "T-Thank you for letting me be here with you while I waited for my wings."

Belle hugged him a third time and he breathed her in. All the flowers, the pines, and everything she was encapsulated in a single aroma he never wanted to forget. Maybe it wouldn't be for the last time, but it certainly felt like it when he left and headed out into the cold.

The dread in his stomach gnawed at him, ate him up from the inside, and he wanted to vomit it out. His life wasn't ending; it had no reason to react like this. Except it wouldn't stop. His breathing became erratic. His chest hurt. He needed to find some normalcy. A reminder his life was not ending.

He quickly glanced up and down the street and found a nearby payphone. He hurried over and dialed the tattoo parlor before he was truly cognizant of his actions. It was already ringing before he thought better of bothering Raum at work.

What kind of boyfriend was he? Dragging Raum away from work just to listen to his imminent panic attack? Before he could convince himself it would be better just to hang up, go home and have the attack in private, the other end answered.

"'Ey, it's Raven Wing Tats and Piercings, how can we stab you today?" the receptionist, Molly, said in her usual boredom drawl. She was the owner's niece and in charge of phones and scheduling people in. She wasn't bad at it, truth be told, she just found it boring.

Her voice became his first anchor. Asher held onto it and counted his heartbeats to calm down before he dumped all his problems on her in a rush. She didn't deserve that. No one did.

"Hellooo?" Molly stretched out the word and sighed. "Look, no one breathes creepily into the fucking phone and expects us to—"

"Hey," Asher said. "S-Sorry. It's me."

"Asher?" Molly's voice brightened. "Oh my gosh! Raum told us the news. Wings!"

Asher cursed Raum's excitement. What was amazing for him continued to lead Asher down a spiral of panic.

"Yes, thank you," Asher said. "I-Is Raum free?"

"For you he *always* is. Lemme snag him before he starts on someone else. Been a mad-house with the sale we're running."

As he waited, still considering hanging up and leaving, passersby noticed him clinging tightly to the payphone receiver. While his wings were an acceptable shield, a few mistook him for another angel wing and actually approached. One look at his face, however, and they quickly excused themselves and left. He wasn't an angel wing they knew or wanted to help.

He just about gave up when he heard Raum

on the phone. "Hey you." Tension eased out of Asher just hearing his boyfriend's voice. The softness to it, the confidence that made Asher believe everything would be fine.

Molly teased Raum in the background and it made Asher smile. She always did that whenever Asher called up looking for him.

"Are you feeling better?" Raum asked.

"I am," Asher lied and hoped it wasn't obvious. What he needed most of all right now was Raum in his entirety. Not as a voice over the phone. Actually present in the flesh.

"Addam, the kids, and Judith will all be out of the house by the time you're free. C-Could you come by today?"

Raum paused. The panic must have been too clear in Asher's voice. He should have tried harder to sound normal.

"Of course," Raum said, his voice suddenly bright, like he was trying to hide his hesitation and concern. "They'll be *out*, huh? What exactly did you—Molly! Screw off, will you? Let me talk to him."

Asher laughed and covered it with his hand. More of the panic ebbed. Raum trying to be suave was always a sight and leave it to Molly to tease him about it.

Raum sighed, exasperated, and Molly cackled in the background.

"Well," Asher said. "I thought you sounded sexy."

"At least one of us does," Raum said. "I'll come by. You rest up until then, all right?" He audibly kissed the receiver on his end and while Asher did not trust a payphone to do the same, he still made the noise. "See you later, Ash. I'll bring something fun."

Fun lit a tiny spark in Asher's stomach. He was glad they bid each other goodbye before Molly could snag the receiver and tell a dirty joke about the *something fun*. Probably not what Raum meant—something new for dinner was more likely—but Asher could dream.

He left the payphone a great deal happier. Dread coiled into something else, something light and soft sending butterflies through him. He ignored all the eyes on him and lit up another cigarette for the walk home, all his cares and worries exhaled in a plume of smoke.

5

A Try For Normalcy

ASHER FORCED HIMSELF to think positively. He was *finally* getting alone time with Raum. Between Raum being busy at the tattoo shop and Asher not wanting to push him if he was tired, it'd been a bit since the last time. Besides, Asher had been in a mood while he waited for his wings.

Now that they were out? He could be better. Fuck all the rejection. He had Raum to pick him up and that was what mattered.

Judith was out of the house shortly after he'd returned. She'd given him a reassuring hug after hearing the bad news and promised she'd do her best to talk some sense into the watchers. Maybe they'd give Asher a chance and not write him off on rumor alone if Judith met with them in person.

Asher didn't mind staying home while she went off to do just that. Rejection to the face hurt.

Besides, walking so much had aggravated his stitches; he needed to let the pain ebb to be ready for his evening with Raum. Although, sitting and waiting was the last thing he wanted to do.

Positive thoughts kept Asher going despite the growing pain as he cleaned his room. Sure, Raum had seen the mess and probably didn't care, but Asher wanted to show him everything was just fine. A clean room would do that.

Addam might have suspected Asher was up to something. He watched as Asher threw all his bedding into the wash and then when Asher gathered all the candles in the house. Before Addam had decided if it was worth asking, it was time for the quartet's baseball thing. Asher saw them to the door and wished them luck.

Asher remade his bed at least three times before he figured they were just going to undo everything anyway, opting for less than perfect. He lit the candles to give his room ambience. They smelled nice too; a medley of vanilla and jasmine. He shoved the rest of his junk under his bed and promised himself that he'd deal with it properly later. Lastly, he set up his small cassette player with one of Raum's mixtapes.

When he was done, Asher looked over his room and nodded. Cozy. Ready for Raum. He'd even had the sense to stop by the corner store on his way home from Belle's to pick up a pack of condoms. The clerk's face had been priceless. The way his eyes had darted from the pack, to Asher's wings, and then to Asher. He'd repeated the motions a few times before he'd gotten over himself and finished the transaction.

The absurdity got a chuckle out of Asher.

Having feathers didn't suddenly make him celibate.

Asher glanced at the clock. Raum wasn't off for another half hour still. Maybe he hadn't needed to rush everything.

Waiting left Asher fretting and he took another quick shower. Couldn't hurt. The hair-dryer's heat made his wings feel better, but after all was said and done and he'd dressed again, they were throbbing.

Nope. Nope. They were not going to ruin his evening with Raum. He could get past it.

He settled on his bed with Amy's *Wing Tips & Tricks* to distract himself until Raum arrived. There wasn't a section about having sex with wings, but he supposed he shouldn't have expected one. Not Amy's area of expertise, and she'd be too shy to ask Raum. Maybe Asher and Raum could write up something together and convince her to add it in.

He'd flipped through most of the book when he heard Raum's motorbike outside. Asher's smile widened, butterflies swirling in his stomach, and soon heard the thunk, thunk, thunk of Raum's boots coming up the trellis. When they reached the top, Asher turned toward the window and rested his chin on his palm, teasingly smiling as Raum pulled himself inside.

"What happened to the door?" Asher asked as Raum slid next to him on the bed. He plopped the plastic bag hanging off his arm into his lap and Asher sniffed.

Dinner. It smelled nice, although Asher

couldn't tell right away what it was.

"Window's way more romantic," Raum insisted, grinning. And it was, because as soon as he'd said the words, he leaned forward and found Asher's mouth for a soft kiss. "I brought you dinner. Growing wings makes you famished."

"I guess you'd know." Asher chuckled and tilted his head. "Is this what you meant by fun?"

Raum blinked and his wings drooped behind him. "Oh." A laugh bubbled out of his throat. "Y-Yeah, but you and Molly thought something *totally* different, didn't you?"

Asher laughed and his wings twitched with delight behind him. His laugh only grew louder when Raum gently shoved him and started laughing himself, flustered.

"You'll like what I brought though," Raum said quickly and Asher swallowed the rest of his laughter. Raum opened the bag, letting the aroma overpower the candles he hadn't even noticed.

Asher's stomach made a petulant growl. He'd skipped out on an early dinner with Addam because he'd been franticly trying to get everything ready. Raum was right; growing wings made a person famished.

Raum extracted the takeout container and settled it between them. He gave Asher one of the plastic forks and took the other for himself.

"It's this new place a block down from the shop," Raum explained as he opened the container. "She blends different cuisines together. This is her rice, peanut sauce, vegetables, and chicken thrown into a tortilla bowl specialty. With her secret spices, of course. She wouldn't tell me what those were."

It certainly looked like what Raum had described. Asher couldn't decide if that was appealing or not, and tentatively took a bite, aware of Raum watching him expectantly. The tastes complemented each other surprisingly well and Asher nodded. Raum's smile widened.

"It opened up over the summer! Molly's taken me a few times after work."

A spike of jealousy cut through Asher's delight and he tried to smother it with another bite. "Why didn't you invite me?" He tried sounding more curious than hurt.

Raum hesitated. "You always seemed tired by the time I was free," he said quietly.

Asher swallowed his bite and cursed his past self. Not going anywhere had just become easy.

"We can go this weekend!" Raum suggested.

"I'd like that," Asher said. "It tastes really good."

Raum perked back up, somehow smiling wider. It was infectious. "And the best part? The owner is a devil wing!"

Asher almost dropped his fork. "Really? How?"

"I'm still working up the nerve to ask her how she managed it," Raum said and happily loaded up his fork. "But man, it gives me hope I can do that too. Like if she went to culinary school or something, maybe I could go to an art school. Always more to learn, you know?" Raum gently nudged Asher with his elbow, too focused on his food to notice Asher's empty expression. "We could go together!"

No, they couldn't. Not if Asher was expected to be an angel wing, shut inside some nest until he disappeared. If anyone wanted him. Maybe they'd all say no and he could do just that. Except no one made funds available for angel wings. They were expected to be cared for already.

"Ash?" Raum asked, worried. The candles made his eyes twinkle. Asher should have found that alluring, beautiful, but a sudden gulf of dread was threatening to swallow him whole.

Asher shook his head quickly. "Sorry, just thinking. I'd love to go," he whispered.

Judith and Addam tried to instill in everyone that life didn't end when you got your wings. It continued, no matter what, and foundlings deserved the same chances everyone else got. But why did it sound so hollow now that Asher had angel wings? He couldn't find an immediate answer and buried it in his thoughts. He wasn't supposed to be thinking so hard.

Raum watched him for a moment, but when Asher mutely continued to eat, he leaned back and wrapped an arm around Asher, mindful of the wings.

"How'd your day go?" he asked softly, resting his chin on Asher's shoulder. "I take it talking to Belle didn't pan out?"

"How'd you know I went to talk to her?"

"Judith might have called to tell me what you two were planning."

Because she'd expected it to fail and wanted to give Raum a head's up that Asher would be out of sorts. Asher bit back another frustrated sigh. No, she'd probably been hopeful.

"I don't know why I thought Belle would say yes," Asher admitted.

"Did you want to talk about it?"

In between slow bites of rice and chicken, Asher did. Raum listened quietly and happily ate the vegetables Asher fed him. Asher was always picky about what vegetables he liked and Raum happily took whatever Asher didn't want, even when they were kids.

A breeze trickled into the room, cooling the pain softly radiating across Asher's back. The candlelight flickered in response. It was the perfect set up for romance, but Asher was too busy drowning in dread. Raum was supposed to look on the bright side of everything, should have been quick with something reassuring to say, but when Asher eventually trailed off, he was silent.

Talking hadn't helped. It left Asher fidgety.

After a moment, Raum spoke. "We'll figure everything out." He was rubbing gentle circles between Asher's wings. It felt nice. "We can ask Harmony tomorrow if she'd mind an angel wing. You're a quick learner—she might like another apprentice."

Harmony owned the tattoo shop and had taken Raum in when he'd answered an 'artists wanted' ad she'd put out. She never minded that he was a devil wing and had quickly made him her apprentice. He knew how to ink skin, pierce ears—and other places—and she'd even begun teaching him more of the business side at his request.

"People might find it disconcerting being stabbed by an angel wing," Asher said.

Harmony made enough to get by and pay her employees, but not much more. The shop was still relatively new and hadn't made a name for itself yet. Losing business for any reason would be hard on her.

Raum didn't answer, but his face was pinched like he was thinking of possibilities. At least one of them was.

Asher wanted to put it so far from his mind, he simply forgot he had wings and the responsibility that came with them. Trying not to think about it, however, left his mind open to imagining pitfalls and he needed something else to do.

While he couldn't change the fact he had angel wings, he could enjoy his boyfriend sitting right there. On his bed. Dense though he was.

Asher set the container aside, and before Raum could ask why, Asher pulled him into a kiss. Many of them repeated after each other, drowning all the negative thoughts. Raum returned the energy eagerly, making sure his sharp teeth grazed Asher's lips in ways that he knew made Asher's body positively shiver.

It wasn't long before Asher tasted more Raum than food between their shared kisses, and it wasn't much longer until Asher was straddling Raum. His boyfriend laid back, bringing Asher down with him, and pressed his fingers to Asher's hips to hold him there. This was the perfect way to simply forget everything. All Asher had to do was please his boyfriend, and if he was good at one thing, it was that.

Their kisses turned sloppy, making up for lost time. Asher's hands trailed down Raum's chest, following the familiar shape he knew so intimately. When he felt the cool kiss of the metal buckle under his hand, he wrapped his fingers around it and tugged. He didn't want to remove himself from Raum's lips, but every attempt to unlatch the belt failed, his hands forgetting motions he'd once had memorized. Raum stopped kissing Asher and tilted his head back.

They were both left breathless, lungs starved, as Asher finally managed to unlatch the stupid buckle. Before he could do anything else, Raum caught his hand with one of his and used the other to tilt Asher's chin so he was looking at him.

"Wait," he said, eyebrows folded in concern. "Ash, hold on."

Fuzzy feelings melted. "What?" Asher asked, trying to hide his sudden frustration with a playful smile. When Raum didn't answer, his mouth working silently like he was groping for words, Asher's face burned.

"*What?*" He dropped all playfulness. "When *you* got your wings, it was two days before you were fucking me and telling me how amazing it was—like you'd been missing something before."

"I know," Raum said quickly. "I know." He repeated it slower. "But I didn't need stitches, Ash. My back healed fast and you—"

"My back is fine," Asher said, voice thick with the lie. It was burning, but he wasn't about to let it get in the way of losing himself in Raum. The one thing right in his life that he wasn't supposed to be thinking so hard about.

He sat up straight and made a show of twitching his wings to prove it was fine. Both motions were a bad idea. More pain etched deep into his back, like someone had stabbed it with a dull knife and twisted.

"See?" he stressed anyway and Raum's lips set in a hard line. "Raum, I want something that's not wrapped up in what I'm supposed to be. I want to forget it all."

Yet Raum still hesitated. The dread pooling in Asher's stomach blossomed, replacing all the warmth and sparks he'd just felt moments before with something that chilled him entirely. Raum's eyes were on Asher's wings, his own devil wings drooping sadly behind him.

"You don't like my wings," Asher said, the very sentence taking whatever air was left in his lungs.

Raum blinked, jolting, and Asher slipped off his lap to stand. "No, Ash—"

"You don't like me anymore because I'm not a devil wing like you." The words spit themselves out too fast. Insecurities and lies he'd told himself bubbling up to refill what the fleeting warmth had left empty.

He stepped back, wrapping his arms tightly around himself, and paced. His hands groped for something to rip. To pull. Do something other than stand there and stare at his boyfriend.

"God, fuck all of this! I shouldn't—"

"Ash, no." Raum was immediately beside Asher, taking Asher's hands away from pulling the only feathers he could reach. "It is not like that. I love your wings. They suit you."

"They *suit* me?!" Asher spun to face Raum, incredulous. "They're *feathers*. They're fucking *white*. How do they suit me?!"

Raum eased out a sigh. "And I like them. I can't explain it, I just like *you* and whatever you come with, Ash." Raum gently put his arms around Asher. "Feathers or not—I like them. They're you."

"Then *what*? You said we could do something when I felt better," Asher said. "I feel better."

Raum released him, frowning. "Move your arms, then."

Narrowing his eyes, Asher moved them as much as he knew he could without causing his back any pain. Raum lifted his eyebrows, giving Asher a knowing look, and nudged Asher's arms higher. Even the smallest amount was enough to remind Asher of the pain knotted up in his back. He couldn't bite back the yelp in time and wrenched himself away.

"We can be careful," he tried.

"Your favorite position is not careful," Raum argued, frustrated. "We should wait until at least the stitches are out."

"Let's do something else, then. Doesn't have to be sex-sex."

"You've seen my wings twitch *a lot* when I get off," Raum shot back. Asher looked away, biting his lip. Raum wasn't wrong. "I don't want to hurt you, Ash, and I know it will." He gently took one of Asher's hands and laced their fingers together. "You know I want to do things to you, but I think it's safer if we hold off just a little longer." He lifted Asher's hand and kissed it. "I don't want to hurt you," he repeated.

Asher stared at their hands, how their fingers looked entwined, their little tattoos almost playing off one another from finger to finger. A moon on Asher's, a sun on Raum's.

Waiting wasn't what he wanted, but waiting was what he'd have to do.

He sighed loudly, giving in, and gave Raum a gentle push. Raum grinned and didn't let go, pulling Asher into him as they did a graceful plop onto the bed together. Asher's shoulder hitting the mattress made his back sting, but he didn't let it show on his face. His wings would not take away cuddling with Raum.

"I even went and bought condoms," Asher said, drawing benign circles across Raum's chest with his finger. "You should have seen the clerk's face. I thought his head was going to explode."

Raum laughed, his entire body rumbling with the sound, and he held Asher tighter. "Oh shit, I should have been there for that. His head might actually have exploded then."

They eased into silence together, their

laughter tapering off. A small sigh slipped out of Asher, this one of resignation, and he rested his head against Raum's chest. At least this was nice. And sure, maybe his wings *were* hurting a little more than he'd ever admit. Maybe this was a better idea.

Raum was always gentle, almost to a fault, but Asher couldn't imagine having it any other way. Even when the devil wings they'd once hung out with teased Raum about how soft he was, he'd let it roll off his shoulders and continued being himself. Asher wished he had the same confidence. Maybe then all the rejection wouldn't hurt so bad.

The candlelight dwindled around them, but Asher was too exhausted to get up to blow them out. Despite the low light, Raum brought over Amy's book and began looking through it.

They were barely a page or two in before Raum was searching for a pen to jot down a few notes in the margins. Some corrections, a funny anecdote, and then also words of praise and affirmation for whoever might be reading the page after Asher. It was sweet.

"That cop was back at the shop today," Raum said when they finished with the book.

Asher made a face. "Again? Does he just like staring at you while you stab people?"

"Wish I knew. He just stayed in the lobby this time until Molly was able to grab Harm to talk to him." Raum shook his head and sagged against the wall. "At least he wasn't asking me about Harv and the others, I guess."

Ever since it became widely known that a devil wing worked at the tattoo shop, a cop came down every few weeks to watch the place from the lobby. Like they assumed Raum would do something unsavory to his clients. It made everyone nervous, but no matter how many times Harmony insisted Raum was a perfect worker, a cop would still come in insisting he had to be sure.

"Why'd they want to know about Harv?"

Harv was the leader of the devil wings that had adopted Raum. Rowdy with a devil-may-care attitude, they usually made themselves a problem because why not? The city already assumed they were, so that was what they did.

Raum shrugged. "Beats me, I try not to ask. Haven't seen Harv since I started there anyway. Apparently, the cops like to watch that restaurant too and she's about as sick of it as we are."

"Pricks," Asher whispered.

"You're telling me."

"Any cool clients lately?" Asher asked, steering the conversation away from the cops. Raum just had to be a 'good' devil wing and, eventually, they'd move on. Just another reality of devil wings trying to play nice and make something of themselves.

Raum smiled and happily told Asher all about a big client he had coming to the shop tomorrow evening. The first one who had specifically booked him by name. Maybe it was simply the novelty of being tattooed by a devil wing, but Raum was excited. She wanted a huge pair of bat wings done on her back. Asher liked seeing Raum passionate about his projects. It fit him better than brooding about cops.

The door opened downstairs and Asher flinched. Shit. He looked at the clock. It was already late. The pitter-patter of four separate footsteps hurried up the stairs as Addam called uselessly after them.

Asher's door busted open before he could untangle himself from Raum to go lock it. All four foundlings tried to squeeze inside at once. Liberty and Caroline held a shiny trophy over their heads, showing it off. Aubrey slipped to the front, a large grin plastered on her face, and she caught Claude tripping inside after her.

They must have wanted to brag that they'd won, but then their eyes fixed on Raum untangling his arm from beneath Asher.

"Raum!" Aubrey squealed and launched herself at him.

Raum was endearingly good with children. He caught Aubrey, hoisting her up with one arm, and easily scooped Claude up with his other. Caroline and Liberty shoved the trophy into his field of vision with a chorus of "Look! Look what we did!" and he gave them the requisite oohs and ahhs to placate their excitement. Aubrey began gleefully telling him all about the game, rapid-fire fast even as her siblings tried to cut in, and punched her fists outward to punctuate her points.

"All right, all right," Raum said, gently edging them all into the hall. "Let's get you washed up and you can tell me more about it while I tuck you all in, okay?"

The cacophony of the four of them trying to tell the story turned into cheers. They absolutely loved Raum and would do anything he asked. Seeing it, though, stung. Asher could never get the same reaction out of them. They didn't respond well to sarcasm or glares. Neither did he have Raum's energy to keep up, nor the ability to fake a genuine reaction.

Then again, Raum's reaction *was* genuine. Maybe the kids could tell the difference.

In any case, romance was over. Completely.

Asher forced himself up, his back protesting the movement, and he slowly made his way around the room to extinguish all the candles. A shadow darkened his doorway and Asher glanced up. Addam peeked inside, still in the coach uniform he wore when the foundlings had a game to play. It suited him.

"Hey," he said softly. "You okay?"

Asher shrugged. "We weren't doing any-thing, don't worry."

Addam frowned. "That's not what I meant," he said. "You know Judith and I accept—"

"I know." Asher blew out another candle. "I'm fine. Judith is still out trying to convince everyone I'm not toxic waste." He swallowed and shrugged again. "I'll be fine. Promise."

There was a pause, an acknowledgment that Asher probably wasn't, but in the end, Addam nodded. "I'll send Raum back your way when the kids unlatch themselves."

Asher smiled. "Thank you."

The smile only held until Addam was gone. Alone, it was replaced by a frown. Tonight wasn't what he wanted. Neither was the direction of his life, if he was being honest. While Raum was so bright and confident about where his life could lead, a bunch of different directions he could go, Asher couldn't muster up the same outlook.

All he had to look forward to was more rejections or, perhaps what was worse: someone saying yes and clipping his wings so he could be the perfect little angel wing with no aspirations.

The last candle snuffed out, leaving him in darkness. For a moment, he considered following after Raum to help with the kids, faking a smile, but knowing his luck, he'd screw it up. Instead, he collapsed in bed and pressed his face into his pillow, so he didn't have to think.

Kiss Off

EVERYTHING PERTAINING TO the city and foundlings was contained to a single building past the downtown boardwalk, across another bridge over the river. It was an unassuming three-story building of rust-colored bricks with white accents around the doors and windows. Ivy clung to the walls, the leaves dry and dark. Pine trees had been planted around the building, secluding it from the rest of the street which housed more governmental offices. Inside, the ground floor had meeting halls and rooms, a few of them Asher had already seen when he'd come a few times with Judith. The second floor had offices for each watcher and the third had a few archival rooms no one was allowed into.

Asher and Raum had tried getting into them once. Judith had taken them and Amy up here before any of them had their wings for a meeting with someone—Asher couldn't remember who— and he and Raum had gotten bored waiting and had gone exploring.

The small bit of comfort the memory brought shattered as the bells in the tower rang out. They could be heard across the city, some holdover from when the whole place was more religiously minded. This close, Asher about jumped out of his skin. It was a reminder that right inside those doors was someone who held Asher's future in their hands. Judith had failed convincing the other watchers to give Asher a chance, so he was meeting with the only one who'd responded: Bartholomew.

Asher sat rooted in Addam's truck, his skin clammy, heart racing, and stared at the main entrance. They were parked in the turnaround in front of the building. The parking lot was off to the side, past the small threshold of pines, and had a handful of cars in it.

Asher had dressed in his best; slacks he'd pressed the night before to give his nervous hands something to do, a white button-up shirt that unfortunately had thin enough sleeves, his black shoulder tattoo showed through, and a sleek black vest over that. He didn't have nice dress shoes, but no one would notice his black sneakers, right? His seldom used overcoat completed the picture, but he already knew inside was going to be too warm, especially since he was overheating now. At least he smelled like the pine spray Amy got him, and not nervous sweat. The scent helped ground him, but it was fading fast.

"Do you want me to come with you?" Addam

asked, breaking the silence.

The poor man was so patient. Asher didn't know how. He hadn't spoken since they'd parked. Didn't rush Asher or anything. If Asher asked, he'd drive him home, no questions asked.

"No," Asher said and cleared his throat. "I-I should do this on my own."

Addam smiled sadly and tilted his head. "Judith went in with Amy for all her meetings."

Judith hadn't taken Asher today because she was trying to get in contact with other cities and their watchers. Asher preferred Addam anyway.

"And she was sixteen still," Asher reminded. "I think I can handle one watcher." He tried to scoff, breathe out the anxiety, but his smile betrayed his fear. "Tell me something about the guy."

The request took Addam by surprise and his eyebrows lifted before he grew pensive. "He's... A traditionalist," Addam said carefully.

"Ah, so I'll hate him," Asher said.

"Asher..." Addam's expression softened, but before he could go all protective dad, Asher unbuckled his seatbelt and opened the door.

"Thanks. I'll try to be open-minded. I'll be back. Hopefully with good news this time."

Addam reached out and squeezed Asher's shoulder. "And if not, we'll figure it out. Just breathe."

Much easier for him to say, but Asher tried as he strode inside.

The woman at the help desk smiled kindly when he introduced himself and she pointed him toward the stairs leading up to the offices.

Just breathe.

He passed a family coming down who gave him curious looks. He tried to smile at them, like he was a real angel wing, but his stomach wanted to revolt. He was a sham. So, he ignored them and kept moving.

Just breathe.

Each step punctuated the words and it felt like forever before he reached the second floor and then, it felt like he should have taken his time.

The hallway would have been silent if not for the soft murmurs coming up from the ground floor of activities in progress. Eventually, the thump of Asher's heart drowned even that out.

Watcher offices lined one side of the hall all the way around. Each door had its own gilded nameplate, a mailbox, and a map of the district the watcher was in charge of. When not dealing with angel wings, watchers tended to focus on their communities, planning projects, and help-ing build networks throughout the city with goodwill and programs. Summer and winter had larger programs, but autumn and spring were still busy.

Amy's watcher, Wendolyn, typically worked with schools to make sure children had access to meals if their families were in need and hosted drives in the winter to make sure the same children had good holidays. It was no wonder Amy had picked Wendolyn as her watcher. Amy loved helping.

As Asher walked down the hall, he took in purposeful breaths. In and out. In and out. He glanced at the doors as he passed. Each one had a decent sized window beside it, letting people peek inside if the blinds were open. Most were closed.

He paused at Wendolyn's office, but it was dark. He could have asked her for advice if he'd just thought about it. Amy would have happily introduced them if he'd asked.

Too late for that now.

Asher continued, mouthing names to himself as he went. He stopped when he reached the door near the back stairwell. Bartholomew Samson. His mailbox was empty and the blinds were closed, but light gleamed from behind the slats.

Just breathe.

In and out. Asher raised his fist and gently knocked. When no answer immediately came, Asher tried again, this time louder.

"One minute," came a voice from inside. "There's seating out there to wait."

Asher bristled, face hot, and checked the watch Addam had loaned him. He was exactly on time. Before he yelled at the door or kicked it to let out his frustrations, he pivoted and sat at the edge of the chair across from the door.

The chairs were *not* made with wings in mind. The armrests were too cramped and the back was too high for the wings to drape over. Pain was already creeping past the meds he'd swallowed during breakfast.

If that wasn't enough, waiting bored into him like screws. Every silent second alone with his thoughts made the pain worse. Made the hallway too stifling. He gently pulled off his overcoat and felt marginally better. Not as hot and his wings were given a reprieve from the heavy fabric. It also gave him something to hold onto that wasn't himself.

Twisting the fabric between his fingers only helped a little. His leg was bouncing with agitation and all the anxiety coiled inside was unfolding into fidgeting. An agitated, fidgety Asher meant a broken window on a bad day. Today was already creeping up on bad.

Just breathe.

Breathe in the stale air of the hallway. It was stuffy with no open windows and the heat from the old radiators was overwhelming. Everything seemed so still. Unreal. Pressing in on Asher, reminding him how unreal *he* was with wings that never should have been his.

It was still pressing in, letting anxious thoughts speed through his head, when the door opened.

Asher lifted his head.

Bartholomew stood in the doorway, the light from within shining around him. The man barely made eye contact before he turned and beckoned Asher in after him.

"Ah, Asher, there you are. Come on in."

Not even an apology. Asher exhaled sharply through his nose and instead of leaving like he desperately wanted to, followed Bartholomew into his office.

Bartholomew closed the door after him and while it made sense—privacy for a meeting to maybe determine the trajectory of Asher's life—Asher felt trapped.

The office resembled Judith's quite a bit. Everything meticulously placed and in order. The large wooden desk a few paces from the door faced the room, and atop was a small handful of books and binders, an old rotary card file next to the phone, and a small desk organizer. In the center was a nondescript folder with Asher's name on it. Behind the desk was a bookshelf with more binders and books, each of them related to theology.

Asher scrunched his nose. Traditionalist just like Addam said, which was a nice way to say religiously minded. That was sure to bode well. Asher gripped the fabric of his coat tightly until his fingers ached. No, it wouldn't do him any good to judge the guy before they'd officially said hello. He said he'd play nice and that was what he'd do.

The wall across from the door had a single window covered in blinds. Tacked up on either side of it were Bartholomew's accomplishments: certificates, newspaper clippings when he'd done something laudable, and framed photographs of himself with others.

Curiously, the pictures included no angel wings of any kind.

Running out of things to look at, Asher

finally studied his maybe watcher.

Bartholomew was past middle-aged with a receding hairline of dusty blond hair he'd kept carefully trimmed. His face bore the weight of his winkles, fine creases that may have been handsome if his expression wasn't purposefully kept blank, like he was hiding his own annoyance with the situation. He wore a simple button-up and slacks, everything subdued. The perfect epitome of a generic watcher.

He sat at his desk and extended his hand toward the chair on the other side. A mirror to the ones in the hall.

"Please, sit. We've got much to go over." Bartholomew looked away and sorted through his piles of city maps and notes in front of him. He paused when Asher didn't immediately sit.

"Ah. My apologies." Bartholomew stood back up, shaking his head. "I should have brought a stool or something. I'll be back. I think Adrian might have one. His angel has pretty massive wings."

A slip of the tongue or something far more innocent, Asher couldn't decide. He watched Bartholomew go. Despite foundlings being divorced from anything religious for at least a few decades, some still held onto the superstitious belief that angel wings were literal angels waiting for their haloes. It was bullshit. Asher certainly wasn't going to be anyone's angel.

With Bartholomew out of the room, Asher gave in to snooping into the files on the desk. On top was the map of where the nest was. Clear across the city from Amy's, but not far from the turn off to the junkyard where he and Raum used to go.

Asher wracked his brain, trying to remember if he'd even seen it before, but nothing came to mind.

The other papers in the folder had Asher's basic profile, likely faxed over from Judith. She'd used an old picture of him, but he hadn't changed much. He couldn't see the scar on his mouth or the tattoos under the corner of his eyes.

Two small face tattoos of simple triangles hadn't been a bad idea at the time. Now he wondered if someone seemingly as straitlaced as Bartholomew would appreciate them.

Didn't matter. It was Asher's face.

Noise from Bartholomew's return echoed from the hallway and Asher backed away. He feigned interest in the framed artwork across from the desk and hid his scowl. An angel wing painted with generic religious imagery. They were wearing white robes, had long silken blonde hair, and a fucking halo. Pink and gold colors reigned, leaving the angel wing suffused in dawn's light as they played a golden harp in their lap.

"Here we are," Bartholomew announced as he plopped the stool down. It had a plain wicker frame with a threadbare cushion, but plenty of space for wings. Asher settled on it, comfortable, and Bartholomew sat at his desk.

With a small smile on his lips, Bartholomew

slipped on a pair of reading glasses and focused on the papers. He looked over one, his jaw working in silent syllables, like he was thinking of where to start. He finally peered at Asher over the glasses.

"Introductions," Bartholomew decided and leaned back. "I am Watcher Bartholomew. Judith sent a message to all of us with empty nests so we could meet you properly."

"Yes," Asher said, nerves leaking through and making his voice quiver. "I'm A-Asher. You-You know that." Bartholomew nodded, glancing at the papers again. Asher twisted his fingers around his coat, holding it taut. "S-Should I say something else?"

"No. No, I'm just glancing through all the paperwork sent over," Bartholomew said, picking one out from the pile. "Give me a moment to compare the information with the young man before me."

"Paperwork from Judith?"

"And others."

Others. *Shit*. A jolt of panic shot through Asher, making his wings twitch. He should have taken a closer look to see what people had said about him. Maybe it was from Belle. *Hopefully* it was from Belle.

He twisted his jacket tighter, palms sweating, and the room grew too quiet to stand.

Just breathe.

Asher's life was in Bartholomew's hands and he was perusing it like Asher was no more than a used car with a lengthy history of crashes.

"So?" Asher asked. "A-Are we a good fit? J-Judith thinks we could be."

"I'm your *only* fit right now," Bartholomew said without looking up and Asher snapped his jaw shut so sharply, it made an audible click.

Bartholomew glanced up. Now, he took the moment to actually perceive Asher. He didn't look pleased.

"There are a few things we should discuss." Bartholomew steepled his fingers together.

"Okay." Asher swallowed and pulled his shoulders together, trying to get his wings to fold closer to his back. "Shoot."

"Your piercings."

Asher touched them. Rose gold studs lined his ear up to his industrial piercing. He'd had most of them since he was sixteen. The group of devil wings that had adopted Raum had done it late one night in the basement of a bar they were squatting at. Probably hadn't been the safest idea. Raum now cringed that he'd let Asher do it at all, especially since he knew way more about piercings now. The industrial had come later, when Raum was at the tattoo shop.

"I like them." Asher settled his hand back down.

"It's unbecoming of an angel wing."

Asher didn't answer, even though he wanted to flip Bartholomew off. He remained still and silent, breathing in deep to stay calm, and Bartholomew's gaze flicked to the scar on his lip.

"Scars not allowed either?" Asher snapped, unable to help himself, and Bartholomew narrowed his eyes. Not an outright glare, but his patience was wearing thin.

"They're... also unbecoming," Bartholomew stressed. It must have been his favorite word.

"It's not like I wanted it," Asher said. "My boyfriend got overzealous after he got his canines sharpened. Not much I can do about it."

Bartholomew didn't answer, but the way his face tightened, there was something about that statement he hadn't liked. Too many possibilities for Asher to guess, each one lighting a fire beneath his skin. He swallowed it down, remembering that he promised that he'd give the man a chance.

Bartholomew's gaze darted downward to the hand left uncovered by the coat, at the moons in different phases dotting Asher's fingers. Asher didn't bother trying to hide them and splayed his fingers to make sure Bartholomew got a real good look. He had nothing to be ashamed of. It was his body, after all.

"Tattoos are also unbecoming of an angel wing," Bartholomew continued, barely hiding the scorn in his monotone voice. His eyes trailed upward to the sleeve, stopping where the black shoulder tattoo was. "What's on your arm?"

"It's tattooed black," Asher said simply and Bartholomew exhaled slowly.

"We can keep it under a sleeve," he suggested.

Asher clamped down on his tongue to keep from snapping. "Why does it matter?"

Bartholomew stared at him like it should have been obvious. Maybe it was, but Asher wanted Bartholomew to say it aloud. Get it over with. Make him squirm spelling out what a judgmental prick he was.

After a silent moment of careful deliberation, Bartholomew straightened. He dropped his hands to his desk, like he was bracing himself. "People except a certain... look from angel wings," he explained slowly and waved a hand in Asher's direction. "They are to be demure, wise, chaste—"

"Wait," Asher spoke, eyebrows high, "wait. Wait. Hold up." Bartholomew stammered to a stop, casting a withering glare on Asher for interrupting him. "*Chaste*?"

"... Yes."

"Like... no sex?"

Bartholomew readjusted his glasses. He must have found talking about it uncomfortable. "Yes, that is exactly what I mean."

Asher blinked. "I've had sex before," he said, laughing, but Bartholomew only slowed, hard eyes on him like he wanted to burn a hole through Asher. "Lots of it, actually."

"We can start fresh. New you. It's not like anyone checks anymore."

"If no one *checks*"—thinking about it at all made Asher sick—"then why does it matter?"

"It's a distraction. To be a good angel wing, you're to have none," Bartholomew stressed through clenched teeth.

Fire blazed through Asher's pulse, his anger ready to blow. "I have a boyfriend that I am very much attracted to." Bartholomew's face tightened.

"You're really telling me I won't be allowed to have sex with him? What, are you going to watch me at all times?"

Bartholomew's face grew a shade redder. Anger or embarrassment, Asher wasn't sure. "Angel wings must carry themselves with a certain amount of *decency*. They look and behave in certain ways or else how are people supposed to look to you for divine inspiration? No. You are not allowed to and, quite frankly, it's a distraction from your divine mission. I suggest you forget all about whoever you've had dalliances with and put yourself fully into being an angel wing. It's all that matters and you need to treat it with respect."

"You just want someone to control," Asher shot back. His body trembled from the pent-up anger, making his words shake. Bartholomew's glare darkened. "That gets you a fucking hard on, doesn't it?"

Bartholomew's eyebrows shot up and his jaw dropped. Asher laughed.

"It's why you gunned for Amy, wasn't it? You saw her as a doll too perfect to ever rebel and you knew she'd listen to whatever religious bullshit you forced on her. And now? Now you're scrambling for favor, thinking that by taming me, people will give a damn about you. You *think* you can convince me to play meek and break up with my boyfriend just to be your perfect little pet in a cage?" Asher leaned over the desk. "Fuck. Off."

Asher was breathless leaving the office, his

lungs catching up to how fast he'd spat out the words. All his anger spilling to the surface, eager to blow up on some asshole who'd pushed him too far.

Bartholomew deserved it.

His ears rang, drowning everything out in white noise. His body trembled so hard he didn't even bother trying to get his coat back on. He focused on getting one foot in front of the other, tearing down the hall, barely hearing the shout of his name.

No. He wasn't going back. He flung himself down the stairs without care, and swung himself around the corner at the bottom to reach the doors faster. The nice clerk at the desk raised her voice in concern, but she couldn't help him. Not with Bartholomew thundering after him.

Addam was waiting in the turnaround. Asher yanked the door open, flung himself inside, and slammed it shut.

Thankfully, Addam didn't need telling and drove. Peeled out without looking back and expertly weaved into afternoon traffic clogging the street. All before Bartholomew managed to come out, red faced, and breathing hard.

It was a while before Asher calmed himself down, until his breathing evened and he stopped trying to tear his coat in two.

And it was only then did Addam speak.

"Well," he said, "I see that went as expected."

Asher jerked to face him. "You *knew* I was going to blow up on that fucker?"

"Language," Addam said and held up a hand

when Asher opened his mouth to tell him where to shove it. "Judith wanted you to give him a fair chance. We thought since he had a whole docket about you, he'd... I don't know... Relax?" Addam sighed and eased them into the turn off lane. "Judith warned him."

"You should have warned *me* beyond calling him a fucking traditionalist." Asher thumped back in his seat and finally remembered to buckle himself in. He missed the latch more times than he wanted to admit between his hands trembling and his vision blurring with angry tears.

"Asher—"

"You both wanted me to see how much I screwed up being an angel wing before I even had wings." Asher wiped his eyes. "I get it."

"No," Addam countered. "We wanted you to go in as your authentic self. We wanted you both to give each other a fair chance."

"He didn't bother."

"I see that. He was supposed to."

An imminent breakdown frayed Asher at the edges, but he didn't want it to happen here. Especially not in front of Addam. It was the kind of breakdown where he'd cry, scream, and break things. As petulant as it was, he needed a physical outlet. Words only went so far. He needed something to do. Something real he could feel.

It helped that Addam was not much of a talker. It let Asher concentrate on not losing it in the truck.

Bartholomew definitely wouldn't want him

now. No doubt, he'd call the other watchers and tell them what had happened and then no one else would want Asher either. Fear welled up in his chest just thinking about it. He was supposed to have his life figured out, like all the other foundlings before him, but he'd fucked it up long before he'd gotten his wings. No matter what loophole Judith found, he was screwed. He probably couldn't stay at the foundling house much longer, but that left him with nowhere to go. If Belle refused to host him, no one else would, especially if there was an angel wing already living in the area.

He was fucked. All possible outcomes came crashing to a halt and the unknown practically suffocated him.

They arrived at the foundling house before Asher lost it, thankfully, and he shoved the passenger side door open before the truck had completely stopped. Asher hurried around to the back for the patio doors, the closest to the stairs near his room. He stormed inside and, of course, Judith was there. She must have heard the truck come up the driveway and was waiting.

Asher couldn't deal with her. Not now. He hardly saw her worried expression through the blur of hot tears welling up again and rushed past where she sat on the couch. She stood, clearly wanting to stop him, but he flipped her off. She let out a resigned sigh and he left her, storming up the stairs alone.

He snagged the small phone from the second-floor hallway table, dragged it into his room, and slammed the door.

He knew he was being a petulant brat. He hated himself for it. All he wanted right now, was to find normalcy. He dialed the tattoo parlor. Just to pretend the world outside didn't exist.

"'Ey—it's—"

"Hey, Molly," Asher interrupted, hearing his voice breaking. "Can I talk to Raum? Please?"

"Yeah, of course. I'll grab him," Molly said quickly, sounding concerned. "He's on lunch. Just hold on a second."

No funny jokes this time. Desperation dripped off Asher's voice and he hated how obvious it was. He paced as he waited, careful not to trip over the coiled phone cord, and began raking a hand through his hair.

"Hey... hey," Raum's voice was soft when he came to the phone. "Is everything all right?"

No, but Asher bit the honesty back and swallowed it. "C-Can we hang out today?"

There was a deafening pause. "Ash," Raum whispered. "I-I can't. Remember? I have that big client tonight."

Fuck. Of course. It had been wiped so far from Asher's mind. Guilt slotted itself right next to the dread, making Asher sick. What kind of boyfriend was he? Forgetting what Raum had told him just last night. He thumped his back against his door, not even caring that his entire back twinged in pain from the impact.

"C-Can I come and watch? Hang out there with Molly or something?"

Raum hesitated.

Silence gave way to frustration and Asher held the phone receiver tighter. "*What*? Are people going to be uneasy with an angel wing there?"

"Asher—"

"Shit, I'm sorry," Asher choked out. "I'll stop. I'm sorry. I'm just angry. I'm sorry for bothering you at work and everything."

"I have the weekend off," Raum said quickly, like he wanted to make sure he got it out there before Asher hung up. "We'll do something stupid then, okay? I promise. I'll be all yours for as long as you need."

Asher exhaled and nodded. "Yeah. I'd like that. Thank you. Good luck with the tattoo. I-I'll talk to you later."

He hung up before Raum could get him to talk more. If Asher spilled everything he was feeling right now, frustration would rear its ugly head and he'd say something he'd regret. Again. More tears slipped down his cheeks and he let them go this time. No use stopping them now.

He slid down to the floor until he was sitting and brought his knees up to his chest to bury his face against them.

Everything hurt. His back. His wings. Curling up to cry made it all worse. Physically and emotionally. Like the universe was punishing him for shit he couldn't take back.

There was a gentle knock against his door and he curled up tighter, gripping his hair. "I'm sorry," he whispered, knowing it was Judith. "I shouldn't have flipped you off."

Judith chuckled on the other side. "I've learned when you do that, deep down, you mean '*I love you*,'" she said and Asher wasn't going to correct her. "I'm sorry I did not adequately prepare you. I didn't think it'd go so badly."

Asher had nothing more to say.

"If you want to talk some of this out," she continued, "I'll be downstairs, okay honey?"

She deployed her mom voice and it stirred some sense of normalcy within Asher. Like maybe talking to her *would* help, but at this point, he didn't want to.

"Thank you," was all he said.

She paused, listening like he might say more, but when he didn't, the telltale creak of the nearby floorboard rang out, purposefully announcing her exit.

Asher eased out a ragged breath. "I don't want to talk," he whispered, drawing his gaze across his room. "I want to fucking do something." His eyes caught the glint of his bag of spray paint underneath his bed.

Weight lifted off his shoulders and his mood went with it. He knew exactly what he could do.

7

Paint Stains

THE FAMILIAR WEIGHT of Asher's bag dug into his shoulder as he climbed down from his window and went in search of a canvas. All the colors he'd collected over the years were stuffed inside the bag, practically ripping it apart at the seams, only safety pins keeping it together, but he wouldn't have it any other way. Having all the colors with him was grounding. He never knew what he was going to do until he found the perfect wall and got to work.

It didn't take him long to find the canvas and, just as quickly, he was absorbed in the act of creation. The sound the colors made as they hit the stucco wall was music. The wall was quickly covered in a sheen of different colors. The whole act of turning something blank and dull into brilliance with his own hands was the most cathartic thing he'd ever known.

The art was transitory, especially when he tagged places without permission, so whenever he painted, he also brought an instant camera to capture the moment. Back at the house, he had a binder full of snapshots of all the pieces he'd done since he began sneaking out.

Transplanting his sketches onto walls and overpasses worked as an outlet—both physically (there was a thrill to it in the dead of night) and mentally (where everything would be out of his head to see properly). Some of the pieces withstood the test of time even now, but others had been graffitied anew or even added to. Those collaborations were the most fun.

When Asher came back to find that another artist had added something, he felt the urge to add more. Sometimes he and the unknown artist would spend days going back and forth on the design until one of them stopped, tired of the game, or when the city inevitably ruined their fun. Even though he'd never met the other artists, it was nice to be connected to them through art.

Although the city never saw it as art. All they saw was blight. They were wrong.

Creation was a fleeting moment. No piece lasted forever, but doing it helped Asher let go of his built-up frustrations because they were fleeting too. The art would encapsulate it, bright and poignant, and it'd be out of his head.

Traffic rumbled by in the distance, but it never came close. Asher was glad. He'd picked broad fucking daylight—a huge risk. Thankfully, the angel wing nest before him was empty and secluded from the street by a hedge grown wild.

Fitting, Asher supposed. This would have been his nest if Bartholomew had his way, though it was clearly neglected. The roof tiles looked weak, the white stucco exterior had cracks along the foundation, and it was a wonder the windows weren't broken just to complete the well-worn image.

More evidence that Bartholomew didn't care about the angel wing he got. Just the notoriety that would have come with it.

That made it all the sweeter to add graffiti art.

The door had been locked, stopping Asher from making a mural inside, but that would have been pushing it. Around the back was a blank wall where he stood with a thousand possibilities.

Normally, he'd find a wall and take maybe a day to sketch an idea for it. Not this time. He was here and so was the wall. His hands guided him on instinct alone. All he knew was that he was sad and frustrated. The emotions sent his hands across the empty space, picking out colors without even glancing at them. He knew his colors and the cans well enough that he didn't need to.

The image quickly took shape, an angel figure standing in the center with one hand up, its pale arm jutting out of a black hole in the white robes. The other hand lay clasped underneath the bright red heart pinned to the chest. The face was sad, eyebrows drawn tight with one eye closed, the other one opened wide. He'd intentionally drawn the eyes larger to bring attention to them. The wings were a pearl white, one of them hung crookedly to the side while the other was perfectly straight. The angel stood against a backdrop of golds and pinks, but instead of being suffused in some holy glow, Asher kept his lines harsh and jagged, letting the angel pop out instead of fading into the background.

The image itself wasn't big, just tall enough where Asher could reach, but he wished he'd lugged his folding stool with him so he could have reached higher. Sneaking out with that was a little harder than just his colors.

Maybe it was better he'd left it behind. The hedge kept him hidden. For once, it paid to be on the shorter side. There wasn't much behind the building, at least. Aside from a street turning into alleys and a creek twisting off from the main river, trees and bushes grew wild. The nest was literally isolated from anything that mattered. It would have been the perfect place to shove an unruly angel wing.

Asher stepped back to consider his art. The fugue state of creation had faded, leaving him in reality. Not bad, all things considered. Maybe not one of his better pieces, but such was art. He dug into his paints, looking for *something* to add to it, and ended up pulling out his bright red again. Perfect. Red accents would make the whole thing pop more.

He was well into the details—a trail of red from the heart to the outstretched hand, a red outline around the arms, and even around the eyes—when he noticed a shadow beside him.

A person.

He jumped with a yelp and spun to face them, spray can raised. Just Amy.

Good thing he hadn't chucked the can and ran like he normally did when caught. Most people didn't bother chasing him once it hit them in the face.

He pressed a hand to his chest, willing his heart to slow, but Amy was studying the art too closely to notice his surprise. She wore a thick wool shawl over her sweater today, a brown patchwork skirt, and neon-yellow stockings that clashed with her usual earthy tones. They were ones Asher had given her when she said she wanted to try bolder colors. She was even wearing the leather studded cuff Asher and Raum had gotten her a few birthdays ago. A contrast to the rest of her image and sized more for Raum than her (the shop hadn't had any smaller sizes), but she loved it.

"You know," she said, tapping a finger on her chin, "they're going to know this was you."

Asher snorted and pulled his facemask down. He'd been wearing it to keep from breathing the fumes. "Really?" he said sarcastically.

His wings ached from being trapped beneath the black hoodie he'd thrown on. Judith had sewn slits into the back, but he hadn't bothered pulling his wings through. One, so no one noticed it was him, and two, he couldn't reach back and get his wings out by himself yet.

"Rumor has it an unruly angel wing blew up on Bartholomew this afternoon," Amy said.

"How do you already know that?"

Amy clasped her hands behind her back. "Old people are very efficient with their gossip. There was an elderly woman who saw you storming off and admonished Bartholomew for chasing after you. Afterward, she immediately wanted to talk to me about this new angry angel wing." She slid a glance at Asher and he sighed. "Your wings hurting under there?"

Asher hung his head. "Like a bitch."

"Want help getting them out? I think your cover's blown anyway."

Especially with Amy literally standing right there with her brown wings. Asher nodded and straightened to let her help. Her hands were as efficient as Judith's, easily prying the wings free of their confines and smoothing them out.

Much better. Asher tested stretching. Pain blossomed, reminding him that was still a bad idea, and he winced.

"It gets easier," Amy said. "Be glad you don't have to maneuver a bra around them."

Asher snorted. "I didn't think that'd be complicated."

"I didn't either!"

"Do you remember when you got your wings?" Asher asked as he rolled his shoulders, hoping to ease some of the residual aches. Amy tilted her head, curious. "And I made fun of them since they looked like featherless chicken wings?"

It was Amy's turn to snort. "*Yes...* I slammed the door on you and you went on cackling."

"Yeah... but in a week or something, all your feathers had properly grown in?" Asher smiled wryly at her. "I think I would have preferred that."

"Starting small probably helped a lot." Amy eased a hand over his shoulder blade and rubbed it. "For what it's worth, it gets easier. You're still healing."

"Do you think if I said sorry now, I'd feel better?"

Amy giggled. "You can try."

"I'm sorry, Amy."

"Apology accepted."

"They still hurt."

To Amy's credit, she tried not laughing. Then Asher started, and soon they were shooing their hands at each other to make the other stop. It was ridiculous thinking the pain would have stopped with a simple apology. But they were laughing, and it made Asher feel like it was years ago before anyone had gotten their wings.

It tapered off pretty quickly. Amy was watching him, like he might start talking on his own if she waited long enough. Judith frequently employed the same tactic, but it never worked on him. Just Amy and Raum.

"Do you want to talk?" she finally asked.

"Not really," he mumbled. "But I probably should."

"I'm told I'm a good listener."

She was. Asher bent and picked up his bag. "Let me just finish this up."

He fished out his camera and eased back to

get the whole thing in the shot. No doubt it'd be gone by tomorrow.

When the photo spat out, he let Amy hold onto it and the camera before pulling out black to sign the bottom of the wall with his middle finger stencil, just in case his message wasn't clear.

Amy bit back a laugh. "Very on the nose."

"They're already going to know it's me, might as well make my message clear."

"Understandable." Amy pointed toward the road. "I brought my bike if you want to put your paints in the basket."

"How'd you even know I'd be here?" Asher asked.

Amy shrugged. "Foundling sibling intuition, I guess." She gazed up at the empty nest and wrinkled her nose. "Seven years without an angel wing here and Bartholomew never saw fit to take care of the place, huh? Seems like a stray lightning strike could take it down. Or a careless match..."

Asher glanced at the grass; it was dry enough. The nest was mostly wood, too. Could probably happen.

"Got anywhere in mind?" Asher interrupted, hoping this wasn't Amy's way of telling him she was thinking of becoming an arsonist. Judith only needed one problematic angel wing. "I should leave the scene of the crime."

"I do, actually." Amy led the way back to her bike. Raum was always insisting he could teach her to ride his motorbike, but she liked the slower pace.

The bike was cute, painted in the same earth tones as most of her clothes. Addam had put it together for her shortly before she got her wings. A wicker basket hung off the handlebars and Asher put his paints inside.

"Well? Where is it?" Asher asked.

Amy took the handlebars and smiled. "The usual place."

The usual place was the grassy incline against the river running between the heart of the city and the road to the foundling house. As kids, when not dashing through the woods with abandon, Asher, Amy, and Raum would lay across the grass on warm days to watch the clouds roll by after school.

It was nice seeing the spot again. Still peaceful and empty. Whenever it rained, the river flooded over. It was intended, though, so the streets wouldn't flood. There hadn't been any attempts to make the incline anything more than what it already was. A paved walkway hugged the shore, in case someone wanted to walk down there, but not many did. There was a bridge farther down for the road where Asher had graffitied the underside with Raum's help once in the dead of night. Some of the paint was still there, pieces of the water god he'd made up lingering, but most had flaked away.

Asher hadn't been by since Amy and Raum got their wings. It was always a place they visited together. When Amy and Raum were too busy, Asher stopped going. It'd felt weird being there by himself. Although now, he realized he missed the place more than he cared to admit.

Amy laid down first, wings tucked around her, and Asher tried to do the same. His wings protested the movement, but he managed to lay beside her, shoulder to shoulder, wing to wing. If Raum was on Asher's other side, he could have believed it was the halcyon days of their youth, silently watching the clouds go by and existing peacefully together.

A breeze ghosted over Asher, making him shiver, and he huddled deeper into his hoodie. Faraway trees rustled, their reds and oranges swaying like distant fire against the clear sky. No matter how cold it was, though, Asher wouldn't have minded lying here all day, watching the sky fade from blue to orange and then finally to purple. It'd be soothing.

Except Amy wanted to talk. He pulled his attention back to her, but she didn't speak right away. She stared at the selfsame trees, hands clasped over her stomach, and watched.

One of them had to start.

"I've been reading your book."

Amy smiled and inclined her head to look at him. "Is it helping?"

Asher turned to get pressure off his wings. They were hurting too much to keep lying there like he used to, and he propped himself up on his elbows. "You didn't mention how decorum meant complete celibacy."

Amy shot up, eyebrows high, and Asher slowly came up to sit beside her. "*What*?"

"When I met with Bartholomew—" Asher winced, cutting himself off from the jab of pain in his back. Amy reached out to help, her hands soft as she righted a few feathers. "He was talking about all this decorum crap and said I can't have sex anymore."

Amy's face scrunched. "He seriously said that?"

The words burned fresh in Asher's mind and he repeated them verbatim for her. Every single one that he'd poured into the paint to get them out of his head. Yet, they persisted still.

Amy's face pinched further and she eased out a breath.

"Wendy did tell me people have this ideal angel wing in their heads," she said slowly. "But she said it's an act you play for the public. All she told me about sex was that if I *was* interested, I was within my bodily rights to engage. It's my body, after all." She crossed her arms as her wings ruffled angrily behind her. "What is he? Living fifty years ago or something?"

"Addam called him a traditionalist."

Amy rolled her eyes. "He should get with the times. You'd think after his last angel wing, he'd be softer or something."

His last angel wing... Asher frowned. "What happened to the last one? You said it's been seven years?"

"It was a big scandal, apparently." Amy pulled her knees to her chest and wrapped her arms around them. "Judith and Addam decided not to let us watch the news when it was all going down to keep us from being traumatized, but from what I can gather, there was... An accident." She stared out over the water in the river. "The angel wing tumbled down the stairs in her nest and broke her neck."

Asher shuddered involuntarily.

"Angel wings are supposed to disappear, not die," Amy said quietly. "So, it unnerved a lot of people. An inquiry was made into what actually happened, but the records were sealed afterward."

"You think Bart did it?" Asher asked.

"Only the angel wings and their watchers have keys to the nests... Bartholomew found her. Officially, it was deemed an accident," Amy said carefully and looked at him. "Wendy won't talk to me about it and tells me not to worry. Although, it's an open secret that Bartholomew has a temper."

"Yeah, saw that," Asher said. "But I guess no one really cared, huh?"

"Well, people are insisting nests have lifts now," Amy said with a dry laugh. "Except no one wants to donate the money, so all my nest has right now is a really nice new stair railing."

Typical. Angel wings were fawned over as something special, but only to a certain extent. Anything that needed actual thought was eventually given up on. The problem transitory.

Asher laid himself back down on his side. "Well, Bart was certainly a dick when I went in. I should have stayed home." He whispered the last part, staring back at the grass instead of Amy.

His shift in mood must have been apparent. Amy's wings drooped and she laid herself beside Asher, facing him this time.

"Raum called me, you know."

Not what Asher wanted to talk about. He tried to roll over, away from her, but Amy stopped him with a hand on his shoulder.

"He said he couldn't get a hold of you at the house, so he wanted me to check on you. It was my plan anyway since, you know, *Bartholomew*. Just tell me, though... What's wrong?"

Everything, but that wasn't a real answer. Just convenient. Asher pushed himself back up and brought his knees to his chest. He tried to get his wings to cocoon him in so he didn't have to look at Amy as she sat up beside him, but they weren't big enough.

"I'm frustrated," Asher said, gripping his sleeves.

"With Raum?"

"Yes, with Raum." Asher shook his head. Leave it to Amy to go right to the heart of the matter. "*Days* after Raum got his wings, we had sex and he said it was like something was *right* with his wings free. But he hasn't wanted to touch me like that since I got my wings." Amy opened her mouth—to argue or refute the point, he wasn't sure—but Asher's mouth kept going. "My wings are *fine*. It would have been fine. And... And, okay, maybe I'm just sensitive right now, but it just feels like he suddenly doesn't want to touch me when he's been all over me for so long. So yes, I am frustrated. Especially now that I'm being told I'm not even supposed to *have* a boyfriend, let alone have sex with him."

His voice was struggling at the end, words uneven and broken, and he hurried to wipe the tears in his eyes. All Amy did was watch, her wings drooping further behind her, betraying her emotion. She didn't know what to say.

Asher immediately regretted saying so much. Back when they were all still in the house, she'd let him and Raum have their space because she knew how they'd felt about each other. It wasn't her thing, though. She wouldn't understand how it felt to have Raum all over him one day—the usual for literally years—and then the next, too afraid to touch him.

"I'm sorry," he said, panicked. "Sex isn't your thing. I shouldn't drop this on you."

Amy shook her head. "No, it's fine," she said. "I was just stunned. You two have always been... Well, you know." She gathered her hands in her lap, never once wavering as she watched Asher. It'd be unnerving if Asher didn't know her so well. She was just thinking. "Perhaps he doesn't want to make your life harder right now."

"I should be making that choice," Asher snapped. "He shouldn't be making it for me. Bart and all this decorum bullshit can fuck off." He looked away, scrunching his shoulders. "I just... I just feel terrible being so frustrated with Raum. But everything's gone sideways so fast and the only thing I could count on isn't there to help me forget everything. And... And I just feel so out of place." He dropped his head into his arms so he didn't have to look at anything. "No watcher wants me. My boyfriend's afraid to want me. I'm actually terrified to just say fuck it and leave. Nothing's right anymore."

Silence greeted his outburst. Too many vulnerabilities he should have kept locked up, now out in the open so fast, and he couldn't take them back. The breeze was the only thing that answered him, throwing a chill across his wings and rustling his feathers.

Amy finally touched his hand. "I know," she said softly. "I easily fit into the mold Wendy made for me. It suited me and I know it will *never* suit you." She leaned in and Asher felt the brush of her wings against his own. "None of that, however, is your fault."

"Then what should I do?"

It stumped her for longer than Asher liked. He lifted his head to distract himself from the silence. The blue sky had darkened, slowly turning into the soft pink and orange streaks of evening. Traffic was louder with the evening rush. Both overt signs of time continuing despite Asher's want for it to hold still so he could think.

Amy's fingers drummed on Asher's arm and he glanced at her.

"Oh!" she said, her eyes practically sparkling with mischief. "I might have an idea. Lately, the gossipers have been talking about this nest-less angel wing that comes to town every so often."

That sounded too good to be true. Asher considered her skeptically.

"Seriously!" Amy waved him off with her hand. "He's been setting up in an alley somewhere on main street and tells fortunes with cards. One even saw him buying groceries recently. Maybe I can ask around, see if we can find him." Her wings perked behind her. "Since he's supposedly nest-less, he might have some worldly advice."

Asher felt his own wings lift. "You think so?"

"The other angel wings will just tell you to fake it until it works," Amy admitted. "It's what so many have done and most of them eventually do take to what's expected of them. I don't want to tell you to do something you'd hate, so maybe advice from this outsider angel wing won't be bad." She pulled her hand away and bounced excitedly in her spot. "I can even put those gossipers to work! Have them keep an eye out."

She was already too into the plan, but it made Asher smile seeing her so excited. Even more so, it made him smile thinking about all those who would probably bury a body for her if she'd asked. She was just that good of an angel wing.

Streetlights buzzed on and the area lit itself in fuzzy oranges. Asher and Amy gazed up toward the street at the same time.

Asher took Amy's hand and held it tight. "Thank you," he said and she beamed at him. "Want me to walk you home?"

Amy snorted, blowing the stray hairs off her forehead. "I have my bike," she said. She bent forward and pecked him on the cheek, her lips warm. "You go on home. Drink some tea with Addam outside."

It was the time of year Addam liked sitting outside on the patio with his firepit. Though it was usually his quiet time, he never minded if someone wanted to sit out there with him. The foundling quartet frequently invited themselves, but if Asher headed home now, he'd get back a little after they were tucked in for the night.

"Maybe," Asher said. "I might go to sleep."

Amy rolled her eyes. "You never go to bed this early." She stood and deftly pulled Asher up with her. "I'll let you know when I find a lead. You stay out of trouble until then, promise?"

"Promise."

Hopefully, the easiest promise of his life. At least the urge for graffiti art was out of his system.

He walked Amy back to her bike and took his paints before he waved her off. She rode into the growing violet twilight, her bike lighting up as she pedaled. Once she was out of sight, Asher turned and fished out a cigarette.

He lit one for the road and though he didn't want to, he began his walk home.

The sky was completely violet when he returned, the sun long since lost behind the city, and stars were peeking out. Asher had planned to head through the patio door instead of the window he'd climbed out earlier—his back hurt too much to scale the trellis—but he hesitated.

Addam was sitting on the patio like Amy had guessed, the last fire of the season blazing bright in the firepit. No foundling in sight and a mug of tea in one hand.

An invitation, loud and clear. Addam even had a thermos and a second mug next to him. Amy must have planned this. Asher hadn't intended to sit down, but after a moment of watching Addam watch him, he gave in.

He set his bag down, and curled up next to Addam on the wicker couch, drawing his wings tightly around himself as a buffer. There was the ghost of a smile on Addam's lips as he poured Asher a cup.

The fire was nice. Always mesmerizing to watch it eat up all the dead twigs and leaves. The smell was even better. All throughout the summer and fall, it would waft into Asher's room, reminding him the day was over and that there was a new one rising out of the ashes of the old.

Addam took a sip from his cup and Asher followed suit. Chamomile and cinnamon tea. It tingled its way down Asher's throat and warmed him from the inside.

"Painting today?" Addam asked, sliding a glance at the colorful stains lingering against Asher's fingertips and then the bag.

Asher drew his shoulders tighter. "Maybe." Before Addam could ask what and where, Asher fished out the snapshot and handed it over.

Like always, Addam studied the picture silently. He liked art, had an eye for it too, but to Asher's knowledge, he didn't paint himself.

"You're getting bolder with colors. I like the red," Addam gave it back. "Do you want to talk?"

"What if I just left?" Asher whispered.

Addam stopped, silent, and remained so for a moment longer than Asher thought he would.

When Addam spoke again, his words were careful and slow. "And where would you go?"

"Would it matter?"

Asher stared into the fire, knowing Addam was watching him, concern leaking through his usual stoicism. Maybe it was too much to say, but leaving *would* solve a lot of Asher's problems and, by extension, Judith's. He wouldn't have to give himself to the city and Judith would be free to move on and focus on the new foundlings.

Except it was the last thing he wanted. It meant leaving Raum and Amy behind. He couldn't ask them to go with him; he wasn't that selfish. And leaving them might kill him. They were all he had.

"Asher..."

"Never mind," Asher cut Addam off, not wanting the vulnerability for either of them. "I don't think I could go through with it anyway."

Asher was glad Addam let it be. They watched the fire and drank their tea, once again silent. When the fire had eaten up all it could, dwindling into a mere glow until only dying embers ghosted into the sky, Asher helped Addam put it out.

When Asher got to his room, he fell into bed fully clothed. The lingering smell of fire clung to him like a blanket and he let it soothe him to sleep.

8

The Divining Punk

WITHOUT THE ENERGY to deal with anyone, Asher kept to himself the next day. Part of him hated it, this limbo feeling of waiting for something to happen, but he didn't know what else to do. Judith checked on him shortly after lunchtime to tell him Bartholomew had come by to talk, but Asher didn't bother replying. He'd already said what he'd wanted to. Besides, if he'd gone out, he'd just yell again.

Judith had taken his silence as answer enough. Shortly after, a car outside drove away, its rumbling engine cutting through the quiet autumn air. Some of the tension inside Asher's back uncoiled. At least Bartholomew hadn't stayed long. Afterward, Judith left Asher entirely alone. Everyone did.

It was a little lonely, but Asher made the most of it. He spent the day listening to cassettes Raum had sent him, sketching tattoo ideas that would go well with the angel wings, and looking through his binder of art snapshots. Addam wasn't wrong; the colors had certainly grown bolder as time went on. Seeing growth like that was nice. Most of the time, Asher wasn't sure if he was getting better or not.

He was glad his room was disconnected from reality at large. Not counting his wings and the occasional throb across his back, it felt like nothing had changed. It let him reorganize himself, if only for a single day.

When evening rolled around, the sun beginning its slow descent out of the sky, a rock knocked against his window. Curious, Asher pushed it open and peeked out.

Raum stood on the patio, dressed in his leather riding jacket, and had a helmet under his arm. He had a large grin on his lips, one Asher knew meant a good kind of trouble.

"Hey you," Raum said, trying to sound suave.

Asher smiled and rested his chin on his palm. "You could have climbed up. Rock throwing is a little cliché, even for you."

Raum bit back a laugh. "Addam told me not to." His gaze slid to the patio doors then back up. He scratched the back of his head. "Something about one day, I was going to take the entire trellis down and break my leg. He saw me coming up. I even parked up the road so I could be sneaky!"

Asher rolled his eyes and chuckled. "You want me to sneak you in? I can come down and unlock the door."

"Sneaking *you* out," Raum said, eyes darting back to the patio doors.

No one would be down there right now; dinner was over and the kids were bathing. It was only a matter of time before one of them finished and stole away to turn on some lights.

"Amy found the guy. Well... Actually, he showed up at the tattoo parlor to get a tattoo from a cool devil wing. Yours truly."

Asher was still hung up on *'found the guy'* even as Raum made a mock bow. Asher's eyes went wide and his jaw dropped. "That fast?"

"Amy's people don't mess around!" Raum said. "Apparently, she told them that if they talk to him, to get him thinking about getting a tattoo from the devil wing tattoo artist as a memento of visiting. I don't think she expected him to show up so soon either." He beckoned Asher. "Come on! When he left, we tailed him to this dive bar near the highway."

"Wait, *we*? Where'd you leave Amy?"

"There was this cozy convenience store on the opposite corner." Asher glared at Raum, but his boyfriend held up his hands. "It was her idea! Let's grab her and find the guy before he disappears into the night."

Asher was in his denim jacket—wings pulled through the slits all on his own—down the trellis, and on the back of Raum's motorbike in record time. They easily slipped through the early evening traffic, weaving in and out of empty side streets to stay on the move and so no one got a good look at Asher and gawked.

The place Raum had left Amy was clear across the city, down streets full of industrial buildings and dingy restaurants that Asher hadn't seen in more than a year.

Raum parked the bike in the alley between the lit-up convenience store and a small pharmacy. They left their helmets with the bike, and before they'd even reached the store doors, Amy was coming out to intercept them. The automatic doors slid shut after her and she immediately pulled them to the corner cross-walk.

She'd dressed down in dark tones for once, purples and blacks, like it would help her appear inconspicuous. If not for the wings. Anyone glancing at her would still know she was Amy, the angel wing. No amount of dressing different would change that.

"He hasn't left yet," Amy said and nodded toward the building across the street. "I was watching his car from the window." She pointed to the silver sedan across the street in the crumbling parking lot. "The clerk helped me watch too since she was bored. No one's come out of the bar since you left to get Asher."

Though Asher was content to wait outside, see if the angel wing would come out on his own, Amy pulled them across the street to the other corner.

Raum was uncharacteristically withdrawn as they crossed and Asher watched him. Normally, he'd be a willing participant, especially since this was Amy's bad idea. He held his motorbike keys tight in his fist and his eyes were darting across the quickly darkening street. Most of the streetlights weren't even working on this stretch.

Amy slowed once they reached the other corner and looked at Raum too, confused. "What's up?" she asked and turned him and Asher toward her to make a protective huddle. It must have been quite the sight. Two angel wings huddled around a devil wing.

Raum shook his head, his eyes darting back to them. His face was drawn tight. "This area's just not so hot with me," he said.

Asher and Amy looked in different directions for anyone watching. A car moseyed on by, and Asher and Amy watched it go while Raum continued.

"Remember the old crew?"

"You mean Harv?"

"Yeah." Raum drew his wings over his shoulders instead of leaving them as the proud stretch he usually had. He was trying to be small. "We... Uh, well, we just don't get on anymore."

Asher studied Raum, frowning. Harv and his devil wings took to the typical reputation with sadistic glee, but they'd felt like a rambunctious family. The chaos was a breath of fresh air compared to the rigidity Asher had been used to.

And then, all of a sudden, Raum had stopped wanting to hang out with them, especially if Asher was with him. At the time, Asher hadn't pried. While the chaos had been liberating, even he'd realized if they'd kept at it, he and Raum would have burned out. And then, the tattoo parlor was taking up much of his time.

It was better this way, but now Asher was too curious not to ask. "Why don't you?"

Raum cut his gaze and glanced around them again. His eyes darted from for sale signs graffitied with bat wings, to the broken streetlights, and then to the bar they were just about to enter.

"He... He was starting to say weird stuff about you," he spoke quietly. "You never heard it—he was real good at making sure only I heard it—but it gave me the creeps."

Asher's skin flushed cold. "W-What?"

"I'm not going to repeat it," Raum said, uncomfortable. "It was weird. And, when I was starting to work at the tattoo shop, Harv decided I'd turned my back on him." He paused, shoulders tense, as a car turned down the street. It passed them and its taillights quickly disappeared into the dark.

"Seriously?" Amy's feathers ruffled around her. "Just because you wanted to do something with your life doesn't mean you're turning your back on them."

"I tried telling him that too and almost got stabbed in the argument." Raum shrugged, nonchalant, even as Amy and Asher stared at him in shock. "Harv and his crew leave me alone now."

"Why didn't you tell someone?" Amy asked.

"'Cause what would that have accomplished?" Raum shot back, angry. "I'm a devil wing too, you know. No one would have cared if one stabbed the other." He shook his head and looked away. "'Sides, afterward, he left me—us—

alone. I figured it'd never matter. Except... Well, except we're here now. On his turf. That he protects really, really well."

Asher suppressed a shudder. "You're not worried for you," he said and Raum was already nodding. "You're worried about us."

Raum turned slightly, scratching the back of his head as if he needed a reason for the turn, and Asher glanced around with renewed interest. The clerk from the convenience store was locking up for the night. The main lights switched off, leaving only a dim lamp illuminating the entryway. Amy waved at the clerk and she waved back, but soon she was gone.

"This neighborhood doesn't really *like* the devil wings," Raum continued, "but they let Harv's crew do what they want since by them being here, they deter worse people. Since it's mostly rundown buildings and businesses, no one cares if there's a nest here or not. 'Sides, Harv hates angel wings and so do his devil wings by association. And now... There's three of you here."

Raum's earlier bravado had been a ruse. Asher saw his unease clearly now. He glanced at Amy and she glanced at him, her wings drawing closer to her back. Too late now to reconsider; they were here and Asher didn't want to let this opportunity pass.

"We aren't going to be long," Amy said and touched Raum's arm. "Let's get inside and get this over with."

Asher gave her a crooked smile. "You're just

excited to see the inside of a dive bar," he said, going for levity.

Amy's cheeks went red and she swatted at his arm. "Shut up! I don't get to go on adventures with you guys anymore. This is going to be a new experience. No devil wing turf is going to ruin that for me."

Stifling a weak laugh, Raum ran his hands down his face. "I think both of you are way more trouble than I'll ever be," he teased. "Well, we going in?"

The three of them looked at the dive bar, but neither of them moved. By virtue of still being underage, Asher hadn't actually been inside a bar, but that wasn't to say he hadn't ever drunk himself stupid. He'd been with Raum then and the very same crew they were now trying to avoid. Raum had a single shot and decided against more since he was driving Asher home. Asher, freshly seventeen, still wingless, and eager to drown his sorrows, let himself be egged on to drink way more than he should have.

He *still* couldn't remember much of the night except the tail end of it. Addam had to come pick them up near two in the morning because Asher was in no state to ride on the back of a motorbike. It had been the only time Asher had ever seen Addam visibly angry. That reaction was enough that Raum and Asher swore off drinking with Harv's crew again. As far as Asher knew too, Judith had no idea about any of it.

The dive bar—Joe's Tavern, according to the flickering sign above the doors—took up the entire corner of the street. The front was a muddy-red stucco with large tinted windows along the sides. Rickety picnic tables lined the sidewalk, but no one was sitting outside tonight. Asher wasn't surprised. It probably would have been packed in the summer with the front doors open. Right now, they were closed and the only hint the bar was even open was the garish neon sign hanging in the window.

Raum took the lead, looking as formidable as he could, and he pulled the doors open. Asher and Amy slipped inside together as a team with Raum right behind them.

Good news: no devil wings inside.

Bad news: everyone near the door stared at them, gobsmacked.

After a beat, most of them went back to their meals, not wanting to get involved, but a good handful continued staring. It made Asher's skin itch. His reputation was already shot, but he didn't want Amy's ruined by association. She was nonplussed, thankfully, and kept a serious look on her face as she peered across the meager crowd. Asher followed her lead and searched for their errant angel wing.

The interior matched the muddy-red paint outside, and the walls were filled with beer advertisements and so many neon lights, Asher doubted the place needed the overhead lights at all. Wooden accents complimented the muddy-red paint, from the bar, to the exposed ceiling beams, and to what looked like an entryway into the other half of the bar where a billiard table sat.

The floor was charcoal black concrete and Asher already didn't like standing on it. The tables and stools were cluttered together, which was going to make walking past them a nightmare with three pairs of wings. It smelled about as expected: stale cigarette smoke, alcohol, and a hint of burger and fries beneath that.

The patrons still looking at them were gathered at the bar, all disbelieving stares and opened jaws. Even the bartender stared, halfway through mixing a drink. Behind him was an impressive arrangement of bottles, taps, glistening glassware, and a pair of standing coolers. A TV hung from the ceiling at the end of the bar with the evening news on, completely ignored. Its volume was so low, it might as well have been turned off.

No errant angel wing in view and Asher bit his cheek.

The bartender's jaw began working again, but no sound came out. Patrons gave him worried looks, searching for what to do about the entrance of two angel wings who had absolutely no business being there.

"For fuck's sake," the bartender finally growled as he finished mixing. It was enough to break the ice. A few patrons went back to their own world of food, beer, and conversation, believing the bartender had it handled.

It wasn't a super busy night, at least. Just a few groups clustered across the bar and then the larger party on the other side of the room. Raum immediately pivoted and walked up to the bar,

Asher and Amy quickly at his heels.

The bartender ran a hand over his cropped hair and steeled his expression into a stormy glare. The patrons around the bar ignored Raum, but a few stole glances at Asher and Amy as they drew closer. While Amy continued holding herself straight, completely impassive, all Asher wanted to do was retreat outside for fresh air.

"I promise no trouble," Raum said, putting his hands up in surrender.

The bartender scoffed. "I ain't worried about *you*. Used to devil wings." He flicked a glance at Asher and Amy. "Those two? Fucking trouble."

Amy startled and put a hand on her chest, absolutely scandalized. Asher had to bite his lip to keep from laughing. Given the way Raum didn't look back at them, he was doing the same.

One of the patrons closest to them sputtered on his drink. "Oh! Hey!" His face brightened and he slapped the counter. "No way. Joe, that's Amy. She's the girl my wife goes to. She's golden."

Amy brightened and her wings perked up. "Oh! Ed? Marie's husband, right? She's shown me so many pictures of you." The man nodded sheepishly. "Does she know you're here? You're pretty far from home!"

Snickers went up and down the bar, further melting the ice, and Ed laughed. "Yes! I swear!" he said more to those around them. "She and the gals are having their wine and book club tonight. I like to give them space. Joe's the best place I know." He turned back to the bartender. "I swear, Joe, she's a real sweetheart. No trouble there."

Triumphant, Amy's wings perked even higher. As Asher tried to ease behind Amy before someone realized that he was the graffitiing punk, the bartender settled his stern gaze on him. Asher froze.

The contrast must have been a sight; one very confident, adorable angel wing in her element and one very nervous and tatted angel wing ready to bolt.

"He's new." Amy nodded at Asher. "Not trouble."

"Promise," Asher said.

Joe didn't look like he believed them. Not that Asher would have. "What do you want?"

"We're looking for another angel wing, actually," Raum said, lowering his voice. "He came in a bit ago?"

Joe trained his gaze to the ceiling and squeezed his eyes shut. "Oh, this is fucking trouble," he grumbled before nodding toward the other room. "He's settled in at the game room."

A blonde waitress swept around Joe, settling an empty tray on the bar behind him, and rung up an order. "Don't complain too hard," she said and went to the cooler to open it. "He's giving me fantastic tips." She gave the patrons around them a knowing look and snorted when they all looked away. "Better than this group here." She plucked out a cold beer and headed back to the floor.

Raum nodded and stepped back. "Promise: no trouble."

The three of them navigated through the

tight path between tables and stools until they reached the game room. Inside was a pinball machine playing a short chiptune, a cigarette vending machine, a jukebox in the far corner playing some old rock tune, and the billiard table in the very center. Tables and stools were along the outer edges, but no one had taken a seat in there besides the angel wing in question.

Asher barely got a good look at the man before Raum was dragging him and Amy into a table on the opposite end of the room, like they were somehow regular patrons. No one would believe that. Too many wings involved.

After the three of them sat down, Asher took a moment to study the angel wing.

He was tall, his long legs stretched out beneath the table, his skin was pale, and he had white hair swept back, hanging past his neck. Asher couldn't tell if it was bleached that way or if it was actually white. His wings behind him were a soft downy gray. He wore black jeans tucked into leather biker boots and had on a long-sleeved black shirt rolled up to the elbows. His leather jacket sat carefully folded on the stool beside him.

One hand balanced a cigarette and the wrist had a square of gauze taped to it, likely hiding the tattoo Raum had given him, while his other lay on the table. More tattoos went up the man's arm; an intricate piece of interwoven black knots and lines.

Finally, Asher studied the man's face. He was younger than Asher expected, strikingly handsome with a sharp jaw and high cheekbones. His eyes were the only soft thing about his face, gentle curves rimmed in long eyelashes. There was a little smile on his lips, almost a smirk, but he hadn't looked at them yet. His gaze was set on the fortune telling cards spread across the table.

Amy swatted at Asher's hand, breaking the spell he'd found himself under, and she huffed when he gave her a look. "You're being obvious," she said. "Stop staring."

Asher's face flushed and Raum palmed his chest.

"Hey," Raum teased, laughter bubbling through the mock surprise. "You don't even look at *me* like that." He cackled as Asher buried his face. "He's hot—I'll give you that—but we're not here to ogle him."

"Shut up," Asher whined. "I'm not ogling."

A shadow darkened their table, making the three of them jump, but it was only the waitress. She quickly passed out three menus and produced a pen and notebook from her apron. Raum balked as he looked at the menu and so did Amy.

"Name's Maggie," she said. "You don't gotta order, I was just giving you some cover while I dish out some advice." She wrote mindlessly on the paper. "I can get y'all some water, though. Look like you need it."

"I'd love water," Amy said. "Can you tell us a little about that angel wing, actually? Does he come here often?"

Maggie smiled, her red lips parting for

perfectly white teeth. "I knew you'd want some gossip." She doodled some more on her paper. "His name's Vale, he comes through town every few months. Always tells fortunes. Got him to do one earlier. A little sharp, but soft, if that makes any sense. And a fucking looker, am I right?" She eyed Asher and he groaned, his cheeks growing hot. No way had he been *that* obvious.

Amy snorted behind her hand. "Do you just go up and ask him to tell your fortune?"

"That's what I did. Sometimes I see him set up in an alley and people flock to him. Maybe they feel comfortable asking him weird stuff they don't wanna burden other angel wings with. I like him, even if some people find him troubling." She collected the menus again and stacked them together. "Joe also wants me to remind you: no trouble. I swear, he thinks you two baby faces gonna cause shit?" She blew air out of her lips and rolled her eyes. "Please. You gimme a holler if you want anything other than water."

She wiggled her fingers at them and was off, leaving them a good view of the angel wing.

At least they had his name: Vale. Asher glanced at Raum and Amy, ready to ask for the next step, but they were watching *him*, expecting the same.

"Well?" Asher asked, dropping his voice.

Raum put up his hands. "He was frosty at the shop. I'm not keen on getting my ass kicked out here if he thinks I mean something bad."

"You gave him a tattoo," Asher said.

"Yeah, but that doesn't mean he's gonna be nice if I start being nosy."

Amy was equally shaking her head. "He's probably realized I had people looking for him specifically. He must have connected the dots by now since you know... We're here."

Hopeless, the both of them. Asher glared at them and slipped off his stool. "Fine. It's my life on the line anyway, I'll do it. I'll just... I'll ask for my fortune and get him talking." Raum started to get up, but Asher waved him back down. "You two watch. Be ready to rescue me if I start running my mouth." He smiled when Raum pulled him down and kissed him on the cheek.

"For luck, then," Raum said as Asher pulled away. "Give the word and we'll swoop over."

It's not like Vale was going to eat him. Hopefully.

More awkwardly than he'd intended, reconsidering if bothering Vale was worth it (it was), Asher made his way over. The man didn't look up. He simply took a drag from his cigarette. Since he hadn't told Asher to scram, Asher sat down.

Vale finally looked at him with ice blue eyes that made Asher shiver. He flicked a glance at the wings, curious. His mouth tilted softly to one side in a crooked smile.

"Hello there," he said, his voice deep and soft. It absolutely gave Asher goosebumps. Vale set the cigarette down in the ashtray and considered Asher. "How can I help you?"

"I want my fortune told," Asher said.

Vale pursed his lips and shook his head. "Don't do that with other angel wings."

Asher frowned. "Why not?"

"You're looking for answers you don't actually want. I don't want you getting pissy."

"What's that supposed to mean? You don't know me."

Vale sat up and propped both elbows on the table. "Word on the street is there's this little angel wing causing a stir. Apparently, he's the same punk tagging the shit out of buildings and notorious for running wild with a devil wing crew with his little devil wing boyfriend." He tilted his head toward Raum and Amy, glancing at them knowingly, and leaned his chin on his palm. "Curious."

"Yeah?" Asher glared at him and gripped the edge of his sleeves under the table to stay grounded. "So what if I am? Doesn't mean I'll be pissy if you tell me a fortune."

Easing out a low sigh, Vale stacked his cards. "What do you want from me, little feathers? Answers?" He picked up his cigarette and took a drag. "For how I got out of all that bullshit currently waiting for you?"

"Yes," Asher said, trying not to sound too desperate.

Vale glanced at him again, up and down, and blew out a puff of smoke. "You got any money? Advice doesn't come cheap, you know."

There was a record scratch in Asher's head. *Money.* His skin went completely cold. He hadn't grabbed the stash he'd squirrelled away from working for Belle. Raum probably had some on him, but Asher refrained from asking. This wasn't Raum's problem, it was Asher's.

Except answers and guidance was right there and the fucker wanted money.

Vale chuckled, setting down the cigarette. "I'd guess no by your face," he said, smirking. "Angel wings usually don't. I'm sure the friend who sent people to find me doesn't have a penny to her name, either. It's by design."

Of course it was by design. Keep an angel wing reliant on the system and they'd never be able to leave. The same problem facing Asher now. Nowhere to go but into a cage. Devil wings had similar problems. Cities didn't like it when foundlings knew how to drive. Didn't like it when they got jobs as they waited for their wings. Didn't like that they could be anything but the mold already rigged for them.

"T-Then why ask for money?" Asher asked and hated the squeak in his voice.

Vale shrugged, a mocking lift to the side of his mouth like he found this whole thing amusing.

Asher internally panicked, coming up with nothing to give in exchange. He couldn't just walk away now. Vale could easily roll out of town and never come back. This was the only chance he was likely going to get for real advice.

An idea occurred to him, but he'd only had it half thought out before Vale was shaking his head.

"No," Vale said. "I know where your head's going. You think you're cute and you can use that. Don't. Don't *ever* suggest that to anyone." He stressed it and Asher felt his cheeks heat up. "People will take advantage of you. Believe me, I know." The mocking expression was gone, and a weary man stared back. One who had gone down that road and regretted it.

"Some think it's a point of pride to fuck an untouchable angel wing. We're so pure and good, they can't help themselves. It'll be another kind of trap. Steer clear of that."

Asher sighed. "I wasn't even going to ask."

"It's an easy out," Vale continued. "Free advice, whether you were thinking of it or not."

Maggie slowly came by, a tray of water balanced on her hand, and she eyed Asher, like she'd swoop in and help if he needed it. He shook his head and she continued through the game room, setting water down for Raum and Amy.

"Want any more advice, you're gonna have to give me something," Vale continued.

"Like what?" Asher snapped.

Vale hummed and shuffled his cards, keeping his gaze on Asher. His hands were quick and fluid, the cards expertly shuffled. He cut the deck and slid it toward Asher.

"Deal me one." He tapped his cigarette off in its ashtray. "Whichever one sticks out to you."

Frustration gnawed at Asher's insides. What good was this going to do? He gazed at the cards and spread them out, hoping for a sign or something. Each card was a little worn around the edges from fortunes told, but all the same sitting facedown.

No sign came. Asher picked one at random and handed it over.

Vale studied the card for a silent moment. He finally nodded and put out his cigarette.

"How about this?" he said. "No fuckery, ain't in the mood."

"Oh." Asher snorted derisively. "Is that it?"

Vale smirked at him. "You're cute, but I'd never put anyone else through that." He set the card face down and stood. "I'll give you advice—guidance—whatever your heart desires to know about freedom for one such as us, you just have to beat me in a pool game."

8

Angels and Devils

ASHER'S MIND WENT blank. "I don't know how to play."

A clatter across the room made Asher jump. Raum had caught his ankle on the stool and almost took the table down from trying to stop himself from faceplanting as he stood. Amy's gaze darted between Raum and Asher.

"I'll play for him!" Raum practically shouted.

Vale tilted his head, amused. "You want to be part of this conversation? Then don't yell across the goddamn room."

Raum glared at the angel wing. He approached, letting his wings stretch out as he did. Tough guy routine, but Asher enjoyed seeing it.

Before Raum opened his mouth, Vale cut him off.

"No," Vale simply said. Asher's heart sank. "I'm playing Feathers over here. You can teach him as we go, but he has to be the one hitting the balls." Even as Raum's glare darkened, Vale grinned and held up his bandaged wrist. "Hopefully you teach as well as you stab."

Vale moved around Raum and looked over the neglected pool table. As he was getting everything out, patrons peeked inside the room. With a glare from Raum and Vale both, the very same patrons scurried away.

All the while, Asher hadn't moved. Panic had him rooted to the stool. Advice and guidance relied on something he'd never done. He was never going to win. The chance was going to slip right through his fingers. The panic only slightly ebbed when Raum approached and touched his hand.

"Hey," he said. The word tethered Asher back to reality. "You good? We can win."

"Yes." Asher quickly nodded and leaned into Raum's hand. "I can do this. I'm sorry, I just..."

Raum smiled so warmly it could have melted the entire world. "One thing at a time." He leaned in and kissed Asher's forehead. "It's not a hard game. Promise."

"Hey." Vale's voice made Asher jump. The other angel wing was making eye contact with Maggie in the other room. "Be a doll and give this angel in here something to drink," he said, throwing a thumb over his shoulder at Amy.

Amy perked up. "Oh, I don't drink alcohol."

Vale gave Amy an exasperated look, but must have thought better about commenting on it given the glare Raum was shooting him.

"Something sparkly then. And gimme a beer—waitress' choice." As Maggie headed off,

Vale beckoned Asher closer. "How old are you anyway?"

Asher frowned and hesitatingly followed the invitation. "Nineteen. Twenty next month."

"Ah." Vale sighed. "Never mind. Was gonna get you something to loosen up, but I don't want you drunk on me."

"I'm not a lightweight," Asher snapped.

Raum squeezed Asher's arm. "You are," he reminded and Asher rolled his eyes. "Focus on the game, Ash."

"Ash?" Vale lifted his eyebrows as he set the cue ball on the table.

"Asher. You don't get to call me Ash."

Vale smiled. "You can call me Vale, then."

He finished setting the table and grabbed a cue stick from its display.

Raum pulled Asher's attention back to the table and immediately rattled off the ins and outs of basic gameplay. Most of it went right over Asher's head, all the information and nuance too much at once. Raum trailed off, biting his lip, and grabbed his own cue stick to demonstrate. Vale didn't seem to mind Raum guiding Asher through a few practice shots, even though he watched them too intently.

That part didn't help. He didn't even look away when Maggie returned with Amy's sparkly strawberry lemonade and Vale's pint of dark beer.

Focus. Asher breathed in and listened to Raum rattle off more about how to play. Maybe a few more practice shots would help.

"All right, enough learning."

Raum straightened his back and flipped off Vale. He was turned away, taking a sip off the top of his beer, and missed it. "You said—"

"You're overwhelming him," Vale said as he set his glass down. "Correct him as he plays." He watched Raum, daring him to argue, but Raum bit his tongue. Vale turned a grin on Asher. "Well? Feathers, you're up."

Asher balked, almost dropping his stick. "I'm starting?" he squeaked.

"Yeah, why not?" Vale came over and shrugged. "Lets me gauge how fast I'll win." He nodded at Raum. "And lets him mellow out by staring at your ass when you bend over the table."

The comment pulled a dry laugh from Asher's throat. He smothered it under his hand, shooting Raum an apologetic look. Raum was glaring absolute daggers at Vale, and Vale continued to meet it with an easy grin.

"He's just riling you up!" Amy called from their table. "Don't let him!"

Raum eased out a long sigh through his nose and turned away from Vale. He raised a hand at Maggie who was walking by again—she must have been doing it on purpose—and said, "Give me whatever this asshole's having. He's buying."

Vale scoffed, but didn't contest it, and Maggie happily went back to the bar for another pint. While she was gone, Asher moved around the table, trying to figure out where to start.

He quickly grew frustrated, warm, and

pulled off his jacket for better movement. He left it with Amy and she was all too happy to have it folded in her lap. Asher returned to the table, hoping to find a new perspective, but all he noticed was the way Vale was looking over his tattoo work, curious.

He whistled. "Didn't think you had that much work done. Must be pissing off the watchers, huh? They tend to be traditionalists here." He tilted his head, eyes tracking Asher's solid black tattoo. "That arm hurt?"

"Not really. Raum's very good," Asher said.

Vale went quiet again, but still watched Asher much too closely. Asher hated it. He wished the man would look away, do something other than stare. He was still thinking too hard about it and where to start when Maggie returned with another beer. Raum immediately took a gulp and left the rest with Amy before even he started watching Asher too.

All Asher had to do was start. Starting meant breaking the balls apart. Should have been easy without all his overthinking. He bent over a spot on the table and tried lining up. Some of them had to hit the edge or it didn't count. Except Asher didn't want to hit them *too* hard and give Vale easy shots.

As he tried to plan just how much strength he was going to push into the stick, Vale released a loud sigh.

How the fuck had Asher screwed up already? He hadn't even *hit* anything.

He glanced over his shoulder, annoyed, and

found Vale's cue stick resting against the table. Vale came up behind Asher and pushed him toward the table as he bent over him to help Asher line up the shot.

Raum's jaw dropped. Asher's brain short-circuited. All he could do was hold still.

"First tip," Vale whispered as he pressed closer to fix Asher's hands on the stick, "is find fucking confidence *somewhere*. I'm giving you an opening to get ahead and you're too neurotic to take it. You will not last long."

Raum got his wits about him. "Hey! Get the fuck—"

"I'm fine," Asher said and Raum gave him a concerned look. "He's teaching me."

Although, maybe not teaching the way Asher wanted him to. This was a little too close. Asher's heart had leapt into his throat, he was pretty sure his face was a bright red, and the ache along his stitches flared hot. Vale was pressed so close, without any regard to Asher's wings.

But it was advice, Asher supposed, and he swallowed his pride to listen.

"Start like this," Vale interrupted Asher's thoughts, and smoothly guided Asher's hand. The end of the stick hit the ball and it clacked into all the others, sending them scattering across the table.

Vale released him, ignoring Asher's wings moving out of sync and him turning to make sure they were fine. The other angel wing's eyes were glued to the table, watching everything transpire. Before Asher could figure out if they'd have to restart, Raum was pulling Asher away from Vale.

It was a clean break at least, if Vale nodding was any indication. None of the balls were pocketed, however, and Asher frowned. Before he could guess which ones Vale was going after, Raum held the glass of beer up in Asher's line of sight.

"Take a sip," Raum said. "It'll calm your nerves, okay?"

Just a sip. Asher could do that. He was trembling pretty bad, now that he thought about it. An actual buzz would help. Something to keep him from getting stuck in his head. A sip would have to do.

He took one and tried not to cringe at the taste. Beyond bitter. When he'd drank with the devil wings, theirs had tasted smoother. He swallowed, and the balls clacked again, shaking him down to his bones. He turned in time to watch a striped ball go into the far pocket.

"Stripes are mine," Vale said and repositioned himself. "Solids yours." He bent over the table again and sent the cue ball forward. It hit another striped ball, but this one missed its mark.

"Shame," Vale said, but it didn't sound like he meant it. Asher wondered if he missed on purpose. "Your turn. Simple rules: pocket something and you go again."

Vale turned to Amy, catching her off-guard, and she sputtered into her drink. He flicked a quarter at the table. "Find something loud to put on, hm?"

Amy shared a confused look with Asher and Raum. Asher shrugged and Raum urged her on. She slipped off her stool and hurried to the jukebox in the corner.

As she fretted over what to pick, Asher peered back at the bar; it was quieter now, chatter a low murmur at best. Maybe Vale wanted to drown out whatever they were going to say to deter the eavesdropping.

"Focus." Vale snapped his fingers in Asher's direction.

Asher gritted his teeth. "Fuck off."

Perhaps the worst thing to say to someone who may have had legit advice. Asher was glad that Vale chuckled.

"Good to see the little bird's got bite," he teased. "But we ain't got all night. *Go.*"

Asher searched the table for an easy shot that wasn't the eight ball. It sat perilously close to a pocket and he opted to give it a wide berth.

While Asher deliberated, Vale stepped closer to Raum, undaunted by Raum's glare.

"How'd you get two angel wings?" Vale asked, leaning against his cue stick. He sounded genuinely curious and it caught Asher by surprise. "It's such an odd sight."

"Uh." Raum bit back whatever he'd started to say—probably some variation of fuck off. "We grew up together in the same foundling house. Me and her got wings first. He was a little late."

A little late. Asher rolled his eyes. Understatement of a lifetime; three years and then some was *not* a little.

"Ah," Vale said, no sarcasm in his voice. "No wonder you're so tight."

"You don't know your foundling siblings?" Raum asked.

"Usually doesn't work like you guys." Vale's voice turned a little quieter. He bent beside Asher and gently took his elbow off the table.

Raum jerked to Asher's other side, likely making sure Asher wasn't about to get wrapped up in helping hands again. Vale slotted a smirk on his lips, hiding away the vulnerable look from before, and raised his hands in surrender.

"I grew up alone," he continued. "The other foundlings were just getting their wings when I came by, and then another foundling came after I got mine, so it was just me. I got on with some devil wings for a bit, but well..." He shrugged and lowered his hands. "Shit happens. All the ones I know now want to beat the shit out of me. Territorial fucks, just like the ones out here."

Raum raised his eyebrows. "You know the ones out here?"

"We've crossed paths," Vale said. "Harv still around?"

Before Raum could answer, music blared out of the jukebox. It was so loud, it made the three of them jump. A brassy number from a band Asher couldn't name. Amy had gone back to her fizzy soda, looking absolutely pleased with herself.

Vale patted Asher's arm. "Enough chitchat. Stop thinking so hard and go."

Asher exhaled and took his shot. The stick

smoothly hit the ball, sending it into the red one he was aiming for. The momentum carried the red ball into the corner pocket.

Vale pursed his lips. "People are assholes."

Asher frowned deeply. "I know that."

"Score another ball then," Vale said, winking. "Easy shots mean easy advice."

"Asshole."

At that, Vale smiled.

As Asher focused on the table again, Raum pointed out another shot for him. Not a straight cue ball into ball into pocket, but rather, it would hit one of Vale's balls into Asher's and sink it.

Raum positioned Asher in front of it and Vale gave the devil wing a look, like he was biting back admonishment for setting Asher up for something trickier. Asher didn't care; he went for it.

The balls clacked, then they did again, and Asher's ball was just shy of the pocket because he hadn't put enough strength into the stroke.

"Close," Vale said and swept his gaze over the table. He eyed a ball and positioned himself differently than how Raum had shown Asher. He'd barely lined himself up before he hit the cue ball at an angle. It jumped over another ball in its way and came down quickly, hitting its real target. The striped ball spun on impact and went into a side pocket.

"Is... Is that even legal?" Asher asked. Raum couldn't answer; he was pressing his face into Asher's shoulder, smothering laughter. "I can *do* that?"

"You try that and you might fuck up the table," Vale said. "Joe will kill you. Don't do it." He walked around the table, thinking. He flicked his gaze up at Asher. "The system is designed to cut off your wings. Can't soar if they take them away, you know?"

Amy scrunched her face, about to say something, but stopped when Vale turned to her. She glared at him instead and sipped her drink.

"They cut off yours too, sweetheart," Vale said and took the shot. The ball just missed the pocket and blocked the one Asher had been intending to sink in next. "Even if you're happy, you can't drive or leave the city. You don't have any money of your own. You're expected to grin and bear all the gawkers. You literally have no talents unless they give them to you."

"Hey," Asher cut in. "Lay off her. You're talking to me."

Vale looked taken aback before a soft smile spread across his face. "All right." It hardened into a smirk. "Your shot then, pretty boy."

Raum pulled Asher to the other side of the table, bodily slipping past Vale close enough, his wings pushed against the man. Asher bit down a laugh. It was cute seeing Raum possessive. Made Asher feel tingly, which he tried to ignore. He had to focus on the game, not what he wanted to do to Raum later.

"Listen," Raum whispered, leaning Asher toward him. "Hit that from this angle. It'll hit those two over there, knock his ball away, and knock yours in."

Sneaky. Asher lined up, letting Raum adjust the angle at the last minute. Asher put a little more oomph behind the stroke and sent the cue ball across the table. It hit the ball Raum had pointed out and clacked into the two closest to the pocket. Vale's ball went spinning and Asher's jumped across the hole. Asher frowned and Raum blew out a sharp sigh. Too much strength then.

Vale swept by them, close enough to Raum to push Raum with his wings. Asher caught Raum's hand under the table and squeezed it. As much as he liked the squabbling, Amy was right. Vale was just trying to rile Raum up and Raum was falling for it. Besides, it was clearly not serious. Vale didn't even look like he cared.

Easing out a slow breath, Raum nodded.

As Vale lined himself up, his wings stretched behind him, like he was showing off. Asher tried not to stare. They were nice, truly an extension of him, working in tandem with his body. Not like Asher's.

It would come in time for him, surely, but it still made him self-conscious of his own twitchy wings.

"You know," Vale began slowly as he leisurely hit the ball. Another of his easily pocketed on the far side. "No one knows *what* we're actually for. Angel wings or devil wings. No one's bothered to compile a real history of when we first appeared or tried connecting the dots." He moved right beside Asher and, though his wings brushed up closely, Asher held his ground.

"No one literally cares about our supposed history." Another ball went spinning across the table, sinking the same. "Their goal is for you to be so content, so full of joy and pleasure from carving out a piece of your soul for the city, you just disappear."

The comment left Asher uneasy. The whole angel wings disappearing always did. "Is that like death, then?" he asked and glanced toward Amy. She'd grown very still, listening.

Vale shrugged. "Of a sort. Regardless, the city washes its hands of you afterward. Who you were and whatever talents you had never mattering." The ball he hit next didn't go in and a flash of annoyance curled his lip.

"No," Amy said and slipped off the stool. Raum eyed her, looking like he debated sliding between the two angel wings. "That's not true."

Vale drew to his full height, his wings stretched out, but she set her feet straight. Raum quickly stood by her side in solidarity.

"I'm not intimidated," Amy said, then added, "whoo, you're taller so your wings are bigger. Big whoop." Asher had to smother his laugh, proud of her sarcasm. "What we do matters. Raum, me, and Asher. The city can't take that away."

"Yes, it *can*," Vale argued, his tone softening. "When you're raptured and gone, you'll be replaced. Maybe you'll be remembered for a little bit—by those that really cared about you—but there'll be no plaque describing who you were and no name in the city's books. Once those people forget, that's it. You play by their rules?

You leave no lasting mark."

"I'm not doing this for fame or accolades," Amy said. "I'm happy helping."

"Then why are you arguing?" Vale asked. "If fame doesn't matter, who cares how little the city remembers of you after you're gone? Everyone wants to be remembered. To go through life content that once you're gone, that's it? That's depressing. Exactly what the city wants. Do you even remember the angel wing you replaced or do they also not matter, so long as they were happy helping?"

All of Amy's idealism faded from her expression and her wings drooped, betraying an answer she probably didn't like. She didn't know the angel wing's name. Sure, she knew the names of her contemporaries and was friendly with them, but they were physically there. The last angel wing in her nest was likely raptured before she was old enough to talk. Raum took her hand, holding it tight.

"Devil wings have it the same," Vale continued as he moved around the table to Asher's side. He set his hands on Asher's shoulders, ignoring Raum jerking toward them, and moved Asher into a position to easily sink a solid. Raum slowed, gazing over the table.

"The city gives you no outlet, no place to call home unless someone extends an olive branch at great risk to be ostracized. And *still* expects you to be the scapegoat for everything. They hardly give you a chance to carve out your own place, unless you work harder than everyone else." Vale made eye contact with Raum. "And, believe me, you have carved your own place. You should be damn proud of that."

Some of the anger melted off Raum, his shoulders relaxing.

"They just hope you disappear. Leave, kill yourself, or get yourself killed—anything so they can wash their hands of you and go back to pretending you weren't ever there. Angel wing or devil wing, the city is not on your side. It wants us both folded into the fabric of the city, never to be heard from again."

The speech was passionate as it mixed with the crescendo of rock tunes spilling out of the jukebox. Asher was more unnerved, hearing all his worries said so succinctly. Amy clearly was too, staring at Vale with thinly veiled frustration, but he wasn't wrong.

Nothing they did really mattered. Rail against the system or play nicely with it, they'd be the same in the end. Gone.

Forgotten.

Asher quietly took his shot and pocketed the ball with ease, but missed the following one. Vale took over the table again, staying silent this time. Just as well; Asher sidled up to Amy, wrapping his arm around her back in a half-hug. She relaxed into him with a sad smile. Raum stayed at Amy's other side with his arm around her too.

"Most of all," Vale continued as he pocketed yet another ball. All of his were in and Asher jolted to attention, his stomach sinking. Only the eight ball was left and Vale positioned himself to easily sink it.

"You—" He looked up and caught Asher's gaze, his ice-blue eyes practically piercing right through him. "You don't owe anyone *shit*. You don't want to bend over for some prick and force yourself into his mold? Then fucking don't. Don't play by their rules if you don't want to."

The cue ball shot forward, clacking into the eight ball and sent it whizzing for the corner pocket. It went in and Vale straightened.

"And, game."

Asher felt he hadn't done badly as he gazed over what he had left to pocket. Though now, he understood Vale could have won much sooner. He'd been playing with Asher as an excuse to talk.

What had talking really done, though? Nothing. Asher felt as empty and aimless as he was before, except now he knew those feelings were valid. Somehow, that made them worse. Amy's hand rubbed circles between his wings, trying to comfort him.

"In the end," Vale said, turning away to return his stick to the rack, "it's your life. All advice is bullshit and no one decides what you do with your life other than you." He faced them with a soft expression. "I know it's scary, but do it scared. Who you are and what *you* want is all you should be going for. Fuck everyone else."

There was a finality there, all advice doled out. Asher remained still, not any surer of what he was going to do than before, while Amy and Raum returned to their table for their things.

After a soft exhale, Asher put his cue stick away. As he did, another question came to mind. He glanced at Vale, hoping to find permission.

"Yeah?" Vale asked.

"Did you ever get a watcher and a nest?"

Vale crossed his arms, gaze growing distant. "Ah. Yep. I set the building on fire and ran. She washed her hands of me real quick after that."

"Just because you didn't want to be there?"

"I wanted to be free. It was the only way out."

Asher glanced at Raum and Amy, too quickly for them to notice, before he asked what he really wanted to know. "Are you happy like this?"

"Are you?" Vale tilted his head. "Knowing what they want from you?"

Bartholomew's words dug deeper into Asher's thoughts. All the expectations he'd heaped onto Asher in one meeting. All that thinly veiled disgust without even knowing Asher.

No, he wasn't happy. Neither was he interested in trying to make it work.

Would it really be that easy? Could he go back to Judith and insist he wasn't going to be an angel wing? She clearly thought he needed to do what the city expected. Would she be on his side this time, even if he tried explaining himself again?

Asking again frightened him; he didn't know what he'd do if she still said no. And if she *did* say yes this time, what would he even do? Would anyone be willing to accept him as they begrudgingly accepted devil wings? Belle hadn't been. Angel wings had purpose. Had a role. The city wouldn't be as willing to let one escape.

All the what ifs rolled together in Asher's head without a clear answer. He drew himself tight. Indecision left his lungs starved and he could hardly breathe.

Regardless, he still had no idea what *he* wanted to do. Cutting and running came to mind, but he just as quickly rejected it when Raum and Amy came up beside him, concerned. They were his stark reminder that unlike Vale, he wasn't alone. Leaving would mean leaving them. Not happening.

The rest of the bar had quieted while they'd played. One of the larger groups had left and a busboy was cleaning the tables, the clink of dishes loud. There was another group near the door, chatting about the news, and a new handful was seated at the bar. Everyone ignored the three out of place angel wings, like they didn't even exist.

The jukebox finally finished the album Amy had queued up, leaving the game room in hushed silence.

"Hey."

Asher picked his head up, dragging himself out of his thoughts, and found Vale back at his table. He was beckoning Asher over. Raum patted him on the back and Amy let him go.

Vale was holding the card Asher had dealt before and he was smirking at it. "This is what you dealt me, by the way."

Death.

The card displayed a skeleton with bone wings laying against a bed of blooming purple flowers. There was a scythe in one hand, glistening silver on the card stock, and in the skeleton's other hand was a newly budded flower.

"It means change," Vale explained before Asher's mind went in an entirely different direction. "The death of one life and the beginning of another." Vale stacked it on top of his deck. "It comes for us all. You have to be willing to take the reins when it happens."

"I wish it was easier," Asher said.

"See, you got pissy when I told your fortune." Vale shrugged on his coat and slipped the deck away. "Angel wings, I swear." He snickered when Asher rolled his eyes. "I'm serious, though. Think about what it is *you* want, not what'll make it easier for everyone else. Meaning and being remembered aside, every life has value, even yours."

The bar doors opened suddenly. It wasn't the gentle push of a late patron, but slammed with the thud of someone wanting to make an entrance.

Harv.

10

Barroom Blitz

ASHER'S STOMACH SANK all the way down.

Harv marched inside, devil wings stretched proudly around him, and faces Asher didn't recognize filed in after him. Some devil wings too, and others not. The very crew they'd been hoping to avoid.

Raum swore under his breath, gaze darting this way and that, but there wasn't another way out of the game room.

Asher hoped Harv wouldn't see them, that he was here for a drink, but that was quickly dashed when Harv stormed toward the game room.

Harv dwarfed most people, his every limb roped in muscle. His smoky black devil wings always stretched behind him like a challenge. He kept his hair buzzed short and it was always dyed some shade of auburn. Up one ear were black spikes, and the other had a large chunk taken out of it from a story that always changed whenever

Harv told it. He wore his black leather vest over a white shirt and black jeans tucked into steel-toed boots worn with time. Along both arms was a collection of tattoos; spikes, devils, and bats. Each varying in quality, but it fit him perfectly.

Harv never did anything by halves; the city wanted a devil and he fully played up the role just to spite them. To remind them that this was what they created.

Once, Asher had liked him for it. Saw himself doing the same. But right now, with Harv's usual scowl trained on them? Asher was terrified.

The others he'd brought inside weren't as memorable. Varying sizes and ages, they practically blended in with one another in their similar dark clothes. Done on purpose so no one *could* recognize them, leaving Harv alone to take the blame for what went down as intended.

One of the non-winged ones had stopped at the bar as soon as Joe started to speak. He shut up faster than what felt normal; the guy must have flashed a pocketknife. The other remaining patrons held very still, like they were afraid to breathe, and Harv's people filled the place unimpeded. There wasn't a lot, but enough to be a problem.

Harv continued toward the game room. To them. To Vale.

Vale had gone still, jaw tight, eyes never leaving Harv's once they'd met.

"Thought I told you not to come back," Harv growled, his wings stretching behind him to block out any escape back into the bar.

"Did you say that before or after I got your ear?" Vale asked, smiling tightly. "You were howling so bad, I don't really remember."

"Hey!" Raum broke in and Asher was too late to stop him from hurrying forward with panicked eagerness.

Harv blinked, like noticing Raum for the first time. His surprise quickly turned into a glare, one that darkened considerably seeing Asher and his new feathered wings trying to pull Raum away.

Asher had a few good memories of Harv, despite what Raum said. The way he'd accepted Raum into the fold and the way he'd accepted Asher too. Nights melted away playing cards with him and his crew, being a menace and laughing all the while. Even the little things like Harv pointing out places for Asher to grace with graffiti art. He'd almost felt like an older brother.

But now Asher saw it for what it had been: another way of control. And now that Raum had moved on with his life and Asher had the audacity to have angel wings, Harv saw them as the enemy. There was real hatred behind his glare, burying whatever lingering good memories Asher had of the man.

"I should have known he'd have feathers. Something wasn't right about him." Harv spat on the floor.

Raum didn't move, even as the glob landed beside his boot.

Amy yanked Asher back and shoved his

jacket at him. Asher pulled it on in record time and let Amy expertly jerk his wings out of the back. None of this was good. They had to leave. This was a bomb waiting to explode.

"Harv," Raum said, his tone collected and cool. All feigned eagerness and fake friendliness wiped clean. "Don't talk about them."

Harv's face twitched and those around him tensed, readying themselves for a fight. There were fewer on the left side. If Asher could just get Amy through there, they might have a chance to escape.

What about Raum? Asher asked himself, biting the inside of his cheek. Asher couldn't leave him.

"The fuck you even doing here?" Harv asked. "Fucked off when you decided you were too good for us. Now you come back 'round here with *them*?"

The others nodded in agreement. Raum remained silent.

"You wanna be an angel wing that bad?" Harv forged on. "Just rip 'em off then, for fuck's sake. Saw some angel costumes on clearance. Might wanna buy one before they run out."

He was trying to get under Raum's skin. Asher glanced at his boyfriend, but Raum's expression hadn't changed.

"We were just leaving," Raum simply said. He threw a nod back at Vale. "Him too." He hesitated and gave Harv a second glance.

No! Asher's thoughts shouted, but he was too late to stop his boyfriend.

"Look, Harv," Raum continued quietly, like he could reach through Harv's anger, "whatever this is, it's not worth it. We'll leave, just—"

And Harv cracked Raum across the face with his fist. Amy gasped, Asher froze, and Raum staggered, eyes wide. Vale shot forward, wings pressed flat against his back, and smashed both his fists into Harv's head so fast, none of Harv's crew had time to react. It sent the big guy staggering, and that was when all hell broke loose.

Shouts echoed through the bar. Some ran for the doors, seeing an escape, but the other patrons rushed in to get a piece of Harv and his crew. The one threatening Joe was quickly overrun and Joe raised his voice above the rising chaos, hoping to gain control over the situation. No one listened; a brawl was going to happen whether he wanted it or not.

And Asher was in the middle of it with Amy and Raum.

Shit.

Asher's first action was getting a hold of his boyfriend and dragging his ass away from those trying to attack Vale. Second, was getting Amy towards the corner to get them out of the way. Raum was dazed, blinking hard as he held his jaw. Asher prayed it wasn't broken.

Vale took charge of the chaos around him; those that tried jumping him went sprawling. With a strong flap of his wings, one was flipped over the pool table and thought better about getting up again. Another smashed against the window and collapsed on the table.

Harv wasn't down for long; he shot up, blood streaming from his nose, and rejoined the fray. His attention was solely on Vale, Asher and Raum all but ignored.

Good. One less thing to worry about.

Asher looked across the room, trying to find an out. Maybe backing into the corner wasn't the best idea. Fuck. A dark shape was coming for them, some sleaze with a crew cut and a knife in his hand. Amy jerked Asher back, her nails digging into his arm, and the swipe missed them.

Raum got his wits back that same instant. He took his pint of beer and smashed it against the guy's face before he attacked again.

Beer splattered across the floor, glass flew, and their assailant retreated, bringing up a wing as a shield. Before he could recover, Raum took a stool and chucked it at the man. As Raum dealt with him, another approached fast, but Asher snagged a cue stick and smashed it over the man's head.

There was nothing dignified about the brawl. Stools were thrown, people were tossed onto their asses, and Harv and Vale were practically destroying the place as they tried and failed to take out the other. There was a vicious-ness between them from a violent past history, making them ignore all else.

Asher could barely keep up with the blur of bodies. His pulse pounded so hard in his ears, he thought he was going to faint. Raum became a wall in front of him and Amy, at least, but they needed out, and this corner wasn't out.

Amy suddenly shrieked, brandishing her mug as a weapon, but Maggie ducked before it hit her head. Undaunted, Maggie shot back up and grabbed Amy's wrist.

"Come with me," she said. "I can let you out the back!"

She didn't wait for an answer before she was dragging Amy through the blur of bodies. She'd kicked off the heels she'd been wearing before, easily maneuvering around the mess in stockinged feet. Raum didn't hesitate and dragged Asher after her. Asher didn't want to leave Vale, but there wasn't much he could do to help the errant angel wing. Just pray he got out.

Joe urged Maggie behind the bar and once they were all safe, he bent low and resumed yelling into the phone. A glass skipped off the counter, smashing as it hit the floor beside them. Maggie didn't look at where it came from and neither did Asher. He was dragged too fast into the kitchen.

A burly cook passed them with a frying pan and Asher didn't want to see the guy that tried to take him on.

Maggie threw open the back door. A breath of fresh air rushed inside and Asher barely had time to appreciate it before Maggie shoved the three of them into the alley outside.

"There," Maggie said. "Go home, now!"

Raum whipped around, worried. "Wait, we're witnesses. We can't—"

"And you're a devil wing," Maggie stressed.

A glass smashed against something inside and she winced. "The police will lump you all together, like they always do. Just go. We'll get this handled. I don't want you three in any trouble. This ain't your fault."

Maybe it wasn't, but Asher didn't feel right leaving. Until police sirens echoed from down the street. Panic shot into high gear and he tugged Raum away from the door. Being witnesses wasn't worth losing him to a misunderstanding.

Maggie disappeared into the dark interior and the three of them ran for the alley they'd stashed the bike in.

Thankfully, it was still there unharmed. Raum jumped on, jamming his keys into the ignition. Amy squeezed in behind him, pressing her wings tightly to her back, and Asher scrambled on behind her.

Riding three to a bike was something Asher never wanted to experience again. From how quickly Raum sped off to escape the sirens and lights descending on the bar, to how tight he took turns to get away, Asher struggled to hold on. The city quickly became a blur. All Asher could do was close his eyes and trust his boyfriend.

When they finally arrived at the tattoo parlor, Raum slowed and maneuvered them into the alley behind it. Asher was shaking like a leaf trying to keep himself together.

Once Raum was parked, the engine cut, Asher let go of Amy. Once he had, he fell off, hitting the concrete with a thump. Amy sank off the bike and settled next to Asher, hand pressed to her chest as she caught her breath. Raum was the only one who didn't fall and kept his bike from tipping. Small miracles. He dragged the bike closer to the building and hid it beneath its usual tarp.

When he returned, he collapsed to his knees beside Asher and Amy.

"Shit," he breathed. "Shit. Shit. Shit."

"T-The place will be fine," Asher said, trying to believe it.

"I just didn't think they'd fucking try to jump Vale like that. I thought they were different."

Amy frowned at Raum. "Were they?"

Raum didn't look at her, his jaw tense.

"Raum..." Asher whispered.

"I know," Raum replied, dropping his head. "I'm just trying to figure out when it all changed. When we first met, he wasn't like that. Not that bad, I swear."

Raum wasn't wrong. At the beginning, Harv and his crew had been family away from the foundling house. Asher knew he wouldn't be who he was without Harv and neither would Raum, for good or bad.

But that was because they'd stayed within Harv's narrow definition of what was acceptable. Maybe it'd gotten even narrower since then.

"What would have changed?" Amy asked.

"Time, I guess," Raum said. "I can see it clearly now. He's older. Really close to that age where maybe he'll disappear no matter what."

"So, he's afraid," Amy spelled out, frowning.

"He wants so badly to make a mark. Go out in a blaze of glory rather than a whimper. He's a fucking asshole, but he's scared."

It didn't excuse who Harv was, how he'd changed, but the fear he must have felt and acted on sat with Asher all the same.

He didn't know what to say and, given Amy's silence, she didn't either. All they could do was sit with the terrifying thought that like Harv and every angel and devil wing, they'd face the same building panic eventually.

Asher wasn't sure if he'd lash out like Harv or accept it softly like most angel wings did, but it didn't matter right now. Asher wanted to scrub it from his mind and not think about it.

Amy broke the silence as she sidled closer to Raum. She squeezed his shoulder. "I'm sorry his panic and rage made him think so much less of you as you made your own life."

"I am too," Raum whispered.

The three of them took another moment huddled together on the concrete to catch their breath before they hauled themselves up. Raum was the steadiest. Asher did not let his pride get in the way and fully leaned against him for support. Amy managed to stand on her own, but she was fretting as her gaze darted to the sky. The stars were peeking out of the streak of clouds and she bit her lip.

"I can't walk home. It's too late," she said.

All her earlier excitement over mischief had washed away, leaving only anxiety. Angel wings were supposed to be safely tucked into their nests this late. Asher doubted anyone would actually punish her if they'd heard she was out all night, but then he thought of Bartholomew. That prick would have definitely done something, he was sure.

"Wendy won't be mad," Asher tried.

"No," Amy said slowly, "but..."

Raum waved his hand. "I'll drive you home tomorrow morning," he said. "Crash here. My bed's big enough."

It definitely was, Asher knew that firsthand. When Amy nodded, Raum led them up the fire escape and into the back door of the apartment.

The three of them together again in the same room, same bed. Almost like their time in the foundling house when they had sleepovers in each other's rooms. It'd be the first time since Raum and Amy got their wings. Asher hadn't known he'd missed cuddling with them both until the opportunity presented itself.

Raum didn't have much room in the apartment; it was a single open space he'd tried to split with a couch and a few room dividers. The windows were along the back and peered out into the alley, but the view of the rising sun would be the same here as it was in the foundling house. Maybe a little more obscured, but still beautiful.

Raum's bed was tucked into the corner beneath the window and had a folding screen to block the view of it from the door to the parlor's stairs. Across from the bed was his dresser, painted with a splash of colors, courtesy of Asher after they'd garbage picked it and dragged it up the fire escape. Above it hung another garbage find: a starry sky painting on canvas. It'd been damaged, but Asher fixed it up for Raum's twenty-first birthday earlier this year. Raum had hung fairy lights around it so it twinkled in the dark, like now, giving the room its softness.

Once they were inside, Raum scrounged up something for Amy to sleep in. An old oversized sweater with bats all over it came out of his closet and she took it into the bathroom to change. Raum and Asher needed no such privacy. Asher was only glad to strip down to his undershirt and boxer briefs before he fully faceplanted into the bed to breathe it in.

None of them spoke as they washed up and situated themselves on the bed. Exhaustion ate the words away, but they didn't need them. Amy curled up on the open side of the bed against Raum's shoulder, her arm around his chest, and Asher took the side of the bed nearest the wall and tucked himself underneath Raum's other arm. Raum's quilt, a gift from Judith when he'd left the house, was pulled across the three of them and it was warm.

It was here Asher knew the world was right. Where, if he had his way, he wouldn't ever leave. The warmth, the way Raum smelled, and Amy's presence made it so nothing mattered.

Except, he had no idea how to keep holding onto the timelessness in the room. The piece of perfection he'd found was slowly coming apart at the seams, no matter what he did to try and salvage it.

11

A Break From Reality

SUNRAYS SLID THROUGH the windows and lit the room in pale golds. Asher had barely opened his eyes before Raum buried his head against him, mumbling something about forgetting the curtains. Amy shot up with a squeak. She was a morning person and usually got up with the sun. For once, Asher wished she'd given in to the allure of sleeping in.

"I should be home," she whispered, pulling Asher further out of the dregs of sleep.

Raum groaned, brushing his hair back, and peered across the room at his clock. "I'll drive you like I said. Just let me open my eyes."

With a tiny chuckle, Amy relaxed and extracted herself from the bed. Asher was sad to see her go. It washed the room out of its fuzziness and anchored him back to reality. The three of them cuddling together wasn't something they did anymore.

Raum pushed himself into a sitting position

and Asher let himself sink into the pillows he'd left behind.

"It's early enough. No one's gonna even know you were out all night with a devil wing." He winked.

Amy giggled, shaking her head. "Would that have been so bad?" She gathered her neatly folded clothes from the couch. "People might think I'm edgy." She held her clothes close and headed for Raum's tiny bathroom. "Let me shower really quick. I can still smell smoke in my hair and *someone's* going to notice that."

"There's a hairdryer in there if you need it."

At least she didn't sound as scandalized as she could have been. Some of her rigid edges were finally softening. Asher smiled. Maybe they could get a shared tattoo to commemorate it. She'd like a flower, he was sure.

He rested his eyes, debating about which kind, and happily breathed the bed in. It felt like a hug in and of itself. He would have drifted off too, if Raum hadn't bent over and peppered a dozen kisses along his jaw, sending a pleasurable tingle over him. Raum pulled away much too soon and Asher pouted at him.

"Shop's closed today," Raum said, searching for the pants he'd discarded last night. He found them, but then threw them into a nearby hamper and went to his dresser instead.

Asher had been too exhausted last night to really admire his boyfriend, but now was as good a time as any. Raum had gone to sleep in just his underwear and they were ones Asher had bought for him. Vibrant orange with little bat wings decorating his ass.

"I'll take Amy home and you and I can hang out here as long as you want. Not doing three on a bike ever again. That was terrifying."

"Fine by me," Asher said lazily, stretching himself across the bed. "Your bed's warm anyway. Not moving."

Raum smirked at him and turned away to change. Asher did not mind the view one bit. The way the muscles in Raum's back moved as he did, the way his wings met his skin seamlessly. No scars there. And, like Asher, Raum had tattoos all over. Asher loved tracing them with his fingers. There was a row of diamonds and triangles following the length of Raum's spine. The spiky wheel rim curved across one shoulder. The scattering of bats among black stars along the other. His forearms had lines creating the beginning of a larger piece he was still going back and forth on.

Although Asher wanted to admire the tattoos more, think of what else Raum could get, there went the underwear. Asher's eyes immediately darted down to his boyfriend's ass. It was nice and toned, but covered all too soon, this time with stars and moons across the fabric.

Asher bit back his complaint. Amy would have been embarrassed if she'd walked in while Raum had absolutely no clothes on.

Next came a black band t-shirt and Asher admired the way Raum's wings effortlessly slid through the slits. It made Asher a little jealous, but he assured himself he'd learn to do it just as easily with time. Lastly came the ripped jeans decorated with patches of plaid fabric, a pair of striped socks, and his boots.

Once he was put together, Raum bent over Asher, nuzzling his cheek. The scratchy stubble made Asher laugh. Before he could drag Raum down for a proper kiss, Raum had retreated to tie his hair back up.

"You cozy up. I'll bring back breakfast." Raum kissed Asher on the head.

No arguments there.

Asher nestled deeper into the blankets. He was being spoiled and wondered if it was because of how he'd stared at Vale. Before he could outright ask—apologize, maybe—Amy had returned. Freshly cleaned and dressed, she had her hair wrapped into a messy bun.

Raum snickered. "You could have taken your time. Harm doesn't charge me that much for water."

Amy rolled her eyes. "If I'd actually washed and dried my hair, it'd take almost an hour."

"All right, all right. If you say so. Give me a sec and we'll be off."

As Raum ducked into the bathroom, Amy approached the bed. She lingered, thinking a moment, before bending over to kiss Asher on the forehead too.

"Don't think too hard about everything," she said softly. "The world can wait. Relax a bit."

"I know," Asher murmured. "Thanks for coming with us."

Amy smiled wide. "It was fun. Actually terrifying... but also fun!"

Hopefully she didn't think all of Asher's and Raum's misadventures ended like that. Sure, a lot of them *had* in some way, but it wasn't all that terrifying. Before he could say more, Raum had reappeared and left with Amy.

Listening to the motorbike drive away, Asher lingered on Amy's words. Telling him not to think so hard had a habit of making him think harder. It would have happened eventually, but he'd hoped to drift off first. Nagging thoughts quickly invaded the domestic bliss he'd been enjoying. Mainly, questions of what to do next.

He didn't know. He didn't *want* to know right now. Ignoring it didn't help. He grew fidgety and had to pace around the apartment. It was small, but he didn't mind the tight circles he made. Slowly, the city woke up around him, the muffled sounds of traffic slipping inside, and time continuing onward.

After a while, Asher focused on the little things in Raum's apartment to distract himself. It was all so very much Raum, touching all corners to make it his home. From the stereo decorated in bat stickers, the stand of curated cassettes, to the underground punk band posters lining the walls, and his trinket shelf near the television. Gifts from patrons, Asher, and probably Amy. Most were little glass bats and devil inspired figurines. Near those was a glass decanter containing the marbles Asher had given him. Raum always liked them, ever since he was a kid, so Asher kept an eye out for them. He was glad to see them on display, glittering in the light. Near the decanter were Raum's books. Some old-school art books, a tattered adventure novel there, and anything Asher had given Raum based on vibes alone.

This was Raum's *home*. It wasn't just a place he stayed; it was evidence of a life he'd made despite the city's distaste of him.

Vale's words crawled into the forefront of Asher's thoughts and he sighed, pacing again. The fear and worry he'd hoped to bury was bubbling anew. All because Vale had confirmed that everything Asher felt about the system was right. It was tailor-made to contain the unknowable. If you didn't fit into its confines, it wouldn't do anything to help you.

Leaving sounded like the only viable option. Yet he feared considering it. Vale clearly hadn't had an easy life before he got his footing. The way he spoke and doled out advice said as much. Asher wasn't sure if he could do the same. Somewhere, he'd break, and that'd be that. Especially if he left his only support behind.

Anxiety made him fidget and before he started pulling at his feathers to give his hands something tangible to do, he grabbed his discarded coat and dug for his cigarettes.

The beat-up pack was deep in the interior pocket and had one final cigarette. Good enough. He popped open the sliding window above Raum's bed and lit it up.

He'd intended to sit there, relax for a change

as the cool autumn breeze fluttered across his bare shoulders, but then he was pacing again, cigarette tight between his fingers like a lifeline.

What was he even doing here? Asher felt like an intruder. He always did whenever he stayed over at Raum's place. Like he didn't belong in this life. Part of him knew that was bullshit, but it gripped him so deeply and fueled the fire of leaving altogether. It would break Raum's heart, especially if Asher told him not to come with. Asher selfishly wanted him to, but Raum's life was here. A life he'd stubbornly worked for to prove he was more than the devil wing title they'd given him. What kind of boyfriend was Asher if he asked Raum to throw it all away?

There was a knock at the door leading down into the shop. Asher ignored it. He paced a full circle again before the lock unlatched itself. He spun to face the door, and caught someone peeking inside.

Harmony, the lady that owned the place, was there and she yelped, eyes wide, and Asher did the same. He threw himself behind the screen, all too aware he was literally still in his underclothes, and Harmony let out a sigh.

"Uh, sorry." Asher swallowed and peeked around the screen. "Raum's not here."

"I see that," Harmony said. She had piercings and tattoos across everything exposed and certainly looked like she owned the place.

"No smoking, okay?" she added.

Asher quickly searched for something to put his cigarette out on. His cheeks flushed as he had to run across the room to the lone empty ash tray on the dresser. Harmony wasn't looking inside anymore, thankfully. She'd turned around.

"I shouldn't have come in unannounced, I just smelled the smoke, and Raum knows better, so I thought someone else got in."

"I'm sorry," Asher said again. "Really, really sorry."

"Let Raum know he forgot to take his tip from last night. It's in the safe."

She quickly left, locking the door as she went, and her heavy boots echoed off the wooden steps as she descended. It was a wonder Asher hadn't heard her coming up, but then again, he'd been so deep in his thoughts.

Asher listened intently as a car engine rumbled to life. He waited a little longer until it drove away before he breathed a little easier.

Lighting up somewhere he wasn't used to was the stupidest thing he could have done. She could have decided to kick Raum out for the smallest thing. Not like anyone would care since he was a devil wing. He was only allowed to stay here out of the goodness in Harmony's heart.

Still fidgeting too much to sit down and wait, Asher grabbed his pants and headed into the bathroom to wash up. If someone else came in, he wasn't going to be caught in just his underwear this time. His shirt could wait until he had help to get his wings through. They were stiff this morning and he wasn't looking forward to it.

He turned on the sink and bent over it to try to wash the embarrassment from his face. The cold water felt nice, so did brushing his teeth. It scrubbed the stale taste of beer out of his mouth. After he'd finished, he tried smiling at himself in the mirror, but it just reminded him how lost he was. His wings folded close, a response to his sudden sadness, and he turned away.

Don't think too hard, he repeated Amy's words to himself. Nothing at all mattered right now, so it did him no good to think so much and stress.

If only he could switch it off like that.

As he left the bathroom, intending to throw himself back into bed, the door to the fire escape opened. Asher peeked around the screen and smiled seeing Raum coming inside. Perfect distraction.

He had a cupholder balanced in one hand with two large coffees within, and in his other was a container of donut holes. Hanging from the same wrist was a small plastic bag.

Asher's curiosity was piqued and he intended to ask about the bag. When he looked up at Raum, however, he found his boyfriend smiling so earnestly at him, the question was stolen away.

Maybe that was all he needed to feel whole again. The simple tilt of Raum's lips made Asher tingly. Worries faded into the background noise. Today was a break from reality and he'd enjoy it.

"Harm came by," Asher said, the burning desire to be honest taking over. He took the drinks and placed them on the dresser. "Said you forgot your tip last night? It's in the safe."

Raum's wings drooped. "Why?"

Asher shrugged. "Sorry. I lit up a cigarette and I guess she smelled it."

Raum's eyes went to the ashtray and he sighed. "She *does* have a nose for it. She quit a while ago and is usually on people to quit with her. Should have warned you not to unless you're outside." He opened their coffees and tore open packets of sugar to dump inside.

"Vale's an ass, but he actually did stuff my tip jar pretty full."

He stopped suddenly, making a face, and Asher had to bite back a laugh as the clearly unintentional innuendo dawned on him. Raum nudged Asher with his elbow and Asher pushed him back.

"That *barely* sounded dirty! Stop laughing!"

Asher had to turn away to keep the laughter from escaping. "I'm trying! If you hadn't made that face, I wouldn't have noticed!"

"I mean... Hey. I wouldn't have minded getting manhandled by him at the bar if he hadn't gone after you first," Raum teased. He laughed harder when Asher pushed him. They continued the nudging back and forth until Raum caught Asher's hands to move in for a kiss.

Asher wanted to melt into it. Pleasure danced across his body, reminding him how much he loved his boyfriend, but the kiss ended too soon to take it any farther. Raum drew away and held the donuts up between them.

"Breakfast. Some have sprinkles and you have to share them this time."

Food was a godsend. Asher's stomach growled

indignantly at his lack of stable mealtimes. He'd happily share all the sprinkle infested donuts as long as he got to eat.

They curled up on the couch together, Asher overjoyed to be leaning against Raum like the old days when he sneaked out to have dinner here instead of the foundling house. It was good to be back.

By the time half the box was polished off and Asher had ingested enough coffee to reenergize him from his earlier panic, his curiosity returned. He poked the other bag Raum had left on the couch.

"So?" he asked. "What else did you bring?"

Raum grinned, like he'd been waiting for Asher to ask, and pulled it closer. Out came four boxes of black hair dye.

"You..." Raum swallowed and paused as Asher looked them over, confused. "You don't like your wings. I can't change them, but I thought it'd help if we dyed them? Give you some control over your life back." His smile softened as he tilted his head toward Asher. "Amy said it should be safe. Just to be mindful of the stitches. So?"

Asher was nodding before Raum finished. "Yes," he said, feeling his wings perk behind him. "Let's dye them right now."

Hair dye wasn't new to Asher. His hair had been a handful of different colors—pink, blonde, neon red, pastel blue—before he decided the bleaching was tedious and dyed his hair back to its original black. Raum always helped and treated it like an art project. His fingers were always been soft against Asher's scalp, like a massage, and he had an eye for detail.

Holding still while Raum did his hair was a soft kind of waiting. Asher's wings? Completely different story.

The joints were still too sensitive for their own good. And when Raum brushed his fingers up against them? Or hell, simply gripped them firmly to move them? Asher grew flustered.

Before Asher told Raum to forget about dyeing his wings and to get back into bed stat, Raum was finished. He gently wrapped the wings in plastic bags, sealing in the color, and that killed the mood right there.

They looked downright ridiculous, like plastic chicken wings. Asher couldn't help but laugh at himself in the mirror. Raum tried to hold it in, but the bathroom quickly filled with their giggles.

With nothing else to do but wait, Raum and Asher laid on the couch again and watched Saturday morning TV. It was almost like they were back at the foundling house. They'd sneak off with Amy to watch cartoons before Judith or Addam shuffled them off to do something else. Asher was sure now Judith and Addam had always known about their early mornings, but their trio had been left to themselves.

Asher laid across Raum's stomach, keeping his wings away from anything, and Raum gently stroked his fingers through Asher's hair.

Benign television led Asher to think too hard again. There was so much he wanted to talk about, to say, but he had no idea where to start. So, he didn't. Raum's fingers in his hair was soothing and the cartoons familiar, that Asher started to drift off.

This was home. That was how he felt when Asher finally let sleep take him.

"Hey," Raum's voice penetrated the haze of sleep and Asher blearily opened his eyes.

The cartoons had shifted to syndicated talk shows, the sun was higher in the sky, and traffic was louder. Definitely later. Asher laid his head back down.

"Five more minutes," he mumbled.

"Hey," Raum repeated louder, and he jiggled Asher's shoulder. He chuckled when Asher gave him an annoyed look. "We should check on your wings. They've gotta be finished."

Asher huffed and propped himself up on his elbows. "Five more minutes would have been fine."

"My arm's falling asleep!"

Getting the wings out of the plastic bags made them ache. Asher barely kept from wincing, but he insisted Raum continue. The pain would be worth it. By the time they'd rinsed off his wings, the bathtub looked like ink had exploded inside it. The towels were ruined and Asher's undershirt would never recover, but it was done. Raum used his small hairdryer to help them dry and the heat was heavenly.

Once finished, Raum helped Asher out of the tub and immediately covered his eyes. Asher huffed, but let Raum place him in front of the mirror on the back of the door. Ridiculous, but cute. When Raum removed his hands, Asher was speechless.

They glistened beneath the bathroom lights, each feather black with a rich blue undertone. Somehow, even though they were still very much angel wings, they looked better. Felt right. Matched Asher in a way pure white wings never would. A cliché, maybe, but they felt more like Asher's wings now.

There might have been tears in Asher's eyes, but he quickly blinked them away before Raum noticed.

Raum was busy moving the wings again, softly touching a washcloth to the stitches. They didn't hurt as much as they had days ago. Maybe the stitches would come out soon.

When Raum was happy with how dry they were, he bent down and settled soft kisses along the skin. The touch sent a shiver up Asher's back. Again and again, until Asher turned to stop Raum.

They stared at each other, both hopeful, but with a sense of something needed to be said. It had to happen. Too many words bubbled up his throat. Asher held Raum's hands tightly.

"We need to talk," Asher said.

"Yeah," Raum said, squeezing Asher's fingers. "I know." He drew Asher out of the bathroom.

Good. More air to breathe. Asher's pulse was

kicking into panic mode, but he knew it had no reason to do so. He was just so bad at all this.

"I've been trying to think of what to say," Raum whispered.

"You too?" Asher tried to laugh, even as his anxiety continued spiking. "I'm the one who was a dick about literally everything since I got wings."

Raum lifted one shoulder in a half-hearted shrug. "I should have said what I was thinking—feeling—and not danced around it."

There was more to Raum's hesitation, but hearing it like this made Asher's heart race. His thoughts filled with every goddamned what if imaginable until they ended up at the same answer: breaking up. It might have been easier for them both, allowing them to move on from whatever they had. In all honesty, Asher was surprised they'd lasted as long as they had.

Thinking about it at all, about accepting that as the only answer, made Asher's throat close. Made him want to curl up and cry.

"I..." Raum struggled, his voice uneven and weak. "I didn't mean to make you think I didn't want you."

Asher paused and then cut his gaze away. "Oh. Amy told you I said that, huh?"

"She wanted to help."

"I know." Asher tried to take in a calming breath and swallow the lump in his throat. "I-I didn't mean to freak out and shove words in your mouth."

Raum's wings drooped behind him. "I was

panicking too, Ash, when Judith said you had angel wings. We based our entire future on you being a devil wing like me. I hadn't thought about what would change if we were wrong."

"I didn't help," Asher whispered. "I kept thinking about myself and what I wanted. I never thought about how hard you worked to get where you were. I just thought... I guess I thought I'd just have my life handed to me once I got my wings and was angry I didn't."

"It's okay." Raum gently ran a thumb across Asher's cheek, catching a tear that had escaped. "When I saw what wings you had, I got to thinking maybe this?" He pointed at them both. "That this would make it harder for you to figure things out. You needed to figure things out for you—not for us—for you."

Asher stared at Raum, struggling with words. "My life *is* you, Raum. I wouldn't have anything beyond the foundling house if you weren't there."

"Yeah, but this is still something you do for you," Raum argued. "I'm part of your life, yeah, but I don't want to be the reason you ever give in to a system you hate. Except I tried to make that choice for you and I feel like such an asshole for that. I should have just talked about it. I'm sorry."

"Don't be sorry," Asher said as thick tears blurred his vision. "I'm the one who lashed out. I'm the one who stayed in bed waiting for my wings most of the time." He tried to blink back his tears, but they continued slipping out anyway. "And being with you makes everything better. Fuck what everyone else thinks I should do. I want to stay here and be with you."

Because fuck leaving to avoid all the bullshit here. Fuck living in a nest and playing the part of a good angel wing. What he wanted was right here in front of him. His supposed role be damned. Raum was the only thing that felt right and that was that. Asher was going to hold onto that for as long as they were both happy.

He pressed his lips softly to Raum's before his boyfriend followed up his declaration with something cheesy and ruined the mood. Raum accepted the kiss eagerly and leaned closer, cupping Asher's cheek with one hand.

Very quickly, one—or maybe both—of them deepened the kiss. Trading breathless sighs back and forth as they drank each other in. Raum's teeth grazed Asher's lips in a way that always sent butterflies straight through his body.

The longer they stood there kissing like it was the only thing they ever wanted to do, the more Asher's body grew sensitive. Raum let his hands roam, the touch reminding Asher how much he'd missed feeling Raum physically. When *was* the last time they'd really touched each other? Months before Asher got his wings. It had become increasingly hard to carve out time for themselves.

And now, Raum was touching him again. One hand found its way beneath Asher's shirt. The other held onto Asher's ass like his life depended on it, squeezing it tight. Asher let his own roam, eager to feel his boyfriend's body. Tracing Raum's chest teasingly. Dancing his fingers across the rim of his pants. Pressing his fingers into Raum's hips. Dropping one between Raum's legs, making it very clear what Asher wanted.

Raum couldn't hide his smile against Asher's lips; he wanted more too. Raum scooped an arm across Asher's lower back and Asher took the invitation to hop up, wrapping his legs around Raum.

The kisses turned sloppier, hungrier, and Raum carried Asher back to the bed. His wings wrapped around Asher's lower back, pressing him as close as they could, and they collapsed onto the mattress as one. Asher's wings ached as he hit, but he didn't care. The pain was quickly lost to the pleasure from Raum's lips. As Raum lowered himself, trailing kisses down Asher's jaw and then to his neck, Asher expertly undid his boyfriend's belt. He almost had the pants and underwear yanked down too, but then Raum stopped him. He pressed Asher's wrists to the bed, pinning him there, and hovered above him.

They were both breathing heavily now. Asher liked the way Raum took the moment to drag his gaze across Asher's body, like he was thinking about what he'd been waiting to do to it. Everything and more, Asher hoped. He flashed Raum a mischievous grin, hoping it would coax his boyfriend back down.

"You'll tell me, right?" Raum asked. "If your wings hurt too much?"

Asher doubted he'd *care*, as long as Raum was touching him. He nodded and rocked his hips up against Raum. "I will. I just want you. I don't want to stop."

Raum finally met Asher's grin, one that let go of all worries and apprehensions. He descended on Asher's mouth with the same hunger as before, pressing Asher into the bed.

It didn't matter what the world expected of Asher. Right now, Asher knew exactly what *he* wanted and it was right here. Losing himself entirely until Raum was simply everything.

Even after they'd explored each other's bodies like they were once again new to one another, even after all the motions were spent and ran their course, leaving them both exhausted on the bed, Asher's body kept on tingling. He was *still* catching his breath, enveloped in Raum's arms like he might have left. Not a chance. Not while thinking about everywhere Raum had touched him, hands and lips both. And all right, sure, Asher's wings were sore, but he wouldn't trade it for all the world. He'd missed Raum so much.

As bliss and elation faded and the autumn air from the window cooled the afterglow, Asher realized he should have gone home. Checked in somehow.

Honestly, he *really* should have left when Amy had. Sure, he was an adult, but he'd never *not* gone home. *Shit.* His eyes flicked to the clock across the room. Dinner time.

Lost underneath the bliss of kisses meant goodbye to any sense of time. There had just been so much to explore, to remind himself of, and then the blissful aftercare and cuddling until they'd dozed off.

Asher was brought back to the room and his very eager boyfriend when Raum's lips found the crook of his neck. He gently nibbled the tattooed skin and Asher giggled, turning his head to catch Raum's lips with his own. Raum's hair was a mess, pulled apart at some point. It lay across him as a soft wave.

"Hey, you," Raum said.

Asher could have melted, but he tried to stay focused. "Hey yourself." He gave Raum a quick kiss. "Probably should go home, huh?"

Raum groaned and dropped his head against Asher's shoulder. "Yeah, maybe. I can drive you." He rolled over and took his warmth away to sit up. His wings stretched behind him, his back muscles tensing with the movement. "I'm sure we have time for a shower, though."

Definitely time if they took one together. Although, in hindsight, maybe they'd spent *too* much time in there. Hands went right back to roaming and they were stealing breathless kisses off each other beneath the showerhead. Shower sex wasn't really something Asher had ever planned on doing, but somehow the motions simply happened. He wasn't ashamed to admit it was his fault. Mostly. Doing it once was definitely enough. His wings were really feeling it by the end, as were his hips. Raum had a love bite on his neck (and many other places) courtesy of Asher, but he'd never minded them.

Though achy and perhaps *too* tingly, Asher would do it all over again. All his doubts and worries were but whispers as they gently dried each other off and dressed. Dinner was quick, leftover donut holes and cold coffee, and then they were on the road.

Asher wanted to drag Raum back to his bed for another round, but he buried the desire. Obligations of going home and showing Judith and Addam that he wasn't dead in a ditch took precedence. Maybe he should have called, but it felt better to show up in person and beg for forgiveness if he'd worried anyone.

Raum weaved through evening washed streets, lights buzzing on as they passed. The cold air whipped through Asher, further grounding him in reality, and he held Raum as tightly as he could. He never wanted to let go.

The ride was over too soon. Raum parked against the curb in front of the foundling house. It was the only building around because the city simply hadn't filled the neighborhood yet. Another car sat down the street, but Asher didn't recognize whose it was and didn't care.

The two-story yellow brick house of their youth stood against the darkening twilight, little electric candles twinkling in the windows. Amy had put them there because they'd made her happy and Judith and Addam had kept them going even after she left. It made the house more inviting in the dark.

No one was rushed out to yell at them, so maybe Asher disappearing for a night and a day wasn't as dire as he thought. He slid off the bike and gave Raum the helmet back.

"You want me to come with?" Raum asked as he secured the helmet to the back of the bike. "Help explain?"

Asher laughed. "Explain what? That we got caught up in a bar fight and then had steamy sex? Twice? Once with actual steam?" Asher barely finished, devolving into laughter at the end, and was glad to find Raum snickering with him.

"I'll be fine." Asher leaned over and pressed a kiss to the side of Raum's helmet. "Thank you for taking me home."

"See you again soon," Raum said and blew him a kiss.

Neither of them lingered. Raum drove away, his bike's engine echoing against the asphalt.

With a deep breath, Asher turned.

No one would be mad. No one was actually worried about him. Everything would be fine. He set his shoulders straight and as he approached the house, he made sure his newly dyed wings didn't hide against his back.

He had nothing to hide, after all. Nothing to be ashamed of. He'd dyed his wings, so fucking what? They were his. Spent the whole night with his boyfriend and then some. Perfectly normal. So was his decision to say fuck it to the city and not lock himself into a nest.

Phantom arguments replayed in his head and those would be his answers. His life. His wings. He'd do what he'd want with both.

He'd hardly touched the doorknob before it

swung open, revealing Judith in the doorway.

Frantic.

Oh, shit. Asher froze. She froze. She was dressed in her usual business attire, but her demeanor was all wrong. Panicked, holding her breath, shaking. She was shaking.

"Where the *hell* have you been?" Judith breathed and didn't give Asher a chance to get over his shock that she'd cussed before she yanked him inside.

She shut the door and as she turned, her face fell, taking in the wings. She covered her mouth.

Asher glared at her. "I just lost track of time," he snapped. "I'm sorry, but—"

Judith met his gaze so suddenly, he lost all his practiced words. "Bartholomew's been waiting for you all day," she whispered.

The warmth, the elation, all the goddamned good things Asher had managed to fill himself with ruptured into a well of dread. He exhaled, barely finding any air to breathe.

"W-What?" he whispered. "*Why?*"

"He went around us and asked for approval from the city," Judith said. "They've agreed to make you his angel wing."

12

Broken Trust

"WHAT?!" ASHER WHISPERED, panicked. "How could you agree to that? You—"

Judith threw her hands up, shaking her head. "You weren't *here*! You weren't *anywhere*. You wouldn't even talk to me! I don't know what you wanted to happen, but ignoring it did absolutely nothing to help your case."

Asher stumbled on his words, everything jamming together as one sound. "Y-You—" He swallowed, trying to breathe evenly. "Of course, I ignored it! Because it's all fucking bullshit!"

There was a little whimper and Asher went cold as he turned toward the small mudroom off the front door. *Shit*. Addam was there helping the foundlings into their coats. Caroline and Liberty were hiding behind his legs, and he'd just gotten Claude zipped up. Aubrey was the only one that watched him with something near fascination.

Asher hated himself for losing his temper

around them. They didn't deserve to see that. Hell, they probably would have thought his wings were cool if he'd come home under any other circumstance, but now they'd seen him at his worst, ready to blow. Addam had probably hoped to get them all geared up and gone before Asher came back. Too late.

"Last ice cream of the season, kiddos. Let's go," Addam announced, drawing all eyes to him.

Judith's, however, were exclusively for Asher. He couldn't meet them again. Not after losing his shit in front of the kids. All he could do was turn to let Addam and the foundlings out beside him.

Addam paused and Asher hoped the man would pull him out with the kids too. Give him an escape. It didn't happen; whatever Addam intended to say stayed with him. Without another glance, he left with the foundlings and shut the door behind them.

Because Asher was no longer a foundling. He was an angel wing. There was no more Addam could do to help him.

"Asher," Judith spoke again as Addam's headlights shined through the windows. Her voice was quieter this time.

"This—" Asher paused as tears blurred his vision. "This is fucking bullshit. Judith, how could you let him do this? I told him no."

Judith put a hand to her chest, eyebrows high. "I did everything I could to give you more time, but you're not mine. I got them to hold off for *three years*. They wanted you out of here as soon as possible and I argued to let you stay." She threw up her hands, frustrated. "Except it never mattered. In their eyes, you kept making mistakes and we were on thin ice. Bartholomew is the only watcher who showed interest, so that's the one they chose for you."

The whole world felt far away. Asher's pulse thundered in his ears. "Mistakes?"

"Their words, not mine," Judith said. "Do you know how close they were to taking away the foundlings because of how I handled you? Letting, you do whatever you wanted? I had no choice but to agree to Bartholomew." She waited and Asher could only shake his head. No, that couldn't be right. "What I want doesn't matter. What you want doesn't matter. You are a ward of the city and they can make whatever decision they want for your future. I'm just here to see you to your wings."

It was such a callous way to put it; said in a stilted voice, like she'd had to be reminded herself. Despite all the love Judith had shown him ever, it was a job. One Asher was fucking up.

He stammered on his words, any argument he could have given Judith already lost to the guilt squeezing his lungs. She shook her head.

"If you'd just *been* here instead of sneaking off who knows where, maybe we could have talked more. When I had no idea where you were, the city decided for us. And Bartholomew was happy to oblige them."

"I wasn't who knows where," Asher whispered, drawing his arms tightly across himself. "I was with Raum."

Judith frowned deeper. "And neither of you could take a break and call me?" She waited for an answer, but Asher had none. "All this?" She waved a hand over him. "This is not helping."

Asher finally picked his head up and glared. "It helped *me*," he said. "Why don't I matter in any of this bullshit? Was everything you ever said about being me and doing what works for me bullshit too? Is it going to be bullshit for everyone after me?" When Judith didn't answer, Asher forged on. "You lied to us, Judith."

Judith closed her eyes, resigned. "Asher…"

Maybe that was harsh. Maybe she'd meant everything she'd said, but when he was the errant angel wing, none of that mattered. They'd played a waiting game, leaving Asher's future in limbo, and now everyone expected him to have no say in it. Judith had been done with him long before he'd realized it, wings be damned.

Except he didn't have to stand there and take it. Neither she nor the city could force him to do anything, no matter what. Asher didn't owe anyone *shit* and fuck standing here and letting everyone make decisions for him. He'd make his own.

His wings lifted, stretching out proudly, and he sped past Judith. She reached out, but he shoved her arm away. Talking to her accomplished nothing. She'd said it herself: she'd had no choice. But there was someone Asher could lay all his rage on and he knew exactly where Judith would have kept him waiting.

Asher slammed open her office door, but Bartholomew wasn't even bothered. The fucker sat leisurely in the armchair across from her desk, drinking tea like everything was peachy with the world.

Papers littered the desk with Judith's flowy signature and Bartholomew's loops underneath hers. Every single one had a stamp from the city.

There was no need to look closer; Asher knew what those papers were. Signing over his life like he was fucking property. Amy had to deal with the same, but at least Judith had let her participate and her sign her own papers.

"You," Asher snapped, bracing himself against the doorframe like it would contain his rage. Bartholomew deigned to glance at him, a smug quirk to his lips like he really believed he'd won. Asher held the frame tighter, felt his fingers ache. "Fuck you."

"Asher!" Judith shouted, but it was drowned out by Asher's pulse in his ears.

"I am *never* going with you," Asher spat the words out. "The deal is off. Stop fucking trying, because no way in hell am I gonna be locked up by you."

He spun and hurried past Judith, using his wings as buffer to keep her away. Soft pleas followed him as he turned and rushed up the stairs, but she didn't pursue. Asher didn't care. If she and everyone else wanted him handed over to some controlling prick, he could leave. It was his life and he'd make sure it stayed that way.

As he threw his door open, his thoughts

descended into a whirlwind of what to take with him. Nineteen years of his life was too much to grab; he had to only take what was necessary. The bag of spray paint went over one shoulder. Clothes were haphazardly shoved into the duffel bag pulled out from under his bed. He shoved a handful of cassettes in, too, the ones Raum made for him. That was when the floorboard creaked. He jerked to scowl at Judith, but it wasn't her.

Bartholomew stood in his doorway.

"Get out," Asher growled.

Bartholomew placed an open palm on his chest like he was offended. "You can't go on like this," he said slowly and stepped inside. "You know that, don't you?" A mean smile jutted across his lips. "I am the only watcher who is ever going to give you a chance. You're too unpredictable, coddled, violent, and rotten to the core. You wouldn't be the first, you know. This is a charity, Asher, and even the city sees that. Frankly, no one *wants* you. Not the other watchers, not any establishments, not even me, not anyone."

Asher struggled to take a meaningful breath. His heart was pounding too fast. It wasn't even the words that did it; it was the abject *glee* Bartholomew derived from seeing Asher trapped in a corner. And that *this* was the man everyone trusted to oversee an angel wing.

"And for goodness' sake." Bartholomew scoffed, coming closer despite Asher's glare darkening. "You painted your wings *black*, and for what? Some chance for so-called meaning? Many people have forgotten, but angel wings are here for a single purpose." He held up a finger. "Divine introspection. You're not here to sleep with people. You're not here to leave a mark. The only reason angel wings even exist is to help guide us to divinity. All you did was taint your divine self. But I can fix that. You can have a place as *my* angel wing. Something that matters. Be what you're supposed to be and guide your waiting parishioners to the divine path."

"Why don't you fuck off?" Asher choked out, trying so hard not to retch from nerves alone. "I don't believe in that religious bullshit and you can't make me do fucking anything."

"Asher, I'm only trying to help you."

"Like you helped your last angel wing?"

Shock held Bartholomew still for a single moment before his face twisted with rage. Asher stepped back, keeping space between them. He had to get out, but Bartholomew was blocking the door. Swinging a bag occurred to Asher, but that meant getting closer to the man.

Cold air trickled across his clammy skin. The window was still open from his earlier escape. Perfect.

Asher flipped Bartholomew off and went for it, knowing he could get out before Bartholomew moved.

"No!" Bartholomew roared.

Bartholomew was faster than he looked. One hand caught Asher's wrist before he'd climbed across the bed. Asher set his feet down and shoved the man back with an elbow, hoping to throw him off balance, but that only made

Bartholomew reach out with his other hand. It latched onto Asher's wing and, after a second, to be sure of what he'd grabbed, Bartholomew clamped his fingers down.

Asher gasped; pain like lightning shot through his wing joints. It was even worse when Bartholomew planted his feet and wrenched Asher backward. The pain raced across his entire back, making Asher cry out. He fell off the bed, crumpling to the floor, and could barely move.

"You see now?" Bartholomew whispered, digging his fingers deeper. "It's easier to just give in. Do us both a favor."

Asher's wing tried to twitch free on its own, but Bartholomew's grip was too solid. Asher hated the whimper that came out of his throat.

"Asher!" Judith called from his doorway, but Bartholomew held up a hand to stop her. She stilled. Her hesitation might have hurt more than this prick's fingers digging into his wings ever would.

"Judith, let me handle this." Bartholomew finally let go, like a show of good faith, and Asher quickly pushed his back against his bed to get his wings away from the man.

"Asher," Bartholomew said, softer than he'd been speaking all night, "stop all this. I'm the only chance you're ever going to get. Nothing's waiting for you out there, so come with me."

"You're wrong," Asher breathed.

Bartholomew's hand shot out so fast, Asher didn't have time to knock it away before the fingers clamped around his wing again. A pained gasp cut off anything else Asher might have said. He tried to push away, but Bartholomew took the chance to grab one of his arms next. He hauled Asher to his feet. Judith remained frozen at the doorway, covering her mouth in shock.

"You're only making it harder for you," Bartholomew whispered. "For us. We can make this work."

Nothing would work. Not with him. Asher gritted his teeth and met Bartholomew's eyes. The man had recovered from his earlier bout of anger. He was calm, in charge, probably loving it. This prick didn't care about Asher or the system. Not one bit. All he wanted was to show everyone he could control an angel wing who was rotten to the core. Tame Asher and he could rake in glory and accolades from his peers. All this spouting of religious nonsense was a ruse. Maybe he believed it, but that didn't matter. That wasn't why he was gunning so hard for Asher now; it was all about control.

And he fully expected Asher to bend over and take it.

He wouldn't.

Asher balled his free hand into a fist and swung as hard as he could. It smashed across Bartholomew's face. There was an audible crack, blood spewed from his nose, and Bartholomew fell to one knee, holding his face in agony.

"Fuck you!" Asher shouted as loud as he could. "Fuck you and everyone else!"

Pain from the yanked wing dug into his shoulder blade and was spider-webbing across his back. His breaths came out in bursts, each one ragged and uneven.

Judith had finally come in, but she was still hesitating, glancing from Asher to Bartholomew like she didn't know who to help. Fuck her too. He ran past her and she didn't stop him.

The front door would have to do for an escape. He was in no state to climb out of his window.

"Asher!" Judith yelled, but he was already down the stairs.

"Come back here!" Bartholomew's voice roared after him, but by then, Asher had the front door yanked open. Cold air accepted him as he was and he bolted out of the house, swinging the bags over the shoulder that didn't hurt. He ran into the street.

The street where headlights shined across. In his haze of panic, Asher hadn't seen them coming. He froze in the center between the two lanes, stunned, and brakes squealed. The oncoming silver sedan shuddered as it jerked to a complete stop, inches away from Asher. He caught himself on the hood of the car, partly panicking and needing to hold himself up.

This close, he recognized the driver through the windshield.

"Vale?" he whispered. It was him. White hair bright in the dark while his wings tucked around him on the seat.

"The fuck?!" Vale stuck his head out of the open window. "What are you doing in the fucking road?"

Asher glanced back at the house. A shadow had darkened the doorway. Bartholomew was there. A splatter of red covering his mouth and jaw. Judith was trying to pull him back in.

Asher looked at Vale. Pleading. "Let me in."

Confused, Vale flicked a glance at the foundling house. Bartholomew escaped Judith's grip and lumbered toward them, hatred twisting his face.

Vale reached over and pulled the lock up. Relieved, Asher whipped around the car, yanked the door open, and threw himself inside.

"Drive!"

Vale floored it. The foundling house, the streak of light cutting across the street from the open door, quickly became small and insignificant. It was over.

It was a little longer before Asher breathed easier and remembered to belt himself in. Once it clicked, he settled his bags at his feet and rested his head against the window.

Vale was going down a street lit up on either side, with soft orange glows, and they soon caught up to late traffic down in the city. The radio was playing some punk indie underground song off a choppy cassette.

From the lights, Asher noticed the stark bruise on Vale's jaw from what must have been the brawl. That was all the evidence that he'd been in a fight. Harv must have looked worse.

Vale still wore what he had last night, but he smelled a little like the woods now instead of cigarettes and cheap beer. Maybe it was his cologne. Relaxing, at least. He had his wings huddled around him, the longest feathers spilling over the sides of the seat.

Asher blinked. "You said angel wings can't drive. How do you even have a car?"

Vale's jaw clenched. "I mean, we technically aren't allowed to, but that's why you don't do anything stupid. No one usually notices the wings unless you get pulled over, but then they just get weird about it since who the fuck arrests an angel wing? They let you go anyway. Car came from a friend." He shrugged and turned down another street. A little emptier than the main thoroughfare, but lit up the same while businesses closed for the night. He glanced quickly at Asher, but instead of answering with another question, Asher stayed quiet.

While Vale focused on the road, Asher peeked behind them. The backseats themselves had been folded down to make room for a charming little nest of blankets and pillows. There were water bottles too and a small leather bag. Looked homey for traveling, at least.

"Do you live in here?"

Vale snorted. "Only when I'm on the road and I don't trust the motels. Got a place."

"Your place?" Asher watched him, raising his eyebrows. "You said—"

"I know what I said. It's not mine on paper. The old lady doesn't mind me staying though. It's in her son's name and he passed away quite a bit ago." There was a sad smile on his lips for a moment before it disappeared and Vale frowned again. "She lives in the building below it. I keep both places fixed up. She likes having a strapping young man like me looking out for her."

That sounded rather sweet. Asher nodded, trying to imagine himself in the same situation, but he wouldn't be able to make it work. He hadn't bothered learning how to fix anything, even when Addam had offered to teach him.

Regret bubbled fast and Asher focused on the bruises growing on his knuckles. They *hurt*, each one throbbing. While he wasn't sure what all he'd managed to hit beyond Bartholomew's nose, he'd really got that prick good. He only hoped Bartholomew was hurting worse than him.

Thinking of that hurt, however, made Asher all too aware of the pain still radiating from his wing. He cleared his voice.

"I take it you don't live around here?" he asked, digging for a distraction.

"Nope. Out by the coast."

That was at least half a day's ride out. "Why do you come all the way out here?"

Vale shrugged. "Sometimes I just want to drive and I end up places. See how they've changed. Make some cash." His voice trailed off and he glanced at Asher. It was quick and concerned, but then his eyes were on the road again. "So, you wanna tell me what happened?"

"I punched a watcher."

Vale whistled, tapping his fingers on the wheel. "Deserved it, I'm sure. Your wing okay? One's been a little twitchy."

There was no ignoring the pain now. Asher reached over to feel it, but all that did was make it worse. He seethed. "Got yanked. It'll be fine, right? Anyone ever pull your wings in a fight?"

"Yeah. It gets better. It's why you keep 'em tucked close before you start swinging," Vale said. "Yours look nice black."

"I'm sure the dye will wash out."

"Not all the way." He rolled his shoulder and Asher glanced at his wings. The soft gray feathers ruffled against the seat. "Mine have been gray for a bit. Started about as white as yours."

Asher raised his eyebrows. "You dyed yours?"

"A few times. Bitch and a half doing it solo. Bet your little boyfriend helped you." He winked at Asher. "But I'm serious; the black really suits you. Even if it's a little on the nose."

Asher snickered halfheartedly, appreciating the compliment. Although now, he wasn't sure about them. What had they even meant? Control over his own life? It was a lie. He had none. With a soft sigh, he eased into silence and tilted his head back against the seat.

Before long, the lack of noise other than the road itched across Asher's scalp, burning deep. It echoed back everything that had happened.

He'd *punched* a watcher. Yelled at Judith. The yelling was worse. Tears welled up in his eyes suddenly again.

He'd fucked up.

Everything piled together, one thing after another, overwhelming Asher. He had no idea where to go. What to do. If he showed up at

Raum's place, would the police be there looking for an angel wing on the run? All that would do was get Raum into trouble. They'd stick it all on him, somehow. Ruin his life.

No answers came. Breathing hurt as his lungs squeezed with panic. He had to distract himself before he lost it. He glanced out the window. The street was too dark to make anything out but the lights flanking the sides.

"W-Where are you driving to?" Asher asked.

"Fuck if I know. You said drive," Vale said and waved his hand out toward the windshield. "I'm driving. I was gonna take the backwoods road out so I could head back to the coast tomorrow, but then you jumped in front of me." He glanced over and inclined his head toward Asher. "Tell you what, there's a place nearby that's good for stargazing. You game?"

Anywhere but home. If it even was a home at this point. "Sure." Asher nodded and pressed his palms to his eyes to quell the tears. "I'd like that."

The cars thinned out as Vale drove them around the city proper. The buildings dwindled until there were lots for sale and even those became open fields. The road led them up the surrounding hills and Asher knew then where they were going. A little park that had an overlook peering out across the city.

Addam had taken him, Raum, and Amy there once on a nature hike and, because they'd been all so small, it'd felt pretty large. The trees packed together, the underbrush left to run wild, but the overlook had been neatly kept, clearly a tourist spot. The three of them had taken turns looking out at the city with the standing binoculars installed there. He'd never thought to come here at night.

It was empty when they arrived, and so much smaller than Asher remembered. The view was still amazing, at least. The sky had turned such a soft violet and the city lights sparkled against it, like a collection of stars. It was pretty. Vale parked as close to the overlook railing as he could and they sat in silence. It was a moment before Vale turned off the engine and got out.

"Where are you going?" Asher asked as Vale stretched his wings.

"I'm having a smoke," Vale said and shut the door. "And I don't smoke in the car. You can stay there if you want."

"No, I'll come out." Asher almost tripped over his bags as he disembarked. "Can I have one?"

Vale gave him a look over the cigarette he was lighting. "I'm stingy," he said, breathing it in, and then he held it out across the hood of the car. "But sure. I'm supposed to be quitting anyway."

Asher snickered and took it. "Me too," he said and took a drag.

Vale pulled himself up on the hood of the car, stretching his legs out, and Asher waited a moment before he slid atop too. He took another drag, breathing it in, and handed the cigarette back. As gentle as he could, he lay back and blew out the smoke. The chill from the windshield was soothing on his wings.

It was a few passes back and forth, watching the stars twinkle out of the darkness, before Vale spoke again.

"Well?" he said.

"Well what?"

"Got a plan?"

Asher crossed his arms, curling his wings around him until the crooked one spasmed. Pain flared anew and he winced, shooting forward. Before he could think of how to dull the pain on his own, Vale's hand was suddenly there. It drew over his back slowly, feeling the wing joints gently, and he frowned.

"You check the stitches?"

"No... How'd you know?"

"You got your wings late and was hard up for advice. I put two and two together. You got them pretty recently and they were too big." Vale pressed in and Asher bit down the yelp of pain. "Sorry. I don't feel blood, at least. That watcher must have been really pissed."

"I didn't think he'd go and fucking *yank* it."

"Easiest way to stop an unruly angel wing."

At least Asher knew that first hand, now. Keep wings tucked before swinging. Solid advice. He only hoped he didn't have to punch anyone else.

Vale retrieved his hand and took a drag on the cigarette. When he handed it back, Asher was glad for a distraction. Doing something familiar helped settle his mind.

"People are assholes, but you know that." Vale drew one knee up and settled his head back against the windshield, eyes trained upward. "Your foundling mom not do shit?"

Asher breathed out and handed the cigarette back. The orange tip left a trail in the dark, bright like an out of season firefly.

"I think she was too shocked," Asher admitted. "I'm just a ward of the city, after all..."

It still stung hearing that from Judith. Tainted every single happy memory they'd shared. Tears prickled Asher's eyes and he wiped them away.

"The problem," Vale said and exhaled, "is you all showed up around the same age and were raised like you were a real family." He waved the cigarette dismissively in front of him before tapping the ash off the side of the car. "City should have honestly split you three up, but she probably thought she could handle it. I'm sure she understands now that it's better if no one gets attached. Especially her."

Asher brought his knees up to his chest. "There's four little ones after me."

"Well." Vale snorted and took another drag. "She's gonna have hell to deal with if they all end up like you."

"I didn't mean to fuck it up."

"Don't apologize for it," Vale said. "You're living *your* life, not theirs, right?" He tilted his head toward Asher, expecting an answer.

"Right," Asher whispered, still not sure how true that statement was.

Asher finished the cigarette off, letting the smoke fill his lungs until it felt like they were burning, and let go. The fuzziness faded, leaving him hollow, and Vale took the butt to put it out on his heel. The motion moved his sleeve up, revealing the wrist he'd had Raum tattoo. Asher smiled. It was a triangle.

"Hey," Asher said and showed off his wrist. "I have that too."

Vale looked down at it, eyebrows high. It was one of the first tattoos Asher had gotten from Raum. Vale laughed and shook his head.

"Should have figured. Told him to do whatever called to him. Was thinking of you the entire time."

Hearing so lit up a little happiness inside Asher, softening the wrong just a bit. Asher pulled his sleeve back down and peered at the sky. A late plane was blinking through the stars.

It was a little longer before Vale spoke again.

"Look," he said slowly. "If you need a place to crash, I don't mind you using mine." Asher snapped upright to stare at him. "If you need time away just to think."

"You don't even know me..."

Vale shrugged, waving his hand. "I know you're lost and I know when I was like you, I wanted options and had none." He smiled at Asher gently. "It's an option. Think on it."

Options. That was one, at least, but that meant leaving. Something he didn't want to do. For good and bad, this city was his home.

Maybe he could stay. Have a place in Raum's

life. Maybe Amy's.

But then what would he do? Bartholomew was sure to tell everyone about the violent angel wing who broke his nose. There was nothing to stop him from using the police to force Asher into the nest. All he'd have to do was spin some lie about how it was for the good of the angel wing. People would believe it, especially if it was a known menace it happened to.

The what ifs tore open old worries and Asher scrunched himself tighter to block it all out. What he needed was for Bartholomew to back off. A bloody nose wasn't going to stop him, Asher was sure.

He sniffled, rubbing the back of his hand under his nose, and glanced at Vale again.

"D-Did you really burn your nest?"

"That's what I said." Vale stretched his legs out and folded his hands over his chest. "They're mostly wood. I even threw some fireworks in there too. Quite the sight."

"All because you felt you had to?"

"At the time, it was literally the only option I had," Vale whispered and his eyes grew distant. "Easiest way to smash my way out of the box the watchers shoved me in. All that they tell you that you're for? Betterment of the city or some divine path? Bullshit." He shook his head. "If that eyesore was gone, I didn't have to go back and it wasn't like they had another one to put me in. So, I'd decided that meant burning it. I'd probably do the same now."

"Were you really alone?"

Vale made an uneasy motion with his hand. "I certainly didn't have what you have. The city devil wings let me pretend to be one of them until fucking me went out of style. Got into divination cards around then, wandered for a while to find different places to squat, and then this old lady noticed me. She offered me a place to stay." He smiled, glancing away. "Better than going back to all that bullshit."

Asher watched him, expecting more, but none came. He squeezed himself tighter. "Amy believes in all of that bullshit."

"And some always will. Better to let those who don't find their own calling."

"You tell fortunes, though," Asher pointed out. "Isn't that similar?"

Vale gave him a tired look. "That's on my own terms, though. I'm not forced to listen to how this prick down the street cheated on his spouse or this asshole asking forgiveness because he gets a hard on when his neighbor tends his garden. All I do is deal cards and let the bastards weave their own lies. It helps they pay me and I get to keep it."

"Do you not believe in your cards?"

"It's all in the interpretation," Vale explained. "They're pretty pictures on cardstock. It's just how the mark relates to what's laid out."

"Then why'd you show me the one I dealt you?"

"Because you wanted a reason to change," Vale stressed. "Wanted a reason to say yes." His gaze flicked to the black wings. "I'm glad you found your change, even if it led you to punching a watcher. Wish I had. Actually…" He grinned wide. "Which one was it?" He turned to face Asher, propping his head up on his hand. "Come on, tell me."

Asher hid his smile. "Bart."

"Ah, *that* fucker." Vale made a face, making Asher chuckle. "Well deserved. Seen him around a few times. Once he stopped to lecture me about the sanctity of angel wings while I was setting up shop. Like I care." He rolled his eyes. "Self-righteous asshole."

"You're telling me." Asher studied Vale and noticed the bruise again. He thought back to the brief conversation in the bar before fists and devil wings started flying. He tilted his head. "You seem to know a lot of our assholes."

Vale chuckled, nodding.

"What happened between you and Harv? In the past, I mean. You seemed to know each other."

The question soured Vale's smile and he rolled over to his back. "His face is worse than mine," he said stiffly. Asher didn't doubt it. "Had a run in with him shortly after I burned my nest. We're both about the same age; probably got our wings around the same time. He likes to fuck angel wings, but he also hates everything they stand for and doesn't shy away from saying so."

Asher frowned. "Ah."

"Yeah. Not the smartest decision I ever made. I stayed with him for a bit because hey, I wasn't alone. In the end, we had a big fight and I thought he was gonna kill me. I skipped town afterward."

"I'm sorry," Asher whispered.

"What's life but a bundle of things we regret?" Vale chuckled derisively. "I'm over it. He's clearly not. Happy to kick his ass again until he gets over it."

"Is that all life is?" Asher asked softly, but Vale didn't answer. Asher slid a little closer to him and dropped his voice. "Are you scared?"

Vale blinked and glanced at him. "Of?"

"You're near that age, right?" Asher asked. "Where angel wings disappear?"

A soft sigh escaped Vale's throat. "I am, but what am I going to do about it?" He shrugged. "Whether it happens or not isn't up to me, if we believe the assholes. I'm going to live the way I want to in the meantime." He hesitated another moment before reaching out to squeeze Asher's shoulder. "Don't let that potential dictate what you do, all right? It's no good living your life terrified."

"All right," Asher said, nodding. "I'll try."

Besides, Asher had years before he had to seriously worry about it.

They fell silent and watched the sky. After a few moments, Vale slipped off the hood. His wings stretched behind him and Asher stared, fascinated. His wings really were seamless, just like Raum's. Working as one fluid unit with his body instead of against it. One day, maybe Asher would have that self-same confidence, regrets but a glib comment buried in his wake.

As Vale went to look at something in the

backseat, Asher wrapped himself up tighter, drawing his jacket closer. It was cold enough to see his breath. He wished he'd thought to bring his overcoat.

"Here." Vale had come up on his other side and handed over a box of cards. "People see me and think I need a dozen packs, so they gift me a bunch. You might like this one."

As Asher took it, Vale sat back on the hood, closer this time, and one of his wings fell across Asher's back, like it wanted to share some warmth. Touching, it reminded Asher of Amy and the way her wings always wanted to do the same.

He opened the box and pulled the cards out. Stiff with gilded black edges that shimmered, the imagery was lavishly painted with heavy strokes reminiscent of those Asher made with his graffiti art. There was also a heavy focus on eyes.

Vale waited, tapping his fingers against the hood, and then sighed when Asher didn't immediately respond. "If you don't like that pack, I got a dozen others you could choose from."

"No!" Asher pressed the box close. "I love them. They remind me of my art. Thank you." He smiled softly, glad to see Vale's wings perking behind him. Maybe he wasn't as stoic as he seemed. "Am I growing on you?"

Vale looked away, laughing. "You know that cute face *will* get you into trouble."

"It already has!" Asher's smile only widened. "Wait, do you really think I'm cute?" He laughed when Vale's wing slapped him forward. He shoved it back, face hot, and the feathers ruffled against him. "Hey! Stop that!"

The wing retracted and Vale hid a smile behind his hand.

"Could you teach me a spread?" Asher asked.

"Hell no. There's a book underneath the cards," Vale said. "Experiment. Do what feels right and tell anyone who says otherwise to fuck off."

That sounded like advice for life. Asher found an interior pocket in his coat and slipped the cards inside.

They sat in silence for another few moments before Asher leaned against Vale's shoulder. He was surprised the man let him, but it was comforting. They stared at the sky together. At the medley of bright stars revealing themselves as time rolled by.

"You better not cry on my shoulder," Vale said, breaking the moment.

With a snort, Asher righted himself. "Could you drive me back?"

Vale raised an eyebrow. "To your house?"

"No. To Amy's nest? I want to talk to her."

"Sure." Vale slid off the hood. He stretched again, wings unfolding wide, and Asher followed suit. His wings hurt too much to fully stretch out, but he tried.

"Look..." Vale faced him and stopped Asher from walking around the car. "I was serious before. You need a place, after tonight? You can crash with me. Just let me know. I'll linger around here until tomorrow morning, okay?"

It almost sounded desperate, like he wanted to make sure Asher understood the offer was genuine. Asher nodded. "I'll remember."

Vale let him go and went around to the driver's side. "Just saying... My place is along the coast. Nice view from my balcony. Even has all these nice blank walls you can tag." He winked as he settled inside.

Biting back a laugh, Asher slipped in. "Nice blank walls are my weakness."

"I figured." Vale grabbed a piece of paper from the dashboard and a pen from the glove compartment. He scribbled numbers across it and handed it over. "That's my number. If you stay and want more shit advice, give me a ring. I'll talk to you if I'm there."

"Thank you," Asher said and pocketed his number.

"Sometimes us rogue angel wings gotta watch out for each other." Vale turned the key in the ignition and the car rumbled to life. The headlights buzzed on and the dashboard lit up. "Well? Where's her nest, little runaway?"

13

Little Runaway

AMY'S NEST WAS on a historic side street where people tried to preserve what the city looked like years ago. Asher didn't see the appeal—he liked modern comforts. The corner her nest was on was away from the main thoroughfare and re-sembled the one Asher had tagged, except it didn't look decrepit. The hedges around the lot were perfectly manicured with late wildflowers trying to bloom among the leaves. There was even a small red maple up against the building, its leaves sparse this close to winter. Asher could just imagine Amy sitting underneath it with a book on warm days.

How many times had she invited him over, planning to do just that? Guilt squeezed Asher again, making him regret how much he'd taken her friendship for granted. So much sisterly advice was right there, if he'd bothered asking for it at all.

Vale drove off, his headlights bright against

the white stucco walls, until he was a dark shape down the street. Asher watched him go for a moment, and then he faced Amy's nest.

With a deep breath, he hoisted his bags over his shoulder and dug into his pockets for his wallet. Amy had given him an extra key she'd had Raum make for her on the sly. Just in case either of them ever needed a place to crash.

The stained-glass windows were pretty and they curved around the tall oak doors. Ivy clung to the walls, reminding Asher of the foundling house. The windows up where Amy lived were normal double panes, covered in sheer curtains. Electric candles sat in each one, twinkling bright.

Just breathe.

Asher let himself in with the key and softly shut the door. He'd missed Amy's late hours by thirty minutes, but he doubted she'd be asleep yet.

Everything was dark down here. It was a small space, especially with a pillar in the center of the room. There was a donation box affixed to it, proclaiming that all money went to the up-keep of the nest in question. Nothing about Amy. Behind the pillar loomed the confessional doors, a shadow stretching from floor to ceiling.

The whole design was a holdover from when it was a more religiously minded time. Town hall meetings liked to proclaim they were going to change the nests so the remaining confessional booths were turned into small rooms, but they hadn't moved forward with the idea. People liked the anonymity the booths gave them.

Besides, this kept the angel wing's privacy intact. The only way into their apartment was on their side of the booth and only the angel wing and their watcher had a key for it.

For some reason, Asher expected Amy's nest to be more modern. Her watcher, Wendolyn, was lauded as a progressively minded woman and well regarded as a result. Maybe it was in her future plans.

Whatever the case, the interior was made of dark woods. Amy had given the place personal touches with the fairy lights she'd wrapped around the ceiling beams. They twinkled even now, light ghosting across the room. It made it feel more like a home.

But that wouldn't matter in the end. When she was gone, so too would be any lasting impression she'd made on her nest. For now, though, it was Amy's place. Nothing would change that. He fished out some coins and dropped them into her box. Not much, but it was customary for visitors to give something.

The coins clinked and Asher headed over to the confessional booth. The door had been left open in contrast to Amy's door, which was shut tight for the night.

Inside, the booth smelled of lavender and cedarwood from the unlit incense sticks in a small tray on the shelf. Beside the tray was a fat electric candle that Amy must have put in there. Asher turned it on to give him some real light to work with. Not much to stare at. Just more wood. Facing Amy's side was a small window; tight lattice gave the angel wing privacy, but still allowed visitors to know that the angel wing was there.

Asher slid the door shut and sat, glad to rest the bags on the floor to give his shoulders a break.

It wasn't long before the soft pitter-patter of slippered feet came down a flight of steps. The interior door on the other side unlatched and opened, letting a wash of light inside. The lattice-work glowed gold as light shined through, almost too bright to look at.

"It's me," Asher said before Amy got too spooked.

"Asher?" She paused on the other side, her shadow darkening the light. "What are you doing here? Why in the booth?"

"I punched a watcher. Seemed pretty confession worthy," Asher said.

Amy sighed. "That *is* pretty confession worthy..."

"You don't sound surprised."

"Well, he had it coming. Judith told me."

"What?"

The other door unlatched and Asher's was open before he could meet Amy halfway. She squeezed herself in, a tight fit with their wings, but it was a welcome squeeze. As she settled beside him, her gaze flicked to his wings. A small smile tilted her lips.

"Aw, Raum *did* dye them." She gently petted the one nearest her.

"Judith was here?" Asher asked, trying to get

her back on track.

Amy inclined her head, frowning. "Of course. She thought you'd run here."

"Why here?"

Amy shrugged. "Maybe she thought it was too obvious you'd go to Raum and figured you'd also think the same. So, she came here. I don't know where she went afterward. Maybe to Raum's." She hesitated and gently took Asher's hand. "Judith told me how terrible she felt. And she admitted she should have done more to make the city wait."

"What do you mean?"

"The city didn't like how long you stayed at the foundling house," Amy whispered. She looked down at their hands. "I don't know what they expected Judith to do about it, though. You didn't have your wings, so it wasn't like she could just throw you at someone and hope for the best. She wanted to wait until *you* were ready. She wanted that for all of us."

"Except you and Raum left so quickly. She'd thought I'd be the same." Asher hadn't meant to sound hurt, but deep down, he was more than he'd ever verbally admit.

Amy picked her gaze up. "Only because we found our stride quickly. If I'd known you would have ended up like this, I would have taken more time to at least set a precedent. Besides..." She gently smiled at him. "I think Judith and Addam liked having you around the house." The smile faded. "But then the city pressured her to offload you. When she wouldn't make the decision, they made it for her."

"That's pretty much what Judith told me," Asher admitted.

"I know. She told me what she said."

"Do you believe her?"

Hesitating, Amy glanced away. It was another moment before she found her answer. "I think Judith believes what she said. Whether she could have fought harder, done something different, I don't know."

Out of the heat of the moment, Asher's anger at Judith ebbed. He sighed and rested his head against the confessional wall. She had a role she performed for the city, just like the foundlings she took care of. See them to their coming of age healthy, and then, let go.

It must have hurt. Sixteen years of love and affirmation only to turn them over to a city that largely didn't care, so long as they fulfilled their role. Judith was the same; as long as she fulfilled hers, the city would let her continue to take care of foundlings.

She'd been so frazzled thinking she'd lose the quartet, she'd had to let Asher go.

And he felt like more of an asshole than ever.

"She feels bad," Amy continued, watching Asher like she expected a response other than him staring at the wall. "I'm not trying to excuse her. What she did was bad. She knew how you felt and let that sleazeball waltz right in." Amy's wings twitched with indignation. "He *deserved* to get punched."

Asher chuckled softly. "I'm glad you agree."

"I think Judith does too," Amy said. "I'm sure Addam would have been proud. He never liked Bart very much."

If Addam hadn't taken the foundlings away, just to spare them seeing everything transpire, Asher wondered if Addam would have been the one to punch Bartholomew.

None of it mattered anyway. His life was still signed over to that prick and it was only a matter of time before someone less agreeable than Judith came looking for him. Asher didn't know what watchers did with rogue angel wings and he didn't want to find out.

They fell silent, Asher unsure what to say while Amy. Eventually, tired of waiting, she ran her thumb across Asher's bruised knuckles.

"Asher..."

"I can't go back," he said.

"I know." Amy nodded. "Judith left a bag of some things she and Addam packed for you. Come on up."

Truth be told, it felt invasive following Amy up the winding stairs to her home. Under no other circumstances should anyone else ever be allowed up there. Angel wings were solitary. If the city even knew she'd let someone up, especially the punk who'd punched out a watcher, there'd be fingers wagged.

Her place was as quaint as the street below, laying itself open just past the doors to the bathroom in the stairwell. The wooden floor had rugs layered overtop, creating a splash of colors among the muted brown. Exposed ceiling beams crisscrossed above, each one with another helping of fairy lights, these in a multitude of colors.

A small kitchenette flanked the left side of the room, the appliances a little old, but carefully maintained. There was a small television on the counter, its antenna twisted to find a signal.

The other side of the room was where she lived. A bookcase separated her desk and bed. The shelves were filled with books, binding material, and knickknacks her patrons must have given her. They were mostly of little birds and flowers. Asher wished he'd given her something too.

Beside the bookshelf was her desk and the plush chair she had pushed underneath it. She had a carefully maintained typewriter already primed with paper and had a ream beside it. It smelled distinctly like ink ribbon and it felt so very Amy. He could just imagine her getting lost simply clacking her latest idea down.

On the other side of the bookshelf was a nook for her bed. She had at least a dozen pillows lining the headboard and against the wall. She always did like to be surrounded by pillows. Blankets piled on top of one another, making it rather nest-like, but it was probably warm and cozy.

Asher liked the place more than he thought. He could have curled up right then and there, as safe as could be, and fallen right asleep.

Amy went to the closet near her bed and pulled a bag out. It was one of Addam's old canvas bags he'd once used for camping. She handed it over.

More of Asher's clothes, the blanket he'd had since arriving at the foundling house, the sketchbook he was using with his pack of pencils, and his camera nestled against his binder of snapshots. It made him pause; he'd forgotten them, but Judith and Addam remembered. Tears filled his eyes.

"Judith really wanted you to have your camera and snapshots at the very least," Amy said. "Both she and Addam know how much they mean to you."

There was no blinking back the tears this time; they slid down Asher's cheeks.

"She also said if you ever wanted to talk, she'd be there." Amy placed a hand on Asher's arm, one of her wings drawing closer to him. "And she'd also understand if you never did."

Asher nodded, unable to form words, and hugged the bag close. Everything he'd said to Judith came rolling back and he wished he'd just talked to her before everything happened. He'd been so focused on the dread of waiting, it never occurred to him to reach out. She might have made a difference if he'd bothered to ask.

Amy wrapped her arm around him, and they stood there together.

Eventually, Amy released him and he hurried to wipe his cheeks. "What *are* you doing here though?" She raised her eyebrows and propped her hands on her hips. "I would have figured you would have gone to Raum first even if it was obvious."

"I wanted sisterly guidance," Asher said.

A shy smile spread across Amy's lips, clearly touched, and she inclined her head. "But you already know what to do," she said. "Listen to your heart, right? Screw everyone else?"

Asher smiled at her. "Maybe I wanted to hear it from you."

"I'm always in your corner, Ash." Amy's wings perked behind her. "Foundling siblings have to stick together, right?"

There was a sudden racket downstairs, surging Asher's heart back into panic, but Amy was just shaking her head, exasperated. She moved around him and peeked down the stairwell. Raum was on the landing below, catching his breath. He picked his head up, wings perking behind him, and his face brightened.

"Oh, thank god," he said, hand on his chest.

"Did Judith visit you too?" Asher asked.

"When she said you clocked that prick the fuck out, I had to stop myself from cheering." Raum collected himself and hurried up the last few steps, immediately swooping Asher up into a tight hug. "I leave you for one night and you straight up punch a guy and run!"

Asher laughed and wiggled to get out of Raum's embrace. "I guess I'm a troublemaker."

"Yeah, *my* troublemaker!"

Raum settled Asher back on the floor. Amy came over and the three of them were together again, like they'd always been. Asher wished it hadn't taken so many years and a bar brawl to be back together.

"Well?" Raum asked. "What do you want? My bike's outside."

What *did* Asher want? He thought about it, chewing on his lip, and finally came up with something. "I want to cause mayhem," he said. "Like we used to."

Raum bit back a snort while Amy laughed, raising her hands and turning away. "I'm not hearing this!" she announced and fussed with something on her desk as a distraction.

"Please?" Asher gently touched Raum's cheek. "I just want to do *something*. Stay out all night, drive around, spray-paint an empty wall, maybe smash something. Can we just... Just forget everything else for a few hours?"

They hadn't been out like that since Raum started at the tattoo shop. Asher had been worried all their mayhem would cause problems for him and stopped suggesting it, but now, with the way Raum was grinning? Asher should have asked. Raum had been waiting for Asher to do so. The grin sent a spark through Asher, lighting him up from the inside.

"Of course I will," he said.

They both looked at Amy. She stopped fluffing her pillows and glanced back at them.

"Come with us," Asher said. "Just this once."

Amy smiled. "One of us has to be the alibi. Besides, three to a bike never again." She returned and drew her arms around them. "Just don't get hurt, and come back here." She kissed them both on the cheek and giggled when they returned the gesture.

Asher left his things with Amy, except for his paints and camera. Soon, he was pressed close to Raum's back as they took off into the city. The streets gleamed as they sped past, the colors and streetlights becoming continuous lines around them without end.

14

Walk the Night

MAYHEM MEANT SO many things throughout the years. Most of the time, it was literally being a nuisance to prove they existed. They'd ride up and down the streets as loud as they could until everyone knew they were there. Alive.

Tonight began the same, the two of them flying down city streets. Then they found a perfect canvas. It became colors blending together into full images by Asher's hands, too quick to consciously control, too free to stop. Walls became art and the moment lasted forever inside a snapshot from his instant camera.

Asher was sure he'd look back on tonight surprised, because everything was blurring together. The only thing in distinct focus was Raum. He was more like his old self again, the carefree Raum that Asher had grown up with. The one he'd fallen so hard for before he understood those feelings.

Every time Asher looked at Raum—beneath

the lights as they drove; the way his grin widened as he took corners a little too fast; after each art piece; when they'd stand in dark corners kissing until they couldn't breathe—the world became right. Pieced together in ways it hadn't been before. Asher wished they hadn't waited so long to return to their mayhem. Both of them had been bursting at the seams to get back to the core of who they were. Maybe they hadn't needed mayhem; maybe it was just an excuse to drive up the adrenaline, but whatever it was, Asher wished he hadn't waited so long.

Their revelry, their loud laughter echoing in the night, how they swung around lampposts on the way back to the bike without a care of *who* saw them, finally led them to the old junkyard they'd frequented in their earlier years. The very same patch where someone still piled up dead fluorescent lights, ripe for the taking.

Raum gathered an armful, like always, and Asher searched for the bat they'd always used. It should've disappeared ages ago, but as Asher bent over to check its usual hiding place, he found it waiting.

"Can you believe it?" Asher laughed as he pulled it out. The familiar weight settled in his hand, flooding his mind with memories. Sometimes they'd beat up old junkers, random trash big enough to hit, or anything else breakable, but mostly the lights. "It's still here."

Raum grinned, one that shot butterflies right through Asher. "Well? You wanna bat first?"

Sometimes, Asher wondered if Judith and

Addam had known all along he and Raum snuck out so often. Not a word was ever said, even when Asher and Raum came to breakfast groggy from staying out all night.

Maybe this was what the city considered mistakes. Judith and Addam let them have their fun, live before the city's expectations weighed them down, so long as they came back in one piece. It must have been easier than trying to contain them.

Glass shards sprayed on impact, each one shattering into tiny stars as they caught the light from Raum's motorbike. Golden glitters spilled out across the dry grass, joining the many more buried from years before. Wildflowers grew despite the glass, each petal some variation of blue or purple. Beauty hidden near the junkyard no one else would ever see.

Each swing bled frustration out of Asher, splitting it between the shards of glass. With each clean strike, the world made a little more sense. It became vibrant. Poignant. Like maybe he finally had a choice.

He grew winded much sooner than he'd wanted, too out of practice to continue. He smiled through the heavy breaths anyway and happily traded the bat to Raum for the remaining bundle of lights.

All Asher could do when he tossed one was stare at Raum in awe. This guy—the one who'd kissed him first, the one who was down for literally anything as long as it would make Asher happy, whose smile melted the ice threatening to close in on Asher—was all Asher's. And he *chose* to be. At any point, he could have left. Asher was a fucking mess. But Raum stayed by his side.

Asher must have been distracted too long between throws. Raum lowered the bat, lifting his eyebrows, and approached. His warm lips found Asher's cheek, bringing him out of his thoughts.

"What?" Raum nuzzled Asher, making him giggle. Raum's wings wrapped around Asher and held him still. "Out of mayhem already?"

"No," Asher teased and wriggled himself free. "Just taking you in."

"Uh huh." Raum chased after Asher, making him drop the lights. The bulbs crashed to the ground, shattering brilliantly, and Asher led Raum away from the glass. "Like you haven't been doing that all night?"

Asher's face went hot, laughter bubbling up his throat. He dodged another attempt to grab him. "Don't say it like that!"

Raum paused suddenly and laughed so hard, he doubled over. Asher's face flared hotter and he covered it.

"Oh my god, I didn't mean it like that!" Raum said between breaths.

"How are you *so* dense?!"

They both laughed, the sounds echoing into the sky, so carefree. Raum recovered first and lunged at Asher. They collided, Raum wrapping his arms and wings around Asher, and they rolled onto the grass. Though Raum had taken much of the fall, Asher's wings still hit the ground and he hated that it elicited a pained grunt out of him.

Raum immediately picked himself off Asher, worried. "Shit!" He pulled Asher into a sitting position and smoothed his arm around him, so he could massage the space between Asher's wings. "I'm sorry. Are your wings okay? I can slow down."

"Please don't," Asher said. "They're fine."

Raum gave him a skeptical look. Asher sighed, resigned to the truth.

"Okay, they ache," Asher acquiesced. "Only a little bit though." The lie was thick on his tongue and the crooked one twitched. "It had nothing to do with you."

Raum watched it, even more worried than before. He gently ran his fingers over the joints. "It wasn't crooked before."

"I know. It's okay." Asher smiled at him, hoping that was enough. He didn't want to re-hash the entire night. Not when he was supposed to be forgetting it.

Raum's face softened. "You sure?"

"I'm sure." Asher cleared his throat. "I've been... I've been thinking, actually."

"About?"

When Asher struggled to piece his words together, Raum sidled up closer. His hand teasingly dropped to Asher's waist and part of Asher wished it would travel lower. Not now, though. Right now, Asher needed to get his words in order.

He forced himself to concentrate on Raum

as a whole instead of his hand. Which was hard. Very, very hard. Raum was close enough Asher caught the subtle hint of his cologne rolling off him. Sandalwood. Asher breathed it in deep.

It was now or never, he supposed.

"What... What do you want?" Asher asked softly.

Raum tilted his head with a cocky grin. "You in my lap, actually."

The one time his boyfriend was actually trying very hard to be suave and Asher had stop him. He slapped Raum lightly on the chest, chuckling.

"I meant... with me." He stopped Raum from repeating his earlier answer with a shake of his head. "I'm bad at this." He dropped his gaze and squeezed his fingers.

The levity and teasing left Raum and worry took over.

"What do you want from me out of our lives? Y-You have so much going for you, and I don't."

Raum gently brushed Asher's hair out of his eyes. "I just like you, Ash," he said and Asher glanced at him. A soft smile greeted Asher. "You're an amazing artist and I like that you don't back down. It's admirable. I don't think I would have had the guts to ask Harmony to let me be there if I didn't have you in my head."

"Really?"

"Yeah. I wanted to be better so you'd have a place to go, too. I knew I couldn't do that with the people I was running with." When Asher looked away again, Raum gently turned him back. "I'm serious. No one knows what they want out of life right away. We just go forward. And I like doing that with you."

The sentiment left Asher speechless and teary eyed. Action drew him forward and he gently kissed Raum. Quick and soft, he parted before Raum could deepen it, and rested their foreheads together.

"Do you think I could stay with you above the tattoo shop? I'll stay out of the way so no angel wings get uppity that I'm encroaching on their space. N-No one will have to know I'm there other than Harmony. W-We could go to art school, together. Maybe. I'd like that."

His words came out as a ramble, too fast to be considered separate words. Like he was afraid of asking Raum for no other reason than he'd already talked himself into a rejection. It made no sense. Not from the person Asher had grown up with, had fallen in love with, wanted to spend his entire life with. He had no reason to fear, yet it was there.

Raum watched him for a moment, silent. When he finally took Asher's hand, he lifted it to kiss the sore knuckles, never breaking eye contact.

"Of course," he whispered. "It's what we wanted, right? Just... You have feathers. I'd never tell you no."

"I won't even be a leech either," Asher added quickly. He fished into his jacket and pulled out the box of cards. "Vale's been giving me some ideas."

There was a flash of jealousy before Raum chuckled. "Are you sneaking off with him too?"

"Not intentionally! He almost hit me with his car. He owed me." Raum's jaw dropped, but Asher pushed the cards at Raum to cut him off. "I got a deck of cards for it though. Look!"

Raum hesitated, but took the hint and dropped the subject. Asher would have to tell him eventually, what all actually happened at the house, but not now. There were still too many raw, festering feelings.

As Raum gently thumbed through the cards, nodding at the imagery, Asher drew his knees to his chest. "Maybe I can tell fortunes for some cash. M-Maybe Belle will have an idea where I can do that. Her wife's into that stuff."

"Want to tell my fortune?"

"Let me mess up a few other people first," Asher insisted, making Raum snicker, "then we can do one for you."

Raum leaned in and kissed Asher's cheek. "I'll be waiting for it." He slid the cards back into Asher's pocket, and gently wrapped his arms around Asher to lower him against the grass.

"All I want is you, Ash," Raum said again, lying beside him. "We'll make this work."

"Thank you," Asher whispered.

They watched the sky together. Stargazing really was soothing with just them and the universe, the stars twinkling like the shattered glass against the deep violet night sky. The hushed silence of everything else faded away until it was just him and Raum.

The closeness of Raum, the gentle sound of his breathing reminding Asher they were existing together, led him to thinking again. He curled up closer to his boyfriend.

"Do..." He swallowed as Raum glanced down at him. "Do you think we'll stay together?"

Raum sat up slowly to look at Asher properly. "Have you been worrying about that?"

Asher cut his gaze away. "Sometimes. I just... I don't know what's going to happen after tonight and..."

Raum took Asher's chin so they were looking at each other again. "Hey," he murmured. "I am beyond happy with the angel wing I enjoy making smile. Ever since I knew what this feeling was, I knew I wanted to share it with you and I still do. We'll make it work. Highs and lows. Nothing will change that."

Before Asher could voice another worry, Raum caught his lips with his own. The words were swallowed in the deep kiss and Asher melted into it.

"Forever's a long time," Raum said when they parted, "but I can't imagine my life without you." He cupped Asher's face. "So let me love you that long. I want to."

Asher leaned into Raum's hand, smiling. "And I'm happy with you. So happy, I can't even describe it. You're the one who's picked me up when I've gone to pieces. I love you, Raum."

"And I love you, Ash. Always will."

He just *had* to one-up Asher's declaration. Though Asher opened his mouth to add more,

Raum's found his so completely, his words were once again stolen away. These were heavy, hungry kisses, complete with hands trailing across Asher's body.

Happy sighs replaced Asher's voice between kisses. The tingling feeling of being wanted shot right down to his core. And it only intensified when Raum tugged Asher into his lap. His preferred place.

Asher let his wings spread around them as a sort of shield from the universe. Raum's wings hooked around Asher's hips, pulling Asher closer until they were pressed together. Asher pushed his fingers through Raum's hair, down his neck, into his jacket. He wanted to pull open all of Raum's clothes to feel all the heat hidden beneath. It wasn't like anyone else was in the junkyard tonight, making it hard to resist.

The thought of doing it here made Asher warmer, his kisses sloppier, and he was happy the same desire whittled away Raum's own defenses. One hand had wormed around to Asher's ass, squeezing it hard, while the other pulled Asher's shirt upward, fingertips cold as they grazed his skin. The feeling was electric and Asher didn't mind it one bit.

Here, Asher could forget about everything except for Raum. The warmth of his breathless lips, the touch of his hand teasing Asher. Raum in his entirety, and what Asher wanted to do to him.

Until an idea struck him.

Asher pulled away, taking a deep breath to

refill his starved lungs, and Raum's teeth grazed his lips as he went. Raum looked ready to pick himself up, nibble on something other than Asher's lips, but stopped when Asher straightened his back.

"What?" Raum asked, breathless.

"I can burn it."

Raum blinked. "Burn what?"

Asher stared at Raum. "The nest they wanted to put me in. They'll keep trying, I know they will. But if I burn it? Where would they put me? M-Maybe they'll take it as a sign to leave me the fuck alone."

Raum was still blinking, confused. Asher pushed him down, pinning him to the grass. A smile twitched across Raum's lips, then widened as the idea settled.

"One last thing," Asher whispered, "to cap off the night."

The grin widened with something mischievous. It made the butterflies in Asher's stomach spread through his entire body.

"You know," Raum whispered. "I've always wanted to burn something."

15

Burnin' For You

THE NEST WAS awash with darkness, nearby lights too dim to matter. The structure wasn't close enough to anything else to fear the fire spreading. Nothing important, anyway. Might char the shrubs, but they looked like they could do with some thinning out.

They're mostly wood. Vale's words sung in Asher's head and he was only disappointed he didn't have fireworks to throw inside. Too late in the year for that.

The crying angel he'd painted was covered by a layer of white paint, but the dark lines still faintly showed through. Mostly the crying eye. It'd go up too.

Raum had gotten a hold of a few punks that owed him a favor and met them a few streets down for two full gas canisters. They were gone once Raum handed over the cash.

Raum shimmied the door open easily—maybe too easily—and they searched the place to make sure nothing and no one was inside. Dusty cobwebs filled every corner. At the bottom of the stairs was a stain, but it was too dark inside to tell what it was.

It made Asher think of Bartholomew and his previous angel wing's fate. She deserved better. Maybe she'd appreciate the place burning up.

The downstairs had the requisite confessional, but in disrepair. Upstairs was empty, the floor groaning under their weight like it begged to give way. That was it. Everything made of wood. Ready to burn.

After thoroughly searching the place, Asher and Raum donned cloth masks from Asher's paint bag to keep the fumes out, and poured gasoline everywhere on their way down and out.

Bartholomew clearly didn't care about the building or the previous angel wing. Hadn't even bothered to clean the place up. He'd intended to shove Asher in here, cobwebs and all. Maybe he'd expected Asher to do the cleaning as a form of penance.

And that was okay. Asher would clean it, all right. With fire.

They coated everything as best they could until Asher had to retreat outside to breathe. They'd used up all the gas by then, at least. It'd have to be enough.

He stood with Raum outside, staring at the building. Asher wasn't sure why he waited for a sign to not to do it. It was going to happen. Raum had a bottle filled with gasoline stuffed with a cloth. For a guy who hadn't burned anything,

Raum knew a lot about getting a fire going. Asher was almost amused.

"All right," Asher said, trying to sound determined even as fear coiled in his stomach. He took the bottle and freed his lighter. "I'll throw it. It's my building to burn."

"All yours, Ash."

This was it. Burn the entire thing to the ground. Free himself from the whole system. It'd be symbolic bullshit, but it would feel real. Couldn't lock him up if there was no place to do so and he stood by that, squashing his fear and doubt.

The cloth wick lit up and Asher threw the bottle as hard as he could. It smashed through a thin, stained-glass window and shattered inside.

The fire began as a flickering ember, not more than a candleflame, but then it found the fuel. It grew and became the blaze it was always going to be, racing through the entire building, eating everything in its path.

Asher wanted to watch as every wooden floorboard and ceiling beam went up, but Raum was dragging Asher further away seconds after the fire caught.

The roof caved in on itself too soon for Asher's liking. His heart caught in his throat as the stark, naked flames stretched up into the sky. More and more of the inside began to fold underneath the flames, crackling and groaning, and Raum continued pulling Asher away. The entire place *leaned*.

They'd wanted to put Asher in a nest barely

holding on.

Burning debris fell into the bushes and sparks ignited, dancing across the dry branches and leaves.

He wanted to laugh at how easily it came down. At how they'd wanted to trap him inside its thin walls and broken roof, but now it burned. A bright flame stealing his breath away in something akin to reverence. The fire destroyed the old and released him. He *wanted* to be elated. Laugh so loud, it mixed with the silent night air.

But Raum dragging him away from the effigy they'd made. Turned him away from its divine punishment for thinking it could cage Asher away.

Sirens echoed across the night, a screech puncturing the silence. Asher took a selfish moment for a photo before he was on the back of Raum's bike. They left so fast, the streetlights streaked across the dark.

They drove, through dark side streets, until the sirens echoed far in the distance. Raum stopped in an alley and if not for the headlight on his bike, it would have been too dark to see.

That was when Asher finally laughed, a breathless sound suffocated by his helmet. He looked at the blurry photo he'd taken; the golden light against the darkness, nothing in focus. That was a building. A whole building he'd torched with a single strike.

Asher ripped off his helmet. "We did it," he said. "Holy shit, Raum, we really did it."

Raum turned to face Asher on his bike and

pulled off his helmet. Concern twisted his face and Asher couldn't stand it. Not right now. Not when they'd done the only thing they could do to ensure Asher wasn't caged up. He gripped Raum's shoulders, turning him farther, and pulled him in for a kiss.

It was sloppy and misaimed, Asher's own anxious eagerness overriding all else so he could cap off the night with exhilaration. He was overjoyed when Raum let go of his concern and pulled Asher over to his lap, his lips just as eager.

As Asher settled there, happily straddling Raum atop the bike, Raum wrapped his wings around Asher, firmly keeping him there. Asher's wings ruffled, attempting to do the same, but all it did was invite a hiss of pain in Asher's throat. Raum stole it away, one hand comfortingly pressed against the crooked wing, massaging it where it met Asher's back.

The kisses aligned, the heat between them chasing away the autumn chill threatening to settle into Asher's bones like a ghost, but then Raum pulled back. There was an awkward chuckle that Asher wanted to kiss away, but Raum didn't let him.

Huffing, Asher crossed his arms. "What?" he teased, smiling, and tried to resist the allure of Raum's lips. Somehow, his boyfriend was more handsome at night. Especially tonight. The shadows played well across his face.

Raum bit back a smirk. "As much as I want to take you on my bike, we should get back to Amy."

"Seriously?" Asher teasingly wrapped his arms around Raum's shoulders and pulled himself closer. "Go back to wanting to take me on your bike."

Raum kissed the inside of Asher's wrist, the center of the triangle inked there, and gently pulled Asher's off him.

"I mean it. After something like that, it's best if devil wings are inside." His voice was serious and Asher's wings drooped. A bit of reality slotted back into place. Raum glanced behind them. The street was silent, but sirens sang in the air still.

"We burned a building, Ash. They'll be looking for who."

Always the sensible one. Asher sighed. "Yeah, yeah. You're right." He slid off Raum's lap with none no more teasing. "And we smell like it too. Back to Amy, then." He tried to smile. "I'm sure she won't mind us crashing there, being our alibi and all."

Then tomorrow, Asher could pick up the pieces of reality that he'd burned and go from there. Tonight wasn't for thinking. Maybe tomorrow wouldn't have to be either, but he'd have to figure his life out someday.

He hid his wings underneath his jacket and clung tight to Raum as they rode down the empty side streets. With his wings hidden, no one would see them as an angel wing and a devil wing when they flew by.

The sirens still sang in the night sky when they returned to Amy's nest. A black cloud clung to the stars, the sight of it coiling unease into Asher's stomach, but he stayed quiet. That thing had been an eyesore. He was doing the city a favor and liberating himself at the same time.

Even if he didn't quite feel it yet.

Amy wasn't at the door to greet them, but she'd left her confessional door open and they went searching for her. As they ascended the stairs, the hum of a television greeted them. Some breaking news story which made Asher's anxieties spike.

When they got to the top, Amy was staring at the tiny television on her shelf, covering her mouth. She blinked, wings perking, and glanced at them, wide-eyed.

"Don't tell me..." she whispered.

A late-night news broadcast showed the smoldering ash of the nest they'd burned. Police and firetruck lights blinked fast as the whole lot was taped off.

Asher shrugged. "Now they can't put me in there."

"You said *mayhem*," Amy hissed. "Not *arson*."

"Almost the same," Asher argued and Amy gave him a look. "It's gone. No more nest, so I'm golden, right? They're not going to rebuild it and no one else wanted me."

Amy continued staring at him, more and more incredulous by the second. "Asher," she whispered, "Bartholomew's going to know this was you."

"And I'm an angel wing," Asher said.

Amy's arm shot towards Raum. "*He* is not."

There it was. The roaring realization of the regret Asher had been ignoring. It gripped him so tightly, so suddenly, he flinched. Raum froze as it dawned on him too, and his eyes went wide.

Breathing was hard. As if Asher was in the nest, burning with it. He forced in deep breaths, trying to even them, but they wouldn't. How stupid *was* he? It was too obviously arson. Too obviously the last-ditch effort of an errant angel wing backed into a corner whose only option was lashing out. An angel wing *known* for having a devil wing boyfriend.

"Shit," Asher forced out the word.

"No one saw us," Raum said, but even he didn't sound convinced. When all Asher could do was shake his head, Raum faced him. "Asher, Asher—it's okay. It—"

"It'll ruin your life," Asher whispered.

Devil wings were scapegoats. Everyone knew that and the city let it happen because it was easy. Everything Raum had built for himself would be burned away as soon as Bartholomew decided to retaliate. He couldn't touch Asher, but he *could* touch Raum.

Asher paced in a small circle, dragging his hands through his hair. His pulse thundered in his ears, panic drowning out everything else.

"Asher..." Amy's careful hands held him still. Her calming presence was a beacon against the waves threatening to drown him. "Let's call Judith. She and Addam can do something."

"No," Asher snapped, harder than he'd meant to. "No, no, no. They'll get the foundlings taken away. I'd be proof they're shit at this. Bartholomew will make sure of it, just to punish me."

What was he supposed to do, then? Amy and Raum stared at him, expecting some kind of answer, but they wouldn't like the one he came up with. *He* didn't like it.

"If... If I leave, if I make sure they see me leaving, t-then maybe they'll take that as its own guilt." The plan sped through Asher's head, then grinded to a halt when he glanced at Raum and found his boyfriend's jaw open in shock.

No. He couldn't look at Raum, or Amy, and stared so hard at the carpet instead. "Everyone will figure it was the punk angel wing who fucking ran away. I'm no good; Bart's already called me rotten, so people will believe it."

And it meant ignoring all the dreams he'd just shared with Raum. All the plans spoken to the stars. Their promises. Burned with the nest. Panic squeezed Asher's insides until he thought he'd be sick.

"You can't be serious," Raum whispered.

"He's onto something," Amy said and Raum whipped around toward her, as did Asher. She was nodding, thoughtful. "The last Bartholomew saw of you, you were almost hit by a car that you got into. A car a lot of people know belongs to another angel wing who also burned down his nest." She looked more sure of Asher's slapdash plan than he was.

"No, Ash..." Raum faced him and Asher couldn't look away fast enough to avoid the despair twisting his boyfriend's face. "Ash, where would you even *go*?"

"Vale offered me a place to stay," Asher said and hated how Raum's face fell.

Amy kept nodding as she reached out and rubbed Raum's arm. "If people see them to-gether—two rogue angel wings—that'll help sell the story," she whispered. "They'll even say Vale helped Asher burn the place, not you."

Two rotten angel wings. Asher only hoped no one thought to come after them.

"Amy's your alibi," Asher continued. "If she says you were here all night..."

"Someone must have seen me on my bike," Raum argued. "It's not that simple—"

"It can be," Amy argued. "We can say I sent you on some late-night errands. I'm not sup-posed to be out after dark, after all, and my word is gold." She turned and grabbed a pack of ink ribbon from her desk. She pushed it at Raum. "You were getting me these from the twenty-four-hour mart. There's the story. You were being a good devil wing and nowhere near the fire."

Amy seemed to hate saying it that way, but it was the truth. It'd keep scrutiny off Raum because her word was gold.

Raum shook his head. "Let me go with you, Ash," he whispered.

"No," Asher said and he hated it. It felt like he was tearing out Raum's heart. "You have an amazing life here. Don't let me ruin it any more than I already have."

Before Raum could insist he hadn't, Asher swooped in and cut him off with a tight hug. It stole the words away and Raum held his breath. Asher stepped back and took Raum's face in his hands.

"Please. Let me go."

Silence spread taut between them. It was a selfish request. Raum had done everything he could just to make sure Asher was comfortable in his own skin, and how would Asher repay him?

By leaving.

It wasn't fair. Asher should have done better.

Raum searched his face, looking for something that wasn't there. Then he glanced at Amy. Even she didn't have a better option. Everything else jeopardized the life Raum had carved for himself. He couldn't throw it all away. Tears slid out of his eyes between rapid blinks.

"You'll come back, right?" Raum's voice was so small, it made Asher's heart crack.

"If you'll have me," Asher whispered. He pulled Amy in as well; she was part of this, too. This huddle of wings wanting to hide from the world. "I'll come back," he promised. He prayed to anything listening that he wasn't lying.

"You will," Amy replied.

"You always will," Raum agreed.

They pulled each other in, their wings failing to wrap around the group. This here, though, was home. Three transient beings huddled together; destined to not matter, destined to be forgotten. But it was home. And Asher promised himself, over and over, that he'd return for it. Let Bartholomew shout and cry all he wanted about his nose and scorched nest. When Asher made it obvious he was on the run, Bartholomew would never be able to hurt Asher's family. No one would believe anyone else had been involved in the fire.

When they parted, Raum tried to smile. It was a broken, a mask to hold himself together. Tears sparkled down Amy's cheeks and she wiped them away with her palms.

"You promised," she said.

"I did." Asher nodded, holding back his tears. "I won't break it."

Raum sniffled. "W-Where is Vale then?" he asked, his voice cracking. "It'll be dawn soon."

"He said if I needed him, he'd be waiting at the overlook in the woods."

"Okay." Raum exhaled a shaky breath. "T-Then, let's go."

Raum headed out first, holding back obvious tears he didn't want Asher to see.

Asher lingered, listening to Raum's footsteps, and struggled to say something to Amy. Something poignant. It never came.

Amy placed his bag at his feet and drew him in for a quick squeeze. When they parted, she kissed his cheek.

"You'll write us letters," she decided for him and he nodded. "And don't break his heart a second time, okay?"

"I know." Asher kissed her cheek in return. "Look, Amy, I'm—"

Amy put a finger to his lips. "It can wait for

when you return.”

It'd have to. Maybe then, he'd know what he really wanted to say. Asher smiled at her and pulled his bag's strap over his shoulder. “All right. I love you, Amy.”

“I love you, too.”

Heading down into the dark was hard. Every step was closer to leaving everything behind. A betrayal Asher hadn't intended. A decision he'd been rejecting ever since he got his wings. He was outside before he could change his mind. Made it to Raum's bike. Where Raum was, hardly looking at Asher.

“Raum...” Asher whispered.

Raum drew him into a tight hug. It was warm, encompassing, and Asher wanted Raum even closer. He wanted to take this feeling with him. Never let it go. Always remember how it felt.

“I will always love you, okay?” Raum whispered into Asher's hair. “That won't ever change.”

Asher nodded against Raum's shoulder. “I know, and I'll always love you too.”

Vale was at the park overlook, like he'd said, sitting on the hood of his car. He was watching the city, amused, and Asher knew why. It was the perfect vantage point to see the cloud blotting out the stars. He must have seen how gold the fire was before it was extinguished.

Vale looked over and nodded toward it. “You

weren't supposed to take that as advice."

"It... It made sense for a split second." Asher pulled off his helmet and handed it to Raum before he unlatched his bags from the bike. Three of them. His whole life, or at least what mattered, contained in three bags.

Vale bobbed his head like he counted them as Asher pulled them over one shoulder.

"Oh," he said, eyebrows high. "You're actually taking me up on that offer."

"It makes sense," Asher whispered. "Bart'll be looking for someone to blame. If I leave with you, a known rotten angel wing just like me, people will think you helped me..." Asher glanced at Raum. "Not him."

Vale slid off the hood and glanced at Raum, worried.

"I'm not going," Raum said. "I've a life here, he says. I just wanted to see him off safely."

Vale let out a sigh. He looked at Asher. "You give him my number, then?"

Asher patted his pockets down and found it. He handed it over.

"Call him whenever. Just... Warn me ahead of time if you're gonna be spicy."

Raum chuckled, but there was no warmth in the sound. He slid the number into his jacket. "I will. Look..."

Vale was waving a hand toward Asher's paint bag, cutting Raum off. "Hey, you got a camera in there?"

"Uh, yeah..."

"It's an instant camera?"

"Yeah. It's still loaded, too. Why?"

"You want a quick photo together? One for each of you?"

It hadn't even occurred to Asher. He quickly nodded and pulled the camera out. Raum slipped off his bike, leaving his helmet balancing on the handlebar, and approached.

He slid his arm around Asher, squeezing him, but they didn't have much time to smile before Vale took the first shot. The flash blinded Asher so suddenly that he laughed. Raum erupted in laughter too, and the second shot caught them just like that.

"There," Vale said and handed over the photos.

Both were a little blurry and crooked, no artistic quality at all, but it was them. Genuinely them.

Raum quickly traded them so Asher got the one where they were laughing. Real smiles, even if the memory would be tinged with all the sadness welling up in Asher's chest.

"If we're heading out, we should get going to beat traffic," Vale explained. "We'll stop at a gossipy gas station I know and make a show that there's two of us errant wings together."

"Errant wings?" Asher asked.

Vale smirked. "I'm certainly not an angel. Are you?"

He slid into the driver's seat. Asher took a moment to linger. Errant wing didn't sound so bad. Fit Asher more than angel ever did.

Before Asher could say goodbye, Raum

wrapped his arms around. Asher turned his head and kissed his boyfriend. Something soft this time. Something that could be broken.

When they parted, Raum's eyes were glassy. His hand trailed through Asher's hair slowly.

"Okay," Raum whispered. "I'm letting you go. Please, come back. I might cry otherwise."

Asher kissed him again. "I promise," he said. "I'll send letters. Postcards. Whatever."

Raum nodded. "And we'll send shit to you, too. Just because you're not here doesn't mean you're really gone."

"I know." He nodded and Raum gave him a third kiss. It must have been the one for luck, even though with each one they shared, Asher felt like his heart was breaking. "I love you."

"And I love you, too. Always."

Somehow, Asher made it into the car. Nothing felt real, like he was floating through a nightmare he couldn't wake up from. The weight of leaving fell across him like a heavy shroud. He managed to buckle himself in, but his jaw was trembled with barely kept back sobs. He watched Raum grew smaller and smaller in the mirror. Memorizing him. Promising him and the wind that this wouldn't be forever.

When he couldn't see Raum anymore, when they had to turn and all Asher could see were the dark trees, tears flowed down his cheeks. Regret bubbled up too fast to hold it back.

Because what if it *was* forever? They hardly had enough years to live and here Asher was, leaving. What if he never got to come back?

What if it took him years? What if, when he did go back, Amy and Raum were already gone?

The questions ate him up inside and the tears continued falling, one after the other.

Vale reached over and rubbed Asher's back. "It'll be okay," he whispered.

"How can you be so sure?" Asher asked.

"I'm not. You just have to believe it," Vale said. "It feels like the end of the world right now, but that's normal. Let it feel like that and pick yourself up afterward. You'll figure out your next step in time. Believe me, I know."

Asher's eyes burned from tears. He tried wiping them with sleeves that still smelled like gasoline. "I'm sorry," he cried. "I'm trying not to cry. I'm trying to keep it together."

"Just cry. Sometimes it helps. Tissues are in the glovebox."

And Asher cried, the weight of everything pouring out of him until his voice was hoarse. Until a headache spiderwebbed across his head. Until dawn streaked across the sky, pushing back the deep violet he'd loved so much.

The world persisted, time continued ever onward, and the sun rose against the horizon, even though Asher wanted everything to hold still.

EPILOGUE
Halcyon Summer Days

RAUM WOULD HAVE drifted off as the summer breeze coasted across him if Amy stopped by. They'd been meeting up more often since Raum's heart broke into a million pieces watching Asher leave. Their meetings filled a void in Raum's heart, and he hadn't realized how much he'd missed them until Amy invited him out. Without them, Raum would have spent much of the last few months in bed, not wanting to get up because Asher was gone.

Whatever dam they'd accidentally built when they grew wings and waited for Asher's was gone. Raum hadn't even realized it'd been there until it crumbled after the bar brawl.

And he hated that when he finally realized it was gone, so was Asher.

Amy had grown a little bolder as the seasons changed, like she was channeling a little bit of Asher to make up for his absence. She pushed back against the city's attempts to isolate her and

Wendy supported her each time.

She got her own phone (Raum gave her a cute frog shaped one), had sleepovers at Raum's apartment (he was teaching her how to play video games), and even had Raum hang out at hers, not caring who knew.

She looked like the same Amy, pushing back against the system while also being cute. Fit her perfectly.

Today, she wore a floral sundress covered in bright pink roses paired with bold red stockings and white sneakers. A sheer shawl completed the look, being tied around her freckled shoulders to keep the sun off them. She had her hair braided over her shoulder, the strands glistening gold.

She settled beside him with her bike's basket in her lap and Raum sat up. They were here almost every week since that day. Summer storms had flooded the river over and covered much of the incline. Raum could see all the way down to the paved walkway under the water. The surface sparkled beneath the sun and the wind pushed little waves across it.

Today was on the warmer side. Hot enough Raum fully considered jumping in river with his clothes on. He briefly entertained the idea of taking Amy in with him, but then she spoke.

"Well?" she asked, eyeing him. "Today the day, you think?"

"Not sure," Raum said. "No one's been answering the phone since before yesterday."

Raum's calls had been more infrequent than he'd liked. He'd worried about harassing Vale.

Asher still managed to miss a lot of them and, while Raum had been worried, he convinced himself it just meant Asher was busy living a life without him. He did his best not to dwell on that.

Every time Asher *did* answer, his voice had the same soft lilt to it that Raum doubted Asher even knew he had. It made Raum melt. Especially when he indulged Asher and they traded, as Vale put it, spicy things. Raum ached over Asher not being here in the flesh, though.

"What did he send you this week?" Amy asked as she pulled a photo and postcard out of her dress pocket. She laid it between them and produced the photo album from her bike basket.

Every week, Asher sent postcards shoved into envelopes and sometimes letters too. It was endearing that Asher didn't quite understand that postcards weren't supposed to go into envelopes. If he hadn't done it that way, though, then Raum wouldn't have received as many photos and those, he cherished. Sometimes, it was a new place Asher had passed on the road, a view from the window of Vale's apartment where you could just see the ocean past the other buildings, what he'd cooked for dinner, and many more of tagged walls as his art evolved over the months he'd been gone. Evidence of Asher living.

Occasionally, another envelope would arrive. Always unsigned with no letter, but it'd have a candid photo of Asher. Raum liked seeing them.

Asher curled up on a bed that wasn't his. Asher eating something delicious and looking shocked as the photo was being taken. And so many more of Asher spray-painting, unaware of everything but the art before him. Vale had sent plenty, but they were as sporadic as Asher's own letters.

Asher wasn't much of a letter writer, but he always made an effort to reply to both of them. Raum kept his letters quick, not sure what to say except that he'd missed Asher (and felt bad saying so because he didn't want to make Asher feel guilty). Amy practically wrote him novels, stuffing her envelopes so full that sometimes, she needed an extra stamp or two.

According to his letters, Asher was enjoying the beach and listening to the waves in the evening when all the tourists had gone home. Winter had been his favorite since no one was out there but the locals. He'd sent a cool rock back, and some marbles he'd found that Raum lovingly kept with the rest. Vale had introduced Asher to the city's underground punk scene and Asher had started painting cool album covers for them. He also told Raum about his misadventures when divining people's fortunes. His brusque nature got him into trouble sometimes, but Vale was there to bail him out.

Raum wished that was him. All the misadventures were supposed to be his and Asher's. He was supposed to be the one bailing Asher out of trouble.

Maybe it'd be him again soon. Earlier this month, Raum had received a shot of Asher and Vale in front of Vale's silver sedan. It was parked on a side street in front of a building someone had painted an ocean wave across (most likely Asher, knowing those strokes). A tree cast its shade across them, making the whole thing picturesque. Asher would have called it cheesy. Except he was smiling so wide beside Vale, like he didn't care. A real smile too, not the one he'd slotted when Judith asked him for one.

What Raum had liked the most though, was how sun kissed Asher looked. Freckles had bloomed across his cheeks, like they'd been hiding his whole life.

It also made Raum smile that Asher's wings had remained jet-black. Maybe Vale helped him keep up the dye. Although thinking of that made Raum a little too jealous for his liking.

No letters had come with that photo, but on the back, Asher had written *want a surprise?* and that was it.

Another photo had arrived since then. He took it out of his pocket and traded it for the one Amy got.

Hers was another view of the car, but inside this time. Asher had gotten a shot of Vale as he was driving. Evergreen trees passed by the window in a blur behind him. Vale's jaw was tight with a forced smile and Raum imagined Asher teasing his fellow errant wing. Raum's photo, meanwhile, had been a shot of a campfire with marshmallows roasting over it.

"Ooh," Amy said, her eyes practically sparkling. "He's gotta be on the move. That photo earlier wasn't just for show."

"He's traveled before," Raum said, trying to keep hold of his expectations. Amy gave him a look. "I know, I know. I just... If he's coming back, I wish he'd told me so I could meet him halfway."

Amy nodded and peered over the rippling river. She drew her legs to her chest and wrapped her arms around them.

"I hope he's coming back," she whispered. "I think it'll do you some good."

Raum huffed. "You think?"

"You've been surly! Have your patrons at the shop noticed?"

"I'm usually stabbing them," Raum joked. "I don't think they notice much else." He followed Amy's gaze across the river. "Harm's probably noticed, but I'm trying, you know?"

"I know." Amy nodded and squeezed her arms tighter. "How's it been with Harmony, anyway? Any changes?"

Life always changed, bit by bit, but she was fishing for something more recent. Raum settled his back against the grass and folded his hands over his chest. The sky was a nice blue today. Not a cloud to be found.

"Harmony finally made it official," he said softly. "I'm a real worker, not just paid under the table. I get all the benefits of a real job. The city'll actually see me as something more than a transient devil wing. All the patrons backed Harmony up. The city had to give in."

Amy grinned and shook Raum's shoulder. "That's so good! I'm glad she was finally able to do it. Is she still helping you look into art schools?"

"Yeah, but I want to wait for Asher," Raum admitted. "He said he wanted to go together. I'm happy right now. I can stick with this a little longer."

"Maybe it'll be soon," Amy whispered. "I really believe it."

Raum wanted to believe it as well.

"Have Judith and Wendy finished conspiring?" Raum asked.

Ever since Asher left, Judith had been having meetings with Wendy. While Addam wouldn't tell Raum what they were about, like he feared it wouldn't work out, Amy had managed to get some details from Wendy. Should Asher return, Judith wanted Asher to have his independence, no matter if there was a nest to be filled or not. Wendy was happy to help and sponsor the idea, especially after hearing the whole tale of what had happened.

"I think so. Wendy sounds hopeful about it whenever I ask," Amy said, nodding. "Not like anyone's standing in the way with Bartholomew gone. Ash just has to come back and talk to Judith so she can finalize it."

It'd be a good time to come back, too. The heat was finally dying down. After the fire, the city had looked for someone to blame. And, like they'd guessed, Bartholomew tried blaming Raum. Amy's word and Raum's own reputation saved him and no one had believed the watcher. Amy had also told Raum about the rumor from her visitors that it'd been the two angel wings seen leaving the city. Just what they'd wanted people to assume.

Except everyone had been quick to scoff at the idea of two angel wings being so rotten, that they'd burn a nest. Then people began adopting the rumor that it'd been a stray lightning bolt. The whole thing made Raum hate that Asher had left even more. He hadn't had to.

Although, perhaps if he hadn't, maybe someone would have believed the rumor. Believed Bartholomew ranting and raving about who was to blame.

Most didn't even care *who* had done it, but rather why it had happened at all.

The nest had been an eyesore for *years* and Bartholomew never took care of it. Those were facts. People had gone on to blame the man because he hadn't been upkeeping the place properly. There was no reason it had burned that fast or spilled its wreckage onto the street.

That buzz had gotten city officials involved and there had been an investigation into Bartholomew and what he'd been doing with the funds he'd raised. It even reignited rumors from the old investigation of his previous angel wing.

While Raum hadn't heard the outcome, it must have been bad. Bartholomew was let go and, last Raum heard, that prick had packed up and left to parts unknown.

Good riddance.

Life moved on once he was gone and funds were raised to put something new there. Instead of building another empty nest, a small park had been planted instead. Everyone had agreed the city had too many nests in general, especially since the population was declining. A park was perfect.

Raum had taken the foundling quartet there with Addam. There was a nice slide, some monkey bars, a set of swings, and a merry-go-round. He'd swung the four of them around and around on it until Claude lost his lunch. They still had fun, at least.

Surely now, with the city having moved on, it'd be safe for Asher to return home. Except though Raum and Amy had both kept him appraised of what was going on, he still took his time returning.

Amy settled beside Raum and took one of his hands in hers. All they could do was wait and hope. Maybe today, maybe tomorrow, maybe another day. But Raum had to believe.

They watched the river ripple in the breeze, the way it glittered against the deep blue sky above. And they waited.

And waited. Like all Sundays, they waited and watched the world move on around them, like it inevitably would when they were gone. The sky changed before their eyes, the blue losing itself to a medley of oranges and pinks. Soon, it'd fade into a soft violet.

In an attempt to break the crushing silence, Raum spoke about the tattoo work he'd done recently. Word got out that a devil wing was working as a tattoo artist, and every month people from cities away arrived just to get something done by him. It was nice, even if he'd done enough bats now to last a lifetime.

When he ran out of stories, Amy began telling some of her own.

Addam was teaching her how to drive, regardless of the city's wishes. She'd also begun writing more. Stories she made up, an anecdote from her daily life that she embellished, and stories based on her past as a foundling. She'd begun giving her visitors zines she compiled out of the stories and they *loved* them. One offered to help her compile them into a full book and made it a point to catch her every month for a new story. Many even gave her money for them, and the funds went right to her. Not to the system that wanted to keep her cooped up, isolated.

She was slowly building a life of her own, spreading wings the city had tried to clip. Maybe not with Asher's bombastic flair, but her life her own way.

The sun drifted behind the city, casting long streaks of gold between the pinks and oranges before it was lost entirely against the buildings. That was their cue.

Amy stood first, stretching her freckled arms over her head, as her wings unfolded behind her. Feathers dusted gold in the dusk sun. Raum stood up next, patting off his jeans, and let his wings stretch the same.

"He did say it'd be a surprise," Amy said, wistful. "Walk me home?"

Raum hadn't brought his bike this time, so

he didn't mind. He let her take his hand again, glad for how steady she always was, and they turned.

She squeaked, dropping her basket, and both her hands flew to her mouth. Raum's thoughts hardly caught up to what he was seeing before she was swatting his arm, words but squeaks behind one hand.

It was a dream. It had to be.

Right there on the road, a stone's throw away, stood Asher. He was grinning shyly, looking as unsure as Raum felt. His black wings glimmered blue beneath the setting sun. One still sat a little crooked, but spread around Asher as proudly as the other one. Dressed in a tank and shorts, he showed off all the ink Raum had lovingly poured into his skin. Vale's sedan was already driving away, the man giving a simple wave as he went. Asher's bags, including a few new ones, sat pooled at his feet.

"Hey," Asher said, his voice sending a shiver down Raum's spine. "Surprise."

It was real. It had to be.

Words stuck in Raum's throat. Everything he wanted to say jammed together in a lump. They didn't matter; nothing needed to be said. He raced up the incline and threw himself at Asher. The force almost sent both of them to the concrete, but Raum caught himself. He wrapped his wayward boyfriend up in both arms and wings and he lifted Asher off his feet. Asher laughed, the sound of it music to Raum's ears, and had his arms around Raum just as fiercely.

Asher was here. Actually here. In the flesh. No longer a soft voice on the phone. No longer a simple smile captured candidly by a camera. He was actually *here*.

"I'm home," Asher said and pecked Raum on the lips. Raum settled his feet back on the ground. "Think I can stay?"

After waiting for this day for months, Raum couldn't find his voice right away. He never wanted to let Asher go. Never wanted Amy to release either of them when she finally moved in, long arms and wings around them both. He didn't know when the three of them had started crying, but their cheeks sparkled. His were the same, no doubt. He tightened his arms around Asher again and he refused to let his boyfriend go this time.

"Of course you can," Raum finally said and Amy nodded enthusiastically beside him, her voice caught in her throat.

Asher squeezed himself in tighter, like he couldn't get close enough. "I missed you both so, so much."

"I missed you, too. Maybe too much." There was more Raum needed to say, but the words bottled themselves up. Amy nodded again, words of her own still stuck. All Raum wanted to do was stand here, arms wrapped around Asher, and really believe Asher was home. That this wasn't a dream.

"I won't leave again," Asher whispered, his voice so soft against Raum's shoulder.

Raum kissed Asher's forehead, unable to

help himself, and Asher giggled. "If you do, you know I'll just follow you next time."

Asher held him tighter. "I know, but I won't. I promise: I won't leave you again. This is my home and I'd have it no other way."

The End

Acknowledgments

Another year, another book! The time really flies, doesn't it? Books are never solitary things, although sometimes it looks that way. A single author toiling away and bam, a book comes out! As I continue my self-publishing journey, however, I have begun to realize just how many friends and acquaintances I've made. More than I ever thought possible!

Errant Wings had a pretty tumultuous beginning back in 2022. Because of reasons, I put it away for years. I just didn't think anyone would be interested. But then I decided, to hell with that. I'm interested in the book and I'm sure there are others like me who can resonate with Asher's story, especially in this day and age. And of course, behind every book is a group of people who help bolster it up even when your own confidence wanes.

As always, I would not be here writing-wise or at all, without my mom. She is still my number one cheerleader who absolutely devours everything I write.

To my early readers for this one, Miranda and MN Bennet. You both read the pretty messy draft that I ended up shoving in a drawer and loved it anyway. Then to M. Rhys Bail for once again providing me valuable insight and helping me fix the ending. To Jake for helping me see the worth in the story after I brought it back out of its drawer and letting me be your friend. To Bri for giving me a lovely positivity pass when I was feeling down about it. And to Vesper Doom for helping me with final edits and for being such a good friend all the while.

And lastly, to all the readers who have stuck by me since I started this endeavor and to all the new ones still finding my work out there. Each and every one of you are grand and thank you so much for reading!

About the Author

S. Jean (they/she) is a queer sci-fi & fantasy author writing whatever strikes their fancy at any given moment. When not writing or dreaming of what to write, they can be found dabbling in game dev and drawing!

For more information,
visit: https://sjean.carrd.co/